CRIME
UNRAVELED

A BUCK TAYLOR NOVEL
BOOK 13

BY

CHUCK MORGAN

COPYRIGHT

This book is a work of fiction. Names, characters, places and incidents are the product of the author's imagination or, if real, are used fictitiously. Any resemblance to events, locales or persons, living or dead, is coincidental.

Printed in the United States of America
First printing 2024
ISBN 979-8-9912740-7-4 (Paperback)
LIBRARY OF CONGRESS CONTROL NUMBER
2024916316

DEDICATION

LAYA

May 17, 2024

We rescued Laya when she was five years old. She came to us when we needed her the most, during the last two years of my late wife's nine-year battle with breast cancer. She made those last two years bearable. She was incredibly considerate, always ensuring I got up in the morning to take her for her walk and get her snacks. She had her own spot behind my desk chair. I've had many dogs over the years, but Laya was at the top of the list. Laya was fourteen when she crossed over the rainbow bridge to be with Jane and all our other dogs. She was loved and is missed every day.

CRIME UNRAVELED, A BUCK TAYLOR NOVEL

Crime Unraveled, A Buck Taylor Novel

CHUCK MORGAN

| 1 |

Chapter One

Colorado State Trooper Marcus Hancock had stopped for breakfast at a small all-night diner at the western edge of Glenwood Springs. He slid out of the SUV, stretched and walked across the parking lot to the front door. This was his favorite place to eat after completing his first patrol circuit on I-70, and he grabbed the seat by the window and waited for the lone waitress to bring him his usual order: coffee, eggs over easy and bacon. At 2 a.m. he was the only customer in the place and enjoyed the quiet. While he ate, he filled out his logbook, noting all the contacts he had made during his shift and the tickets he had issued. He had little to show for the first five hours of his shift. It had been a quiet night.

Marcus finished his breakfast, paid the check and left a nice tip for Sharon, the overnight waitress. He said good night and walked to his SUV. After sliding into the seat, he logged back in with the dispatch center and began his second circuit back east through Glenwood Canyon.

Glenwood Canyon is a twelve-and-a-half-mile-long canyon running between Glenwood Springs, Colorado, on the west and the town of Dotsero on the east. The walls in the middle section of the canyon are as high as 1,300 feet, and the canyon is narrow. Cut by the Colorado River, it is the major east-west route through Colorado and contains both railroad tracks and I-70.

The I-70 portion through Glenwood Canyon is an engineering marvel and cost almost $500 million to complete. Because of the narrowness and fragility of the canyon, the interstate highway was stacked to minimize the footprint through the canyon, and the construction included three tunnels. The entire project took twelve years to complete.

Marcus enjoyed working this section of I-70 during the early mornings, when traffic was minimal and he could enjoy a leisurely drive. He reached Dotsero, exited the interstate, turned under the overpass and reentered the highway heading west. The drive was uneventful, but as he exited the Hanging Lake Tunnel and rounded the curve, he spotted a large eighteen-wheeler stopped in the right lane.

Breakdowns were not uncommon along the interstate and were a regular part of Marcus's job, but this was different. The truck did not have any lights visible, and the driver hadn't placed any cones or signal flares behind the trailer to alert oncoming cars and trucks of the hazard ahead.

Marcus flipped on his emergency lights and stopped behind the trailer. He notified Dispatch that he was exiting the vehicle a quarter of a mile west of the Hanging Lake Tunnel and gave the dispatcher the license plate for the trailer. He checked for traffic, slid out of his SUV and approached the trailer. He pulled the Maglite flashlight from his belt, and, to be safe, he checked down both sides of the trailer and looked under the chassis. He also placed his hand flat on the back left door near the latch—a habit learned from many years on the job, to identify the vehicle if something terrible happened. He shined his light on the trailer as he walked towards the driver's door of the tractor. Using the end of the flashlight, he tapped on the door, figuring that the driver was likely sound asleep in the sleeper section.

Getting no response, he climbed up onto the running board and tapped on the window. The cab was dark. He tried the door, but it was locked. "Hello, state trooper. Anyone in there?" he yelled as loud as he could. He jumped down from the running board and pushed close to the tractor as two cars drove by. He appreciated that they went as wide as they could and slowed down as they passed him. He tapped his hat to thank them and walked back to his SUV.

The explosion vaporized the eighteen-wheeler, Marcus, his SUV, and a thousand feet of both the east- and westbound levels of the interstate. The pressure wave ricocheted off both walls of the canyon, and both canyon walls sheared off and dumped hundreds of thousands of tons of rock into the Colorado River, creating a solid dam more than three hundred feet tall. The pressure wave hit the two cars that had passed moments before, flipped them onto their sides and slammed them into the wall of the canyon. Several cars on the lower eastbound level were thrown around like toys and buried under the rockfall.

Inside the traffic monitoring station in the Hanging Lake Tunnel, the two Colorado Department of Transportation workers on duty saw a white flash on their monitors and abandoned their stations as pieces of the roof fell on top of them. They raced down the service tunnel and crashed through the door at the Dotsero end of the tunnel, looked down the now darkened tunnel and couldn't believe the wall of dust and debris flying towards them. They narrowly escaped out the end of the tunnel as the debris cloud blew through the eastbound entrance. They covered their faces and heads and turned to face the wall as the dust cloud engulfed them, and they could hear large pieces of concrete hitting the floor farther back down the tunnel. When the dust settled, they turned, checked each other for injuries and high-fived. Then they pulled out their phones, knowing their boss would never believe them without photographic proof.

The pressure wave continued down the narrow canyon until it reached the sleeping town of Glenwood Springs, where it shook buildings, blew out hundreds of windows and set off car alarms. Residents, awakened by what they thought was an earthquake, ran outside but couldn't see anything in the dark.

Glenwood Springs Chief of Police Gabe Molina, his wife, Marsha, and their two German shepherds were thrown from their beds as the pressure wave hit their house at the end of the canyon and lifted it off its foundation. Moving through the dark and tilted house, Gabe made sure his wife and the dogs were okay, grabbed his radio, which he found lying on the floor across the room, and called his dispatcher.

"Police one to Dispatch. What the hell just happened?"

"Not sure, Chief," said the dispatcher. "Phones are ringing off the hook. Lots of calls for ambulances, and we've got at least two buildings on fire."

"Okay, call in everyone, call the sheriff and get some deputies up here. Put out a mutual aid request and have our guys set up a temporary command center at Vogelaar Park. I'm gonna head downtown and see what I can find out."

Gabe threw on some clothes, grabbed his badge and gun and ran to his SUV. He slid in and backed out of his driveway. He flipped on his lights and sirens, turned off Lincoln Avenue and headed west on Eighth Street towards downtown. He slowed as he turned north onto Highway 82 and drove over the bridge that crossed over the Colorado River. Something caught his eye, and he stopped at the top of the bridge and slid out of his SUV. He looked down at the river. The water level had dropped significantly since yesterday.

"What the fuck?" he said as he ran his fingers through his hair.

He jumped into his SUV. "Police one to Dispatch. It looks like there might have been another mudslide in the canyon. I'm going to check it out. Call CDOT and have them close the gates eastbound."

"Roger, Chief."

Gabe followed the bridge, turned onto I-70 eastbound and stepped on the gas. Eight miles from town, he had to slam on his brakes when he came to the first cars on the road. He left his SUV and walked up the interstate. A small crowd had gathered at the front of the traffic jam, and he was shocked to see what they were looking at. The highway was gone, and in its place stood a mountain of rocks and boulders. Ignoring questions from the other motorists, he raced back to his SUV and grabbed his radio.

"Dispatch, police one."

"Go ahead, Chief."

"Dispatch. Call CDOT, tell them the highway is gone in both directions and is buried under a mountain of rocks, and to close the interstate at Dotsero. I'm turning around and heading east in the westbound lanes to see if I can get a better view. Call the state police dispatcher and the Eagle County and Garfield County sheriff's offices and tell them what I just told you."

He clipped the mic back on the dashboard holder, made a U-turn and headed back towards town. He exited at the Grizzly Creek Rest Area and headed up onto I-70 West. Five minutes later, he passed two cars smashed against the canyon wall. He didn't see any movement, so he decided to get to the end of the road before checking on the victims. Three minutes later, he came to a dead stop as the road disappeared in front of him. There was a large gap between the end of the road and the mountain of rocks. He slid out of his SUV, walked to the edge and shined his flashlight on the mountain of boulders, some the size of school buses, and the ravine that used to be the highway. It looked like both sides of the canyon had sheared off, and he wondered about the power required to cause something like this.

He raced back to his SUV, turned around and drove back to the two crashed cars. He slid out and ran to the first car. The car was trashed. He looked in the shattered windows and spotted one male, the driver. He checked for a pulse and found nothing, so he ran fifteen yards down the road to the other car and found a man, woman and young child in the second vehicle. They were all dead. He ran back to his SUV, called and told the dispatcher to send an ambulance when one was available.

He sat for a minute to control his breathing and calm his hands. He was confused. Over the years, the interstate had had to be closed numerous times because of mudslides, but this was something different. An entire stretch of highway was just gone. "How the hell could that happen?" He put the SUV in drive and headed back to Glenwood Springs.

Chapter Two

Ramone Velasquez stood on his front porch overlooking his vast property. From the stone porch that was connected to his huge glass-and-steel mansion, he could see several hundred head of cattle moving through the valley both north and south of Dotsero. He loved this land, most of it having been in his family for several hundred years thanks to a Spanish land grant given to his eight-times-great-grandfather. The family had been protective of the land since the late 1500s and protective of their privacy, so much so that little was ever written about them.

Ramone and his sisters had turned their family into one of the largest landowners in the United States. They owned several hundred thousand acres of land on both sides of the Colorado River and held the rights to almost five miles of river frontage. They were the largest producer of rare earth metals in the United States, with a small mine in Wyoming; only one company in China supplied more of the metals than they did. They owned hotels, casinos, mines and a media empire that spanned the globe, and yet very few people had ever heard of them.

Ramone's father had been the driving force, for decades, for electing Republicans to state and national offices, and he held sway over many politicians who owed their careers to the family. When he died, many of them breathed a sigh of relief until they realized that Ramone and his sister, Gabriella, were even more demanding than their father. It was rumored that the vast, high mountain desert land they owned contained the graves of many people who had crossed them over the years. No one except for their immediate family knew the size and scope of their empire, and they liked it that way.

Ramone stretched his stocky five-foot-ten frame and leaned against the porch rail. He was in top physical shape and looked ten years younger than his forty-seven years. He sipped from the large mug of coffee and pulled his shearling coat tighter against his chest to ward off the morning chill, his tan Stetson snug against his head. He turned as his sister, Gabriella, two years his junior, walked onto the porch, holding another large mug of coffee. She was a striking woman with radiant red hair, and she filled out her jeans and flannel shirt in a way that drew attention wherever she went. She pulled her sunglasses from their position on the top of her head and put them on, protecting her eyes from the morning glare. She stood next to her brother and held up her phone, hitting play.

The quality of the video, even though it was taken in the pitch blackness of the early morning, was worth every penny he had paid for the ultra-high-tech drone. He watched as the blast destroyed the highway and smiled as the walls of the canyon collapsed on both sides. He replayed the video several times.

"It worked better than the engineers said it would," said Gabriella with a smile. "We should give them a bonus."

Ramone laughed. "The only bonus they will get is that we may allow them to live. What's the news and the internet saying about the landslide? The slide was much bigger than we ever anticipated. Going to be difficult to plead our case."

"That's where you are wrong, Ramone. The opportunities for us just increased a dozen fold. So far, the news channels are reporting it as a possible massive earthquake. They say that the Colorado River has been closed off and a new reservoir is forming behind the massive rockfall," said Gabriella.

"We got everything we wanted and more. The dammed river and reservoir will give us all the water we need to expand mining operations. It will take them years to clear the slide and reopen the river. And that reservoir is on our land. We know the canyon is rich in rare earth metals, so we will call the governor and offer our services to crush all the rocks and boulders they remove from the rockslide, and we offer to do it at no cost to the state. This will save the state a fortune in haulage costs because we will offer our fleet of dump trucks to haul the debris. We will do it for the good of Colorado, and we will keep all the minerals we find without having to mine anything right away. It's a win-win for us."

"You are diabolical, little sister," said Ramone. "Let's make sure our media outlets keep pushing that story. I don't want any mention of our failed negotiations with the Army Corps of Engineers to dam the Colorado and create a huge reservoir on our property. Let's keep that out of the news."

Gabriella shoved her phone into her back pocket as Tina, their younger sister, stepped onto the porch. "What's got you guys all smiles this morning?" she asked.

Tina, thirty-seven, was petite and pretty, with a round face that reminded everyone who saw her of her late mother. She wore jeans and a black T-shirt under her short leather jacket, and her black ponytail hung almost to her waist. When she visited the family home, she spent most of her days tending her collection of animals and had little involvement in the business, which was the way Ramone and Gabriella liked it. The rest of the time, she lived in Denver with her husband, Peter, and their two teenage sons.

"We were just talking about how fortunate we are that you are our little sister," said Ramone, and he gave her a one-armed hug so as not to spill his coffee. Tina giggled. "Why don't you guys head in for breakfast and I will join you in a few minutes. I need to make a call."

Gabriella and Tina headed into the house, and Ramone stepped to the far end of the porch. He pulled out his phone and dialed a number from memory.

"Sir," said the male voice on the other end of the line.

"Great job on the video from the drone. Looks like everything worked better than we ever expected," said Ramone.

"Thanks," said the voice.

"Just like we talked about," said Ramone. "Both engineers and the two drivers."

"You don't have to worry about the two drivers. They're under a million tons of rock. I'll take care of the engineers. What about their families?"

"Stop and see Gabriella later today or tomorrow and she'll give you cash for the families, enough to keep them quiet about their missing loved ones. Let me know if anyone complains, and we'll deal with them one-on-one," said Ramone.

The voice on the other end of the line clicked off. Ramone finished his coffee, smiled and headed in for breakfast. It was a great day, and the day had just begun. He looked at the directory on his phone, found the number he was looking for and hit the green button.

"Governor Kennedy, please. Ramone Velasquez calling."

| 3 |

Chapter Three

The helicopter landed in Vogelaar Park and Colorado Governor Richard J. Kennedy climbed out and shook hands with Glenwood Springs Mayor Laurie Powell and Police Chief Gabe Molina. The mayor, dressed in jeans and a leather jacket, looked older than her forty-one years. Her red hair was pulled back in a braid, and she looked like she hadn't slept in several days. Chief Molina was forty-four years old, thin, with wavy black hair and a mustache. He wore his police uniform. They walked away from the noise of the rotors and stepped into the parking lot, where they were met by Colorado Director of Emergency Services Helen Hughes, Major Scott Devonshire from the Army Corps of Engineers, Garfield County Sheriff Paul Weaver, County Commissioner John Fallbridge and Tom Holland and Rebecca Jorgensen from the local CDOT office.

The governor looked around. In just a few hours, the town had erected a large tent in the parking lot of the park and set up an emergency command center and triage center. He could see a small army of doctors, nurses and emergency personnel caring for the injured before they were placed in a waiting ambulance to be taken to the nearest hospital. The parking lot was full of emergency vehicles from numerous state and federal agencies, and several volunteer groups were handing out food and drinks. The governor was impressed.

Helen Hughes had served as the state director of emergency services since Governor Kennedy had first been elected and had stayed on following the second election. She was fifty-seven years old and was short with short gray hair. Major Devonshire wore jeans and a flannel shirt. He was tall and fit, and his dark skin worked well with his short silver hair.

"Okay, folks. I've seen the damage from the air, and we've got a big problem on our hands," said the governor. "The interstate is gone, replaced by a pile of boulders several hundred feet high. The flow from the river has stopped, which will not make our friends to the south happy, and I'm concerned that if the rock pile lets go, the new reservoir forming behind it will destroy Glenwood Springs. We've got ourselves a real pickle."

Governor Kennedy was a multimillionaire, a businessman and a seasoned politician, having spent twenty years in the Colorado legislature before running for governor. For most public appearances, the governor wore a stylish three-piece suit. Today, he was dressed for the people, wearing jeans, western boots and a denim shirt, open at the neck with his sleeves rolled up. The governor was fit for a gentleman of seventy-five years old. He had won reelection a year and a half ago by one of the largest margins in state history and was popular with the people because he talked straight and never backed down from a fight. Due to term limits, his time as governor would end in a little more than two years from now.

Major Devonshire was the first one to speak up. "We've closed the dams at Lake Granby, Williams Fork and Green Mountain. That's only a temporary fix because at some point, those reservoirs are going to fill up. We are at the end of summer and the water levels statewide are down, so closing the dams should buy us a couple of weeks. The big question is, what are we going to do about the damage in the canyon? My team estimates there could be as much as a million tons of rock in the canyon. It could take years to move that much rock."

"Thank you, Major," said the governor. "Helen, do we have any idea what happened? Was it an earthquake or what?"

"We're not sure yet, sir. The engineers are up there as we speak, trying to figure it out. We have reports from people who said it sounded like an explosion, but when that much rock moves, that's a good description. We should know more in a few days. The sides of the canyon are still unstable, and we may have to remove more rock to make it safe to work."

"Thanks," said the governor. "Chief, how are things in town?"

"Lots of broken windows and injuries from flying glass. Thank god no one died, although there are a couple of folks with broken bones from getting thrown around by the pressure wave. Lots of houses, mine included, are unlivable. The only deaths we know of so far are the two cars that were smashed on this side of the collapse. That's four dead. We assume that there were other cars on the lower section that were buried under the debris pile. We were lucky this happened at three a.m. and not at four in the afternoon."

The governor looked at Mayor Powell and Commissioner Fallbridge. "Folks, things are gonna get crazy around here. We've mobilized a lot of people, both state and federal, and they are gonna be here in the next day or two. We have some hard decisions to make, and we need to move quickly. Not only are we up against all this damage, but we are fast approaching winter, which means we need to move at an incredible pace. We are not going to have years or months to deal with this. We may not even have weeks before winter rears its ugly head." He looked at each person individually. "Tom, until CDOT can mobilize a team from Denver, you and Rebecca need to hold down the fort. That will mean working with the major on a plan to bypass I-70. We have been working for years on a plan to use Cottonwood Pass as an alternate route because of all the mudslides. Well, the time has come to stop talking about it. We are going to have to put together the largest highway project seen in this country in decades, and we are going to have to do it through the winter and keep the existing road open. We need a four-lane highway from Gypsum to Glenwood Springs, and we do not have time for any political bullshit. For all intents and purposes, I-70 is gone. It's up to us to fix that.

"Towards that goal, I have mobilized the 947th National Guard engineering company. I have called the president and requested as much of the Army Corps of Engineers and the Navy Seabees as I can get. We are going to need every heavy equipment company and every highway construction company we can recruit to get this job done, and we're going to work through the winter, but by the end of the week I want to see dirt being moved and asphalt being laid. At the same time, we need to start moving a million tons of rock to get the Colorado River flowing again. Helen will be in overall charge of the project. She will coordinate with all your teams, but she reports directly to me, and if there is any problem with getting this work done, then you will have to deal with me. You all have my number. If you need anything or feel you are not getting the help you need, you reach out to me, and I'll make it happen. One piece of good news. I received a call this morning from Ramone Velasquez. Most of you know who he is. He has offered us his fleet of trucks and his rock crushing facilities at no cost to the state. I don't need to tell you it will save us a huge amount of money. Helen, we'll need to coordinate with him and his company to get things rolling, and we need to clear the canyon, ASAP."

He looked at each person. "You all have a lot of work to do, and the weather is going to turn to shit soon. I like working with small groups, which is why I am here talking to just you folks and not a huge team. That will come over the next couple of days. What I need from you in the next two days is an action plan, but I was serious when I said I want to see dirt moving by the end of the week. That interstate is critical for our and the nation's economy, as is the buried rail line. You bring in any people you think you might need, and the state will cover the costs. I don't care where they come from as long as they have the expertise to lend a hand. We'll reconvene here in two days. I'm going to be asking a lot from you and your teams, but I know you all, and I am confident if anyone can make this happen, it is you folks."

The governor shook hands and was walking back to the helicopter when his phone rang; he walked across the field and answered.

"Colonel," said Governor Kennedy.

"Sir," said Colonel Mike Prentiss. Colonel Prentiss was the chief of the Colorado State Patrol. "We may have a problem."

"Mike, I'm in Glenwood Springs and all I've got is problems. What's up?"

"Sir, I just found out we're missing a trooper. Trooper Hancock was on patrol last night and was supposed to be off today and tomorrow, but he never returned home after his shift. His patrol area was Glenwood Canyon. Here's the problem, sir. We checked the video from his patrol unit dashcam, which feeds to the cloud, and, well, sir, there was a white flash at about the time the canyon collapsed. Our IT guys say it could have been from the pressure of the rockfall frying his equipment, but it could have also been something else. Something scary."

Governor Kennedy stopped walking and asked Colonel Prentiss to repeat what he had said. He listened without saying a word.

"Mike, are you telling me you think this wasn't a natural disaster?"

"No, sir. I have no idea what caused the rockslide; it could have been anything, but his last call to the dispatcher indicated he was checking a truck that was stopped right near where the landslide occurred. We lost all contact after that."

"Shit, Mike. That's all we need. If this was some kind of terrorist act, we're gonna have the Feds crawling up our asses. Lock down all the video from the dashcam and from his body camera. And Mike. Keep this information tight until I can get someone on this."

"Yes, sir."

The governor disconnected the call and walked back to the group in the parking lot. Major Devonshire had stepped away from the group and was speaking with his other officers, who would get the logistics organized. The others could see the concern on his face.

"We may have a bigger problem, and what I am about to tell you does not leave this group," said the governor. He told them about his call with the head of the state patrol about the missing trooper.

"We could be looking at a terrorist act?" asked Mayor Powell.

"That's one possibility of many," said the governor. "This will not interfere with the action plan you need to work on, and until we know more, we keep this quiet." He looked at each person, and they each nodded. "I will make a call and get some folks out here to take a look before we decide if this was more than a natural disaster."

He shook hands all around and headed for the chopper. He pulled out his phone and dialed a number. This day had gone from bad to worse.

| 4 |

Chapter Four

Buck Taylor had taken advantage of the nice day and hadn't stopped working since breakfast. First, he raked up all of what he hoped would be the last of the leaves in his yard and his neighbor's yard. Then he cut the grass for what he hoped was the last time, winterized the lawn mower and locked it in the shed in the backyard. Now he was changing the oil in the snowblower and getting it ready for the coming season.

This was one of those bittersweet times in life. It was the end of the summer season and the start of the getting-ready-for-winter season. The trees were bare, the flowers were all but gone and any day it could snow. This morning, when he started working in the yard, there was a light coating of frost on the grass—a harbinger of things to come.

Buck had just plugged in the grinder to sharpen the blades on the snowblower when his phone rang. He checked the number and answered.

"Yes, sir?"

"Afternoon, Buck," said Director Jackson. "Hope I'm not catching you in the middle of a river somewhere."

Buck laughed. Everyone knew about Buck's love of fly-fishing, and people calling him always expected to find him knee-deep in some river. They were usually not disappointed.

"No, sir. Just getting some end-of-summer chores finished. What's up?"

Kevin Jackson was the director of the Colorado Bureau of Investigation, and Buck's boss. He had been the youngest person to ever run the bureau when he was appointed by Governor Richard J. Kennedy six years ago. He'd had a stellar career with the Colorado Springs Police Department before being tapped for the top post at CBI. He was more bureaucrat than cop, having spent most of his career on the administrative side at CSPD, but he was a seasoned investigator and was well respected in the law enforcement community, and so far, Buck was impressed with him.

"I take it you haven't been watching the news?"

"No, sir," said Buck. "What have I missed?"

Buck put the bottle of engine oil on the workbench and wiped his hands on the white shop towel.

"This morning at around three a.m., there was a landslide in Glenwood Canyon."

"Well, that's not unusual, sir," said Buck. "That happens several times a year."

The director interrupted. "This time it was bad. A section of the interstate, several hundred yards long, is gone. It's been replaced by a huge rockfall to the west side of the Hanging Lake Tunnel, and it dammed up the Colorado River."

Buck leaned back against the workbench, trying to absorb what the director had just said. His phone chimed with an incoming text, and he opened his messages and clicked on the photo the director had sent him. He stared at the picture, trying to comprehend the magnitude of what he was looking at.

"The governor took that picture this morning when he flew over the damage. He told me he had never seen anything like this. The damaged area is huge and is going to take years to clean up."

"Sir," said Buck. "What's our interest? This looks like a job for engineers and road crews."

Buck Taylor was an investigative agent for the Colorado Bureau of Investigation. He was assigned to the CBI field office in Grand Junction, Colorado. Somehow, he had become the favorite "go-to" guy for the governor of Colorado, Richard J. Kennedy, who was in fact one of "those" Kennedys. The governor was in his second term in office, and Buck had been instrumental in closing several high-profile investigations during that period, which made the governor look good. As a result, when a situation came up that might get a little hairy, the governor always asked to have Buck assigned.

"Yeah. That's what I said when the governor called me. As far as the world is concerned, this appears to have been a natural event. Possibly an earthquake. But here's the issue. We have a missing trooper. His patrol route was Glenwood Canyon. He reported to Dispatch that he was leaving his vehicle to investigate a semi parked in the right lane. That was the last anyone heard from him. According to the governor, when the state patrol checked his dashcam footage, they saw a white flash at about the time of the landslide. He hasn't been heard from since. The IT folks at the company that stores all the dashcam video said the flash could have been from the shock wave frying the electronics in the vehicle."

"Or it could have been from something else," said Buck. "Maybe an explosion?"

The director was silent for a few seconds, and Buck waited. "Yeah," he said. "Or it could have been an explosion. It could also be a bunch of other things, but the governor needs answers. He is mobilizing an army to start removing the rocks from the canyon and to get Cottonwood Pass ready to handle large amounts of traffic. He wants to understand what happened in the canyon this morning so as not to put anyone in harm's way. This work is going to be dangerous enough without having to deal with something unnatural."

"Understood, sir. I'll call Bax and Paul and have them meet me in Glenwood Springs. Can you call Franklin and roll the forensic team? I'll meet him in the canyon on the west side of the damage."

"I'm on it, Buck," said the director. "Listen, Buck. For now, this is a need-to-know operation. Anything you and the team discover goes through me and the governor. No one else. You okay with that?"

"No problem, sir. We'll be as discreet as possible. One last thing. Can you have the state patrol give us authorization to review all the dashcam and bodycam footage for the trooper? We'll also need CDOT to give us access to the video from the tunnel monitoring station."

"You'll have it by the time you get to Glenwood Springs," said the director. "Buck. Be careful."

The director disconnected the call, and Buck stood for a few minutes looking at the additional pictures the director had included in the text. The damage was incredible. He finished what was left of his bottle of Coke, dropped it in the trash and made several phone calls.

"Hey, Buck. What's up?" said Bax.

Buck explained the conversation he had with the director and told her to meet him in Glenwood Springs.

"I was watching the report about the landslide on the news this morning. So, the governor thinks this might have been terrorism?"

"That's what we need to figure out," said Buck. "Head out that way and see if you can get us a couple of rooms. That might be tough, but see what you can come up with."

"Anything else?" she asked.

"No, I'll call Paul next. The director is calling Franklin to roll his team. Since you guys will be there before me, check in with the chief of police and the sheriff. I'm guessing they have a command center set up someplace."

"Okay, Buck. I'm on my way. See you tonight."

Buck disconnected the call and dialed Paul Webber. Buck could hear kids yelling in the background.

"Hiya, Buck. Hold on a sec."

He could hear Paul talking to someone in the background.

"Sorry about that," said Paul. "Kids are having an end-of-summer swim party. I think there's twenty kids in my back-yard. What's up?"

Buck went through the same speech. When he was finished, Paul asked him what else he needed, and Buck told him what he'd asked Bax to do.

"No worries, Buck. I'll get on the road right away. I could use a couple of hours of silence after this swim party. I'll see ya when I see ya."

Paul disconnected the call, and Buck speed-dialed another number.

"Hey, Buck," said Mel. "Bax called and filled us in. What do you need us to do?"

The "us" Mel referred to was herself and her partner, George. George Peterman and Melanie Hart were the CBI cybersecurity team based out of Grand Junction, Colorado, and they couldn't be more different.

Melanie Hart was about five foot two, with shoulder-length black hair; she wore black jeans and dark gray hood-ies and had several piercings. Anyone meeting her for the first time would think she was a high school kid, but she had received her doctorate in computer science from MIT about a dozen years ago. She'd joined CBI right out of college.

George Peterman could have passed for her father. He was about the same height as Buck, a shade under six foot, but where Buck still weighed what he'd weighed when he played football in high school, George had added a few pounds over the years. George had joined CBI after retiring from the navy, where he'd spent his entire career working in cybersecurity. As far as Buck was concerned, George and

Melanie were two of the best computer people he knew. Paul Webber was good. Ashley Baxter was better, but these two were world-class.

"The director is getting us access to the state patrol's cloud storage. Get the trooper's ID and pull up his bodycam and dashcam footage for his entire patrol. Also, call the CDOT IT team and get access to all the traffic camera footage for the canyon. Let's go back to around midnight."

"What are we looking for?" asked George, who had come on the line while Buck was talking.

"Not sure," said Buck. "More than anything, I want the unvarnished footage in our possession."

"Got it," said Mel. "We'll pull it and archive it all. Is that it?"

Buck thought for a minute. "You know what, this may be a waste of time, but start checking social media and news feeds and let's see if anyone is talking about the landslide. You know what I'm looking for."

"Will do, Buck. We'll connect with you when you get to Glenwood."

Buck disconnected the call and walked towards his back door. He needed a quick shower, fresh clothes and his badge and gun. Once inside, he called his daughter-in-law Judy, who lived around the corner, and told her where he was headed and that he had no idea when he would be back. Judy promised, as always, to keep an eye on his house while he was gone. She told him to be safe.

Buck finished up, grabbed his go bag, locked up the house and threw his gear in the back of his Jeep Grand Cherokee, next to his tub of fly-fishing gear. He wondered where this investigation would take him. He had seen a lot in his thirty-six years in law enforcement, and he was no longer surprised by anything he encountered, but blowing up an entire canyon and destroying a highway? Well, that would be a new one on him, if they found out that this was not a natural disaster.

He started his Jeep, connected his phone to the entertainment system and pulled out of his driveway. He had a long drive ahead of him and a lot of time to think.

| 5 |

Chapter Five

Buck Taylor was six feet tall and weighed 185 pounds—very little flab for a sixty-two-year-old man. Buck's hair was salt-and-pepper, with what seemed like a lot more salt than pepper, and he wore it longer than was the fashion of the day. Buck was always pleased when he looked in the mirror since, other than getting older, he was in as good a shape as he had been when he played defensive linebacker for the Gunnison High School Cowboys, what seemed like a long time ago. Except for a couple of sore knees coming from age, Buck was in good shape, which was important in his line of work.

Buck had been married for thirty-four years before breast cancer stole the one person he cared about most in the world. He missed Lucy every day, even after all this time.

If you asked Buck, he would tell you that he fell in love with Lucinda Torres on the first day of their senior year in high school. On the other hand, Lucy always told people that Buck stalked her the entire senior year before she gave in to shut her friends up and agreed to go to the movies with him. She had always considered him just another jock, another football player who was too full of himself.

What she found on that first date was a shy, unassuming gentleman who cared more about pleasing her than bragging about his prowess on the football field. She would tell people it was love at first sight that had taken a year to develop. After that, they were inseparable.

During senior year, Buck had been approached by several college football scouts who wanted to sign him to play for their schools. Gunnison High School was a small school back in 1978, and Buck and his family were amazed at how many schools had recruited him, but for Buck, college wasn't in the cards.

Buck hated school and spent a lot of time getting himself out of trouble instead of getting an education. When he found something that interested him, he had no problem learning all he could about the subject, but regular schoolwork just bored him. After several long, heartfelt discussions, first with Lucy and then with his parents, he decided to join the army after graduation. No one was surprised.

Buck spent four years after high school in the army, and by the time his enlistment was up, he had been promoted to first sergeant. He spent three years of his enlistment in the military police and took to police work. That was when he decided to apply for a position with the Gunnison County Sheriff's Office.

Since he was already well known in the county, he had no trouble getting a job as a deputy. He proposed to Lucy the night he received the call that he had gotten the position. His life and career were set. He made the most of his time with the Gunnison County Sheriff's Office, becoming the undersheriff in charge of the Investigation Division and coming to the attention of the Colorado Bureau of Investigation.

Buck had worked with the Colorado Bureau of Investigation on several cases inside the county and had earned the respect of the investigators he had worked with.

As twilight started to fall on Buck's career, he knew that unless he wanted to go into politics and run for sheriff, he had reached the highest position in the sheriff's office that he could obtain. He loved his job, but when the first offer came in from CBI, he sat down with Lucy and had a long heart-to-heart talk.

He'd spent seventeen years in the sheriff's office and had always figured he would retire from that job. They had three children, two in high school and one not far behind, and he was a well-respected member of the community. Did he have the right to disrupt their lives, pick up, move someplace else and start all over? The kids had friends. Lucy owned a small deli/ice cream parlor, and they had a nice life.

He could stick it out for another ten years and retire, and they could travel and see the world as they had always planned. Twice he turned down the offer from CBI, although more and more, he felt trapped behind a desk instead of doing what he loved, which was investigating crime.

The last offer came from Tom Cole, then-director of the Colorado Bureau of Investigation. Buck always remembered that day. The Denver Broncos had just lost another game, the third one in a row, and his friends had all packed up and headed home when there was a knock at the front door.

Now, anyone who lives in a small community knows that no one ever uses the front door, and no one ever knocks. So, who could this be this late on a Sunday evening?

Buck answered the door and was surprised to see the director of the Colorado Bureau of Investigation standing on his front porch. The director smiled and said, "Before you close the door in my face, please listen to my offer."

Buck invited him in, and he and Lucy sat on the couch and listened as the director laid out his plan. He was opening a new branch office in Grand Junction, Colorado, that would house five agents and a small forensic unit. Buck could continue to live in Gunnison but would have to report to the office in Grand Junction twice a month. Otherwise, he would be free to work from his house. There would be no disruption in his life other than spending time on the road as his investigations warranted. He would work alone but would have all the branch office's resources at his disposal.

Before Buck could say a word, Lucy said, "Buck, this is what you have been waiting for, a chance to be a real investigator again. You have to take this." That was one of the things that made him love Lucy every day. She always knew what he was thinking and understood what drove him. She had nailed it this time. Buck looked at the director and replied, "Well, I guess it's settled; looks like you have a new investigator on your team."

That was twenty-three years ago, and Buck had never looked back. He had made the most of those years and was one of the most respected and feared investigators in the state, but all that work couldn't make up for the loss he suffered.

Lucy was diagnosed with metastatic breast cancer following a routine mammogram, and they set off together on their next adventure: the quest to beat the dreaded disease. After a double mastectomy and five years of chemo, they knew their time was drawing to a close when the cancer returned several times to her brain and was no longer controlled by the radiation.

Together, they decided to stop all treatment, even though they had always told the family that the decision was Lucy's alone to make. Lucy spent the last couple of months of her life taking care of her small business and spending as much time as possible with her children and grandchildren.

The end came one spring night. Lucy had been sleeping on and off for twenty or so hours a day in the end. The night she died, Buck had been lying in bed next to her, reading a report, when she snuggled into his arms and rested her head on his shoulder. Sometime during the night, Buck had fallen asleep. When he woke up, Lucy was gone, and his world was shattered.

They say that time heals all wounds, but Buck wasn't sure that was the case when you lost your closest friend. And even now, all these years later, he missed her more and more each day.

Buck always thought back to that Sunday morning when the family had gathered for a private ceremony at the little dock along the Gunnison River to scatter Lucy's ashes. Each family member got to say a few words about Lucy, and when they finished and turned to go, they were stunned to see several hundred of their neighbors and friends standing behind them in the park. Word had gotten out about their private service, and everyone turned out to pay tribute to Lucy. The affair turned into a huge party, with plenty of food and drinks. Lucy never wanted any kind of service, but Buck figured she would have loved this spontaneous outpouring of love.

| 6 |

Chapter Six

Buck stopped at the roadblock and waited as the deputy on duty approached his Jeep.

"Sorry, sir. Road's closed ahead due to a mudslide. You'll need to exit here and follow the detour signs."

Buck held up his badge and ID. The deputy lifted his digital notepad, ran his finger down a list and nodded. He walked over to the makeshift gate and pulled the board out of the way so Buck could pass through. Buck nodded to the deputy, drove up the ramp and headed east on I-70 westbound.

Eight miles into the canyon, Buck stopped behind several emergency and government vehicles. He shut off the engine, grabbed his backpack off the passenger seat and slid out of the Jeep. He stretched and tried to get rid of the kinks in his back. It had been a long drive, and it felt good to be on the ground again. He looked at the enormous wall of boulders spanning the canyon and was astonished by the size of the rockfall. The pictures the director had sent him did not do the destruction justice.

Buck walked around all the vehicles and stopped at the yellow crime scene tape that had been stretched along the end of the road to prevent folks from walking off the edge. He shook hands with several of the people standing near the edge and introduced himself to a few of those he didn't know, which was not a lot.

People who knew Buck always joked that there wasn't anyone in Colorado that Buck didn't know. Although that wasn't true by a long shot, the number of people Buck knew and who knew Buck was astounding.

Tom Holland separated himself from a large group of folks wearing hard hats and yellow safety vests and approached Buck.

"Buck Taylor, as I live and breathe. Looks like you drew the short straw." He shook Buck's hand.

"Tom," said Buck. "Looks like you got the bigwigs from Denver here." He looked over the edge of the road. "Hell of a mess."

"Got that right on both counts. Hell of a mess, and this is only part of the bigwigs. Tomorrow, the secretary of transportation arrives with his entourage. Can't wait." Tom laughed. "Gonna take a lot of brain power to get this all figured out." He got a serious look on his face and looked around before speaking.

"What have they told you so far?" asked Tom. "The governor clamped a lid on the whole thing, but he made it sound like this might be more than a natural event."

Buck looked over Tom's shoulder at the group at the edge of the road and leaned in. "For right now, I'm here to figure out what happened to a missing state trooper. Anything more will depend on what we find out about that. How much do they all know?"

"At this point, all indications are that this was a massive earthquake or some other natural phenomenon. Anything more than that will depend on what you find. So that's the story we're sticking with. I need to get back to the group. You need anything, let me or Rebecca know."

Buck turned around and spotted Franklin Williams walking towards him. Franklin was the lead forensic tech based out of the CBI office in Grand Junction. He was a distinguished-looking Black man who stood about four inches taller than Buck but weighed about the same. He had short gray hair and a gray goatee. He had been with CBI for more than thirty years. He shook hands with Buck.

"Buck. Looks like a big rock pile. What are we looking for?"

Buck laughed. "Yeah. Our job is to determine what happened to a missing trooper."

"Right," said Franklin. "So, what's our real job?"

Buck looked back towards the group at the end of the road. He turned back to Franklin. "We need to determine if this was a natural disaster or a man-made catastrophe."

"I'm guessing the governor has some doubts about the origin of the slide?"

"He wants to cover all his bases, but there's a question about what the trooper's dashcam captured that could lead us down a different path."

Franklin nodded. "We'll start collecting samples. It's not gonna be easy, but we'll see what we can find."

"Okay," said Buck. "Let's get some samples from the other side of the rockfall as well. I was told the Hanging Lake Tunnel has suffered some serious damage, but you might get some dust samples at the Dotsero end. You're gonna have to send someone over Cottonwood Pass to get there, and the eastbound lanes below us are open to this point as well. You can use the Grizzly Creek Rest Area to stage. Let me know what you need."

They shook hands and Buck walked back to his Jeep, stopping to talk with some of the emergency personnel he passed as he went. He reached his Jeep, tossed in his backpack and took one more look at the massive rock wall that used to be the canyon. He slid into his Jeep and backed up until he could turn around. He stopped next to the two smashed cars along the side of the road and sent Franklin a text to check the cars for explosive residue, then continued to meet Bax and Paul in town.

Buck pulled into the parking lot of the Riverside Lounge, parked his Jeep and headed into the restaurant. He found Bax and Paul sitting at a table in the back that had a great view of the Roaring Fork River and slid into the seat next to Bax. He looked out the window and wondered if he'd have a chance to get in some fishing.

Paul Webber was over six foot four with a muscular physique. He had joined CBI seven years earlier after spending ten years with the Dallas, Texas, police department. His last post had been as a homicide detective. Paul may have seemed like a giant, but those who knew him knew he was a pussycat. He was one of the most soft-spoken men Buck had ever met.

Paul had been instrumental in helping Buck find the hiding spot of Alicia Hawkins, a young serial killer who had returned to her hometown of Aspen, Colorado, and worked hard to fulfill a promise she made to her grandfather, an unknown serial killer from the late sixties who had murdered fifteen young women before an accident ended his career. Alicia had discovered the identity of her grandfather's sixteenth victim, a woman who was still alive and living in Aspen, and she had decided to honor her grandfather's death by killing his sixteenth victim, who would also be her sixteenth victim. If not for Buck and Paul, she would have succeeded in creating a sick legacy that would have long outlived her and inspired others.

At thirty-four years old, Ashley Baxter was the youngest agent in the Grand Junction Field Office. She'd joined CBI straight out of college, and, having had no experience in the field, she valued the time she got to spend with Buck, who became her mentor. Bax also became a kind of surrogate daughter to Buck and made sure he got enough sleep and food while they were on an investigation. She was fond of Buck, and he felt the same way about her.

Bax stood about five foot six with blue eyes and blond hair that she often kept tied in a ponytail that hung through the hole in the back of her CBI cap. Some people would describe her as husky, or what used to be called having a "mountain girl" figure. She wasn't gorgeous, but she was pretty enough to turn men's heads when she entered a room, until they spotted the badge and gun clipped to her belt. She had been with the Colorado Bureau of Investigation for eleven years and had earned the respect of her team-mates.

Buck sipped from the cold glass of Coke that sat on the table in front of his seat. Buck's Coke drinking was well known around the CBI office, but it also seemed that no matter where he went around the state, someone always had a cold Coke waiting for him.

They waited to talk until the waitress had taken their orders and then Bax started.

"We checked in with Sheriff Weaver and Chief Molina. They have a command center set up in Vogelaar Park. Right now, they appear to have all the help they need, but once the governor's plans are settled, the town is going to be overrun with contractors and more. Paul was able to get us rooms in Carbondale at a little B and B and they have a small conference room we can set up in. We have the place all to ourselves for as long as we need it."

Paul nodded. "The woman who owns it went to school with a friend of my wife's. We won't be disturbed. Since we are now part of the governor's conspiracy of silence, how do we want to start?"

The waitress brought over their dinners, set them on the table and asked if they needed anything else. Bax thanked her and she headed to another table. They talked while they ate.

"I've asked Franklin to take air and dust samples from the rockslide. There're two smashed cars down from the destruction area that could have some trace on them. He's going to send someone over to the other side to check for samples at the tunnel entrance. I've asked George and Mel to pull all the CDOT video from the canyon and from the trooper's dash and body cameras. Paul, work with them and see what you can see and check to see how far they've gotten with social media."

"You think someone may be bragging about blowing up the canyon?" asked Paul.

"It's one avenue we need to look at, but here's something to consider. If it was an earthquake that brought down the canyon, why have there not been any aftershocks? Seems odd to me, but I have a call in to the National Earthquake Information Center in Golden to get some answers."

"What do you want me to do?" asked Bax.

Buck finished his cheeseburger and pushed his plate to the middle of the table. "Tomorrow, you and I are heading over to Gypsum. I want to see if we can get into the monitoring station in the tunnel."

Buck called for the check and they each left money on the table, including a nice tip for the waitress. They headed for their Jeeps. Tomorrow would hopefully give them some direction.

| 7 |

Chapter Seven

Buck and Bax were sitting on a park bench outside the command center tent, eating breakfast burritos from one of the local food trucks. Bax had her morning coffee and Buck was drinking from the first of what would be many bottles of Coke.

"So, what are we looking for in the tunnel?" asked Bax.

"Not sure," said Buck as he walked over to the trash can and dropped in the wrapper from his breakfast. "I'd like to try to get to the west end of the tunnel so we can see the damage on that side, and I'd like to get into the traffic monitoring station. I'm not sure if all the cameras are connected to the cloud, so I'd like to see what they might have picked up."

Buck checked his watch, pulled out his phone and dialed a number. Max Clinton answered on the second ring.

"Hey, Buck. How's my favorite cop?"

"Great, Max. I'm looking for some help and thought of you first."

Dr. Maxine Clinton was the director of the State Crime Lab and one of Buck's oldest and dearest friends. She was a matronly woman in her late sixties, about five foot five, with short gray hair. She thought she carried around an extra fifteen pounds she didn't need, but she was still a handsome woman. Married for forty years, Max had four children, eleven grandchildren and six great-grandchildren. She lived in a 150-year-old farmhouse in Pueblo, where she liked to tend her garden, sit on her porch and drink iced tea. She was also a bourbon girl and could drink most people under the table. She was loud and outspoken, but she knew her job.

Max had received her PhD in biology from the University of Colorado and worked as a biology professor for twenty years before joining CBI. She was a tough taskmaster with a belief system that didn't allow for defeat. Her goal was to give the crime investigator, no matter which department or municipality they worked for, all the information they would need to solve any crime. She held that as a sacred obligation to the victims. She was dedicated to her job and her staff, and the team at the lab worshipped her.

Buck would have been included in that group. Many times, during a challenging investigation, it was Max and her team that lit the spark that led to a breakthrough. Max was one of Buck's favorite people, and she felt the same way about him.

"So, what's up?" she asked.

"We're working on the rockslide in Glenwood Canyon, and I need some expertise. I was hoping you might know someone close by who can meet me at the slide and help me understand the geology of the canyon and whether this was natural or something else."

The people Buck worked with always joked that there wasn't anyone in Colorado that Buck didn't know. But Max was way ahead of him in that department. She had contacts worldwide and never failed to get him the answers he needed.

During one recent case, Buck was looking for information on infrasound weapons and their effect on the body. Within a couple of hours, Buck was on the phone with a colleague of Max's, who was an expert in those types of weapons.

"Let me make a call. I know just the person, if he's available. I'll have him call you. Do you think this was a man-made event?"

"Not sure. We just got here last night, but the governor wants to cover all the bases. So far, nothing jumps out that says this is anything but a natural event, but I want to make sure, and with all kinds of state and federal people running around, I'm guessing we are gonna get a lot of differing opinions. That's why I need my own expert."

"Got it. I'll make that call." She ended the call the way she always did.

"You're a good man, Buck Taylor. God will watch over you."

Buck wasn't much of a religious man. He hadn't been to church in forty years. He had been raised Catholic but left the church right after confirmation. He always had too many questions about the teachings and too many people telling him that he had to have faith. That wasn't the answer he was looking for. He had a lot of friends, Max among them, who had always offered a prayer when Lucy was dying. He never once rejected any of those offers, often smiling and thanking them for their kind thoughts.

Buck had realized long ago that it wasn't God and faith he had a problem with; it was organized religion. In his many years in law enforcement, he had seen too many times the aftereffects of someone's religious beliefs. It amazed him that so many people of faith could cause so much hatred and crime. But then, nonbelievers created just as much havoc.

Buck always believed there was a higher power, but he didn't believe that whatever that power was, it cared about one individual over another. His football coach always offered a prayer before each game, asking for help in defeating the other team. He always suspected the other team's coach was doing the same thing. So, how did God decide which team should win?

He knew a lot of people who said a lot of prayers for Lucy over the five years she was sick, but in the end, she still died. And she was the last person who should have gotten cancer. But Buck didn't carry any hatred. Whom could he get mad at? Whom could he blame?

Buck believed that there are spirits or a force all around us, and he always thanked them for allowing him to enjoy the hike, catch fish, or see the sunrise and the sunset. It wasn't religion. It was something deeper. Something Buck didn't understand. He just accepted it. But no matter what, he always appreciated it when Max told him God was watching over him. After all, what could it hurt?

Buck set his phone on the table and took a drink from the bottle. His phone rang and he checked the number and answered.

"Hey, George. What have you got?"

"Well, good morning to you too." George laughed. "Wanted to give you a quick update. Mel has been surfing the web and so far, there is no one claiming responsibility for the rockslide. She set up a crawler that will alert us if anything pops up. Second. We sent the trooper's dashcam video to the State Crime Lab to see if their guys can clean it up better than we can. I just got off the phone with the camera manufacturer and he is of the same opinion we are. It's possible that the pressure wave fried the circuits and that's what caused the white flash, but he's leaning more towards an explosion. He told me that if it was pressure, the circuits would have fried slowly, and the screen would have gradually turned white. He said the windshield would have prevented a rapid pressure-based failure. Mel just uploaded the footage from the traffic cams in the canyon and we will start on those now."

"Great work, George. Keep me posted. Bax and I are gonna see if we can get into the tunnel control room and see if they have other videos that might not be on the cloud. I'll let you know."

Buck disconnected the call and looked at Bax.

"Looks like an explosion just moved to the top of our list," she said. She stood up and walked over to the trash can. "The governor will not be happy," she said as she returned to the table.

Buck nodded his head. "No, he won't. Let's get moving so we can see what we can find."

Bax grabbed her backpack and they headed for Buck's Jeep. They slid in and Buck pulled out of the parking lot, turned onto Highway 82 and headed for the turnoff for Cottonwood Pass Road. Despite it being just after sunrise, the traffic on the pass was slow and they speculated about the governor's plan to turn this into a four-lane highway bypass. As it was, CDOT was stopping all trucks and buses from using the pass, sending them either south and west to Highway 50 or north to Highway 40. Either way the detour would add hours to any trip. Cottonwood Pass made sense, but as it stood today, it was nowhere near ready for heavy traffic.

Buck hated wasting time sitting in traffic, so he made a mental note to see if he could get the governor to assign a Colorado Air National Guard helicopter to his team. He turned onto Cottonwood Pass Road and started the long slog to Gypsum.

| **8** |

Chapter Eight

Paul sat in the small community room in the B&B and stared at his laptop screen. He was connected over a secure internet link to the office in Grand Junction where Mel and George were looking at the same images. They had received the traffic cam video from the Hanging Lake tunnel monitoring station and were working frame by frame from midnight until the rockslide occurred.

Paul stopped the video. "Guys, here is where we pick up this semi entering the tunnel. That's just before three a.m. according to the time stamp. We have video of the semi leaving the tunnel a minute later and then nothing. If we look at the Grizzly Creek Rest Area camera for the following ten minutes or so, we never see the semi pass by. This must be the semi the trooper stopped to investigate."

"We agree, Paul," said Mel, "but look at the eastbound camera. We pick up an eastbound semi at around the same time passing the Grizzly Creek Rest Area camera, but we never pick it up on the tunnel cameras."

Paul watched the video feeds for a third and fourth time. "You're right, so where did that semi go, or did he get caught in the rockfall?"

"If you look carefully," said Mel. "That SUV in the outer lane was traveling right alongside the semi as it passed the camera. Four minutes later the SUV enters the tunnel, but no truck. He had to have stopped on the highway."

"Did one of the tunnel cameras capture the SUV's plate?" asked George.

Mel flipped through several more camera feeds. "Yeah, the mid-tunnel camera got a good view of the plate."

Paul checked the video Mel referenced and wrote down the plate. He entered it into the Colorado Department of Motor Vehicles website and found the information. He then did a license check and found the name and address of the SUV's owner. A few more clicks and he had a phone number for the owner. He disconnected his phone from the call with Mel and George and dialed a number. A man answered the phone.

"Hello," said the man.

"Sir, my name is Paul Webber and I'm an investigator with the Colorado Bureau of Investigation. Is this Robert Holmes?"

There was a moment of hesitancy on the phone. "Yes, this is he. What can I do for you, Officer?"

"Mr. Holmes. Were you driving through Glenwood Canyon night before last at about three a.m.?"

"Yeah, that sounds about right. Is this about the earthquake? My son told me about it. I must have just missed it."

"Yes, sir," said Paul. "A traffic camera captured your SUV passing the Grizzly Creek Rest Area and at the time, you were driving alongside a semi. Do you remember that?"

A moment of silence. "Yeah. That's right. Why do you ask?"

"We have you entering the Hanging Lake Tunnel a few minutes later, but the semi never appears. Do you remember anything about what might have happened to the semi?"

"Yes, sir," said Mr. Holmes. "A little after the rest area, his brake lights came on and he slowed down like he was pulling off onto the shoulder." Another moment of hesitation. "You know, it's funny now that I think about it."

"How's that, Mr. Holmes?"

"There was a black SUV on the inner shoulder, and I remember thinking that it was nice of the trucker to pull over and see if they needed assistance. I was beat and just wanted to get home or I might have stopped, but by the time I saw them, it was too late. It was odd. They didn't have any lights on. I only spotted them when I came around the corner, and my headlights caught them. It's like the trucker knew they were there, because he wouldn't have seen them either on that curve."

"Sir," said Paul. "You keep saying them. Could you see how many people were in the SUV?"

"Yeah, there may have been more, but there was one guy standing behind the SUV and there was a passenger in the front seat. The window was down, so I could see him. Don't know if anyone else was in the SUV with him."

"Mr. Holmes, I appreciate you helping me out with this. We're trying to account for anyone that might have been caught in the landslide. Your information has been very helpful."

Paul hung up and dialed Mel and George. He relayed the conversation he had with Mr. Holmes.

"What are you thinking?" asked George.

Before he could answer, Mel came on the line. "Got it," she said. "I have a black SUV entering the tunnel eastbound moments before the landslide." She put the image up on the laptop screen and Paul enlarged it.

"There's only one person visible through the front windshield. Any chance we missed another SUV?"

"I wonder what happened to the passenger," said Paul. "Can we capture his plate?"

George enlarged the photo and they all stared at the image. "Part of the plate is obscured with tape or something," said Mel.

Paul's mind started working through different scenarios, but he kept coming back to the same conclusion. One he was not comfortable with, but that fit what they were looking at.

"Mel, can you dig through the tunnel video and see if you can pick up the same SUV entering the east entrance to the tunnel heading westbound?"

Paul sat for a few minutes while Mel looked through the videos from the tunnel traffic cameras.

"Got it, Paul. Came through a few minutes ahead of the semi. Same color, one driver, no passenger and the same obscured license plate. What the hell is going on?"

"I have an idea," said Paul. "See what you think. The SUV driver passes through the tunnel a few minutes ahead of the semi. He's alone. The semi comes through the tunnel but never gets to the Grizzly Creek Rest Area. We know the SUV turned around at Grizzly Creek and headed back eastbound, because Mr. Holmes spotted him parked on the side of the road. A second semi stops on the eastbound road by the SUV, per Mr. Holmes, and the SUV now has a driver and a passenger. We pick up the SUV a few minutes later, but no semi, and this time the driver is alone."

"I don't think this was an earthquake," said George.

"Right," said Paul. "I think we have two semis that parked on the highway, right above each other or at least close to each other. I think the SUV was waiting for the upper truck and picked up the driver, turned around at Grizzly Creek and waited for the second semi on the lower level."

"But," said Mel, "what happened to the semi drivers? The SUV only had the driver when it passed through the tunnel going eastbound."

"I think the drivers are dead," said Paul, "And buried under a mountain of boulders."

"Fuck, Paul," said George. "This was terrorism."

"Yeah, my thoughts exactly," said Paul. "Do me a favor, package this all up and send it to me. Any chance we can get facial rec on the driver?"

"We can try," said Mel, "but it's not a great picture."

"Okay, please try. Great work today, guys. I need to call Buck."

Paul disconnected the call and sat for a few minutes, looking at the picture of the black SUV on the laptop. "Who are you, you fuck, and why would you do this?"

He picked up his phone and dialed Buck.

Chapter Nine

The SUV driver parked in front of the Velasquez Enterprises headquarters building, slid his six-foot-four-inch frame out of the SUV and stretched. He reached in and grabbed his black Stetson off the front seat and placed it on his head. He looked at the company headquarters building. Ramone Velasquez had spared no expense to build his modern metal-and-glass monument to his empire. With glass windows running floor to ceiling, the three-story masterpiece was an incredible display of his wealth and business acumen. The driver thought it was a waste of money, but then money was no problem for his employer.

He strode across the parking lot, used his employee badge to pass through security, and waved to the two guards at the front desk. They waved back. They had all heard of the driver, but he rarely showed up at the headquarters building.

There were a lot of stories about the mystery man, from the close-to-real to the absurd. Rumors circulated that he had been a criminal befriended by Velasquez, and one version of the story portrayed him as a former military special operator hired to address any potential issues. Another story said that he was the lover of either one of the sisters or of Velasquez himself.

The truth was much simpler. Dutch Heinrick and Ramone Velasquez had been friends since they were born. Dutch's father was the mine foreman in one of the early Velasquez mining ventures and the ore he produced made the Velasquez family a lot of money. When Dutch's father was killed in a cave-in, Ramone's father promised to take care of Dutch, and when Ramone took over the company, Dutch came with him.

Dutch had been in the marines, but he wasn't a special operator. He had been dishonorably discharged for beating another marine into a coma. After serving time in a military brig, he was sent out into the world, but now he was a lot stronger and smarter than when he first joined up. Ramone saw the potential and Dutch became his problem solver.

For Dutch, the arrangement was perfect. He was paid a lot of money and all he had to do was make sure people did what they were supposed to do or face the consequences. Dutch loved his job.

Today was a good day for Dutch. He liked keeping busy, and today was a busy day that had started very early and was not done yet.

Dutch checked the directory in the lobby, ran his finger down a long list of employees and found the one he needed. He pushed the up button and stepped into the elevator.

Dr. Timothy Woodman sat behind his desk in the small office that looked out over the high desert behind the headquarters building. He never liked the view, found it too stark for his tastes. He preferred to look at the mountains and lakes and trees. From his office, there wasn't a tree to be seen, and the mountains were too far away to enjoy.

He picked up the latest report from the mine and studied the notes from the on-site geologist. His first review of the rare earth metals discovery several months back indicated a large field. This new report was so much better, and surprising in a good way. The find was vast and would take years to develop. He knew this would make Ramone Velasquez very happy.

He had set the report aside and started an email to Ramone when his office door opened. He looked up and froze. He had never met the boss's enforcer, but there was no doubt that the monster of a man standing in his doorway was none other than Dutch Heinrick.

"Dr. Woodman?"

Timothy nodded. Dutch stepped into the office and closed the door.

"The boss wants to thank you personally for the extra work you helped him with. Everything worked as planned, maybe even better. There might be a nice reward coming your way since you have been discreet. But first, he wants me to take you up to look at one of the fault lines. He thinks the landslide might have caused some damage that might impact the new mine site."

Timothy pushed back in his chair. "Right now?"

"Yes, sir. You know Mr. Velasquez. He wants what he wants when he wants it. Sorry for the inconvenience."

Timothy stammered and stood up. "No inconvenience. Let me just shut down my computer."

"By the way," asked Dutch, "have you seen Dr. Mortensen? I stopped by his office, and no one has seen him today."

Timothy placed his laptop in his shoulder bag and looked at Dutch. "He called in sick this morning. Missed an important geology department meeting about the new finds. Why?"

"Mr. Velasquez asked me to bring him along since he helped you on the special project. I'll just catch up with him later."

Something about the way Dutch smiled when he said it sent an icy shiver up his spine. There was nothing threatening about the way he said it. Just a feeling. He slung his bag over his shoulder, and they headed out the door. Timothy stopped at the front desk and signed out, and they headed out the door and across the parking lot. As he walked around the SUV, he never noticed the black tape that obscured part of the license plate. He slid into the passenger seat and Dutch pulled out of the parking lot.

Dutch followed the main driveway away from the building and turned onto an old dirt road that led farther up into the dry, dusty hills.

Timothy tried to make small talk with Dutch, but he was focused on the drive, so he sat back and pulled out his phone. Half an hour later, Dutch stopped along a small ridge and killed the engine.

"Follow me, Doctor," he said as he slid out of the SUV.

Timothy slid out, slung his bag over his shoulder and ran to catch up to Dutch. He looked around as they walked. He knew there were several small fault lines throughout the area, but he didn't recognize the area they were walking through, and he wondered how the boss would have seen something this far from the landslide.

Dutch stopped at the end of a small crevice, more of a split in the crusty ground. Timothy stepped up next to him.

"What am I looking at?" asked Timothy, trying to catch his breath from the climb to the ridge.

Dutch pointed to a small crack at the bottom of the crevice about thirty feet down. "Mr. Velasquez doesn't remember that crack being here before the landslide."

Timothy set his bag on the ground and stepped closer to the edge, holding the shoulder bag strap in one hand. He shaded his eyes with his hand and stared into the abyss.

"I don't see anything that looks fresh," he said. He hadn't noticed Dutch take a couple of steps back from the edge.

The bullet made almost no sound as it entered his skull behind his left ear, and he never felt his body land on the hard ground at the bottom of the crevice. Dutch had grabbed for the shoulder bag, not realizing Timothy still held it, but he was a second too slow and the bag went into the crevice with Timothy. He walked to the edge and looked down.

"Fuck. How the hell am I gonna get that?"

He stared into the crevice. Not finding an easy answer, he removed the silencer from the black pistol and slid it into his back pocket. He put the pistol back in the shoulder holster under his leather vest and walked away.

"Ah, screw it. I'll tell him I destroyed it."

He pulled out his phone and speed-dialed a number.

"It's done, but Mortensen wasn't in his office," said Dutch when the call was answered.

"Find him," said the voice on the other end of the call.

"No problem."

He disconnected the call and headed back down the trail to his SUV. He would have preferred to finish this job and head home and get some sleep, but he knew that wasn't going to happen just yet. He slid into his SUV, pulled out his laptop and searched the company directory for Dr. Jack Mortensen's address. He found what he was looking for, put the car in drive and headed back towards the office and then on to Gypsum.

| **10** |

Chapter Ten

Buck stopped at the checkpoint just east of the Hanging Lake Tunnel and signed in with the sheriff's deputy on duty. He pulled forward and parked next to the tunnel entrance. He and Bax slid out of the Jeep and approached several men and women in hard hats and yellow safety vests. Buck recognized some of the people, shook hands and introduced Bax to several people she didn't know.

Tom Curtis was the senior construction engineer with the Colorado Department of Transportation, his white hard hat highlighted by his dark skin. He was younger than Buck by a few years and was tall and thin.

"Tom," said Buck. "Hell of a day, huh?"

Tom smiled weakly. "Could have been worse. Had this happened in the middle of the afternoon, the death toll could have been huge."

"Yeah," said Buck. "Tom, we need to look at the videos in the control room. Would that be okay?"

"The tunnel has suffered some damage, but not as bad as I was told to expect. We haven't checked it all. My guys are in there now doing that. I can't guarantee your safety, but if you're willing, then have at it. The tunnel still has power, so everything in the control room should still be working. Let me know if you need anything."

Buck thanked him, and he and Bax walked back to Buck's Jeep and grabbed a couple of yellow hard hats, yellow safety vests and N95 dust masks from the back. They grabbed their backpacks and a couple of bottles of water and walked into the tunnel.

The dust from the landslide had settled several inches thick on the floor of the tunnel, and Buck spotted numerous footprints as they walked. He was glad they were both wearing dust masks because a lot of the dust was very fine. They could hear Tom's team of engineers talking farther ahead. Halfway through the tunnel, Buck spotted the door to the control room and pushed it open. The sealed door had kept most of the dust and debris from entering the room.

The control room was larger than Buck expected, with concrete walls painted a light green color and lots of fluorescent lights. Despite its stark appearance, the room was pleasant, with a white concrete floor that shone as though it had just been polished. There was a restroom off to one side, and a long desk along one wall that was covered by monitors. Buck looked at the bank of monitors and was surprised to see that some monitors still had live images from the cameras. A lot of the images were blurry from the dust, and many had images at odd angles. Several of the monitors were blank.

They set down their backpacks and Bax pulled out her laptop and an HDMI cable and connected to the computer system. While she keyed in the access codes she had been given by CDOT, Buck pulled his big Maglite out of his backpack.

"I want to walk a little farther down the tunnel. I'll be back," he said. Bax nodded and went back to her laptop.

Buck pushed open the door and headed towards the west exit. He passed several teams of men and women checking the walls for cracks and taking measurements with some laser-guided equipment Buck had never seen before.

"Buck Taylor," said a voice from in front of him. Buck looked at a small group of people looking at a large crack in the ceiling.

"Hey, Cory. Been a long time." Buck shook hands with Cory Whitman. Cory was a bear of a man with red hair and a long red beard. He had been a tunnel engineer with CDOT for more than thirty years.

"You runnin' this show?" asked Buck.

"Tom needed the best of the best on this, so he called me away from my nice cushy desk chair and here I am. What brings CBI out on a landslide . . . or wasn't this just a landslide?"

"Nothing to worry about, Cory. The governor wants to cover all his bases. You know how he is." Buck and Cory laughed. Buck looked at the crack above them.

"That doesn't look good," he said.

"Nah. Looks can be deceiving," said Cory. "We sound tested it this morning and it's solid. The tunnel construction held up. Of course, if the slide had triggered closer to the tunnel, then all bets would be off."

"Any thoughts on why the canyon walls gave way? You guys have done a lot of work to stabilize things," said Buck.

"We've had a lot of slide issues over the past couple of years, as you know, but all our testing said the slides were mostly dirt and mud washing down the face. We thought the walls were tight. Seems we were wrong. The first report I got was an earthquake. I don't know about that. We've been working in the canyon one way or another for a long time and we've never had a quake that could cause this kind of damage."

"I'll let you get back to it," said Buck. They shook hands, and Buck walked through the rest of the tunnel and out into the canyon. Buck spotted more teams of government folks checking the roadway and the side walls of the tunnel. He walked out of the tunnel and headed down the roadway, stepping around various-sized boulders that littered the road. He stopped once he could see the huge wall of boulders and just stared. He walked over and looked down at the Colorado River below. The water level behind the rockslide was ten feet below the roadway he was standing on. They wouldn't have a lot of time to get their work done before the river level overflowed the road and flowed into the tunnel. He pulled out his phone and took several pictures of the damaged roadway, the canyon walls and the river below.

Buck spotted something metallic near the broken edge of the road, walked over and kneeled next to it. He pulled a pair of black nitrile gloves out of his pocket and put them on. He pushed a couple of small rocks aside and brushed off the flat piece of metal. He pulled out his phone and took several pictures, then pulled an evidence bag from his back pocket and placed the small metal piece in the bag. He knew what the piece was. The red-colored background with the white flame and the partial number could be only one thing. He was looking at part of the hazmat placard from the back of a trailer. He stood and was turning to walk back to the tunnel when he spotted two men in hard hats and vests waving at him.

The men approached. "Agent Taylor," said the first of the men to reach him. "Glad we found you." He stuck out his hand. "Dr. Jeremy Ratzenberger, USGS." He shook Buck's hand and pointed to the man behind him. "Todd Quinlin, my chief engineer."

Buck shook both their hands, but he couldn't take his eyes off Dr. Ratzenberger. The doctor was on the portly side and shorter than Buck, but it was the purple ponytail sticking out from under his hard hat that caught Buck's attention. Todd Quinlin appeared to be fresh out of college and was muscular with dark hair. They both wore jeans and heavy work boots, and their boots were scuffed and scraped. Both men walked past Buck and stood looking at the rockslide.

"Incredible," said Dr. Ratzenberger, pulling out his phone and taking a series of pictures of the rock face.

"Max Clinton asked us to track you down," said Todd, "and the folks in Glenwood Springs told us you were on this side of the slide. That's quite a drive without the highway."

They stared for a minute at the pile of rocks and did the same thing Buck had done: looked over the rail at the rising water.

"That's gonna make a mess," said Todd. Buck nodded.

"Gentlemen," said Buck. "What can I do for you?"

"Sorry," said Dr. Ratzenberger. "Max said you were looking for an earthquake expert. That's why she called me. We work for the U.S. Geological Survey, and we've been studying earthquakes all over the world for more years than either one of us cares to count. We were in Denver at a meeting when I got the call, and we hotfooted right over."

Buck looked at the massive rockslide behind him. "At first glance," said Buck, "what do you think?"

Dr. Ratzenberger stared at the side wall of the canyon. "We'll know more once we take a look up top, but if this was an earthquake, it's one of the strangest we've seen."

"How so?"

Dr. Ratzenberger looked at the rockslide and then at Buck. It was like he was trying to figure out how to say what he was thinking without getting too technical. He moved closer to the edge of what was left of the roadway.

"There are several fault lines that run through much of this area. None of them appear to traverse the area that collapsed, so an earthquake along a specific fault is unlikely. The other thing that's odd is the construction reports for I-70, which we pulled up on the way over. Experts stated in the reports that this rock wall was considered stable and hadn't moved in decades or even centuries. Now, decades of freeze-thaw cycles could have changed that, but that will require putting our eyes on the faults."

"Okay," said Buck. "So, what's the plan?"

"We are going to trace some of the faults on both sides of the canyon and see if we can determine what moved. With any luck, we should be able to give you a preliminary assessment in the next day or two."

Buck reached into his back pants pocket and handed them each a business card. "Thanks for your help," he said. "Let me know if you need anything."

Dr. Ratzenberger and Todd gave Buck their business cards and headed back the way they came. Buck stood for another minute looking at the canyon. He'd just turned to head back to the control center when his phone chimed with an incoming call.

| 11 |

Chapter Eleven

Buck pushed open the control room door and stepped through. He walked over to Bax, who was typing away on her laptop. She looked up.

"Did you talk to Paul?" she asked.

"Yeah, so we've got one, possibly two disappearing semis and an SUV that started out with two people and left with only one. He thinks it might be terrorism, but like I told him, there could be several other explanations. Let's not jump to any conclusions until we've had a chance to look at everything."

"Yeah," said Bax. "I picked up the SUV entering the tunnel heading westbound, followed a few minutes later by the first semi. He's right. The semi must have stopped, because it didn't get picked up on the Grizzly Creek camera. Also, as you can see, there is something obscuring the license plate, maybe tape. Who knows at this point. In this picture, we can only see the driver, and he has his hat pulled down like he's avoiding the cameras. No clear facial view."

"That must be the semi the trooper stopped for," said Buck.

"I would agree," said Bax.

"Did any of the cameras pick up any marking on the truck or the trailer?"

"Not that I've found so far. I'll keep looking," said Bax. She pointed to the monitor next to her, which showed a still picture from the Grizzly Creek Rest Area camera. She clicked a couple of buttons on her laptop.

The picture changed to a night view, and she advanced the camera until a semi came past. She froze the frame.

"This is the eastbound semi Paul was talking about. It passed the Grizzly Creek camera a few minutes before the rockslide. It never reached the west entrance to the tunnel." She paused the video. "Here is the SUV that was traveling alongside the semi." She clicked on another monitor and pointed.

"Here is what looks like the same SUV coming through the tunnel entrance a few minutes later. The license plate on this one was clear, and the owner of the SUV was the guy Paul spoke to, who remembered the semi stopping for another SUV on the side of the road."

She clicked on a third monitor. "This is the Grizzly Creek camera a few minutes later."

Buck watched the video as the SUV exited the westbound lanes, pulled through the rest area and reentered the highway heading eastbound. He could see a person sitting on the passenger side, but the back windows were too dark to see anything else.

Bax clicked her laptop, and the eastbound tunnel entrance appeared. "This video is four minutes later and only two minutes before the rockslide. The SUV from the Grizzly Creek camera enters the tunnel." She froze the video.

Buck got closer to the monitor. "Can you move this feed to one of those larger monitors?" he asked.

She clicked a few keys, and the image covered the entire wall. Buck looked at her, and she smiled. "Wanted to make it large enough so you wouldn't need your reading glasses."

Buck laughed. "You sure did that."

He walked to the front of the room and looked at the still photo. "There's definitely only one person in the front seat."

She backed up the video until the camera caught the license plate and froze the video. "I can't improve this any further, but as you can see, someone has used tape or something to partially cover the license plate and obscure the numbers and letters."

Buck stepped closer to the wall of monitors. "Okay," he said. "This is going to sound funny coming from me, but can George and Mel use some of that AI magic and give us some possibilities on what the plate might say?"

Bax laughed. "We're gonna make a tech geek out of you yet. Yeah. I sent this over to them and asked them to do just that. It's a long shot, but there may be just enough of each letter and number showing that we might get some options."

She clicked another button and the picture on the screen changed to the front windshield of the SUV and a clear picture of the driver's face.

"Where did you get this view?" asked Buck. "Paul said he didn't have a clear view of the driver."

"Paul didn't have access to this camera because it's only local. The camera is attached to one of the highway barricades. There's been a road crew in the tunnel for a couple of weeks, replacing lights and doing general maintenance. They have had several instances of drivers not paying attention to the work and almost hitting them, so CDOT put another camera on the barricade. The barricade had been set up earlier, and the camera was rolling. Looks like the driver wasn't aware of this camera."

"You think we can get facial rec from this?" asked Buck.

"It's possible. I sent the video to George and Mel to work their AI magic." She smiled. "They'll run the image through all the databases and then run it through social media."

She sat back from the desk. "What do you think? Was Paul right?"

Buck sat in one of the office chairs and looked at the monitor. He tented his hands in front of him and rested his chin on his outstretched fingers. He was silent for several minutes, and Bax sat back in her chair.

"Something's bothering me," he said. "Why didn't the cameras shake?" He looked at Bax. "Whenever they show earthquake videos on TV, the cameras always shake. These cameras didn't shake before the rockslide. If the rockslide was caused by an earthquake, I would think the cameras would have started to shake prior to the slide. The cameras didn't move until most of them glitched out when the slide hit. It's like nothing led up to the rockslide. I might be crazy, but that seems weird to me."

He looked at Bax, who ran a couple of the cameras back to just before the rockslide. She ran them forward at normal speed. "You're right. The cameras didn't move until they did. No preliminaries. Just wham and the lights went out."

"I think Paul might be right that this was human caused, but let's not jump to that conclusion until the geologists get me their preliminary report. I met them outside and they were heading up top to check on some fault lines. Let's wait for them."

"Anything else you want to look at while we're here?" asked Bax.

"No, let's head back to Glenwood Springs."

Bax put her laptop back in her backpack and slung it over her shoulder. They put on their dust masks and pushed open the control room door. They walked through the tunnel and put their gear in the back of Buck's Jeep. They took a minute to clear their throats with water and then slid into the Jeep. Buck pulled out of the parking lot, and they headed back to Gypsum to begin the long trek back over Cottonwood Pass.

| 12 |

Chapter Twelve

Jack Mortensen enjoyed his work with the Velasquez Mining Company, a subsidiary of Velasquez Enterprises. He'd started with the company right after graduating from the Colorado School of Mines with a master's degree in mine safety and a PhD in geology. His fascination with rocks and minerals began when he was a little kid, and he still possessed the very first mineral collection his father had given him when he graduated kindergarten. It was made of cardboard and had twenty small mineral specimens under little plastic bubbles. The description of each mineral was written under the sample, and he would spend hours reading and rereading the information. He was keeping it safe so that someday he could pass it along to his own children.

The sun shone through a gap in the bedroom curtains as he opened his eyes in the small bedroom in his house in Gypsum. He reached behind him and found the other side of the bed empty but still warm. He picked up his phone off the nightstand and looked at the time. It was early, and he was thinking about maybe grabbing another half hour of sleep when his wife pushed open the bedroom door. She held up her phone.

"There was a landslide last night. The highway through Glenwood Canyon was destroyed, and there's a huge rock dam across the river. We may have to evacuate if the water gets too high."

Jack grabbed his glasses off the dresser and opened a local news app on his phone. He read the article and looked at his wife. He was as white as the sheet he was sitting under.

"Jack, what's wrong?" she asked.

"N-n-nothing you need to worry about."

He threw off the sheets and slid out of bed. "I need to get going. The article said it was an earthquake. I need to get to the mine and make sure everything is okay."

He walked into the bathroom and closed the door, leaving Betty, his wife, standing in the doorway, dumbfounded. After a quick shower, he dressed in jeans and a flannel shirt and slid on his steel-toed work boots. He walked into the kitchen and Betty placed a bowl of cereal and a cup of black coffee in front of him.

"Jack, what's going on? You turned white as a ghost when you read the article. What aren't you telling me?"

"It's nothing, Bet. I have a few things to check on at the mine, but I may end up working late tonight. I'll try to call you if that happens."

"But Jack. What if . . ."

He stood and grabbed both her arms. "There's nothing to worry about. I'll call you later and we can talk about it, but right now, I have to get going."

Jack finished his breakfast, stood, kissed Betty and headed for his pickup truck. He climbed onto the seat, threw his backpack on the passenger seat and sat for a few minutes, his mind racing.

"They didn't tell me it was happening this morning. What the hell is going on? I should call Timothy. He should be in the office right now."

He pulled out his phone and clicked on the number for Timothy Woodman, but the phone went straight to voice mail. He hung up and dialed the security desk at the office.

"Security. How can I help you?"

"Hi, Marty, Jack Mortensen."

"Hey, Dr. Mortensen. Did you hear about the earthquake this morning? Dammed up the whole Colorado River. What a mess."

"Yeah, Marty. Listen, did Timothy Woodman check in this morning?"

"Yeah, he must have come in early, because he was already checked in when I got here for my shift."

"Is he still checked in, Marty? I tried his cell phone, but it went straight to voice mail."

"No, Doc. He left about an hour ago with Mr. Heinrick."

"Thanks, Marty."

Jack hung up, his hands shaking so much that the phone slipped and fell onto his leg.

"Shit, why would he leave with Heinrick? That guy's a creep. What the hell is going on?"

He closed the door, started the truck and backed out of the driveway. He didn't notice his wife watching him out the front window with her arms wrapped around herself and a concerned look on her face. He turned onto the interstate and headed for the office.

After passing through a state patrol roadblock, he pulled onto the road leading to the office but stopped short when he spotted Dutch Heinrick sliding out of his SUV, alone, and talking on the phone. He wondered where Timothy was, but he decided he wasn't going to wait around to find out. Something wasn't right.

He turned around and headed back the way he came. He needed to get Betty, and they needed to take a vacation someplace away from here. He drove onto I-70 Eastbound, drove the twenty minutes to Gypsum, and exited onto US 6. He cruised down Valley Road, turned left onto Chatfield Lane and headed for his house on Springfield Street. At the end of the block, he stopped.

Parked in front of his house was a jacked-up yellow Ford F-150 with huge all-terrain tires, the tailgate covered with bumper stickers. Two burly guys with bald heads and wearing leather vests were walking up his front walk. "This isn't good," he said out loud to no one. He watched as his wife opened the door. She spoke to the two men for a moment and started to close the door when they pushed their way in, and the door closed.

Jack pulled back out of his street and headed back to the interstate. He figured his wife would be okay since they were looking for him and wouldn't hurt her. He turned onto the interstate heading east and hit the gas. He had no idea where he was going, he just knew he needed to get away from Gypsum as fast as possible.

Chapter Thirteen

Dutch Heinrick pulled his SUV to the curb and parked behind the yellow pickup truck. He shook his head. "Fuck. They could have driven something less noticeable."

He slid out of the truck, looked around the quiet neighborhood, didn't notice anyone watching and walked up the sidewalk to the front door. He pushed open the door and stepped inside.

Betty Mortensen was sitting in a high-backed chair in the middle of the kitchen with her hands duct-taped behind her and her legs duct-taped to the chair legs. Her pink robe was open at the top, exposing her petite breasts, and her left eye was closed and turning purple. She had a split lip and blood had dripped onto her chest.

Dutch stepped into the kitchen and looked at the two guys sitting at the kitchen table drinking coffee.

"She says she doesn't know where her husband is," said goon number one.

He walked over, placed his hands on her jaw and looked at her lip and eye. He reached down, pulled her robe closed and looked at the two guys.

"I told your boss that she wasn't to be hurt."

"We were just having a little fun, that's all. She'll heal up just fine," said goon number two.

Dutch kneeled in front of Betty. "Mrs. Mortensen, I'm sorry about this. You were not to be touched. Did they hurt you anyplace else?"

She shook her head.

"Betty, may I call you Betty? I'm Dutch. We met at the office for a Christmas party a couple of years back. I need to know where your husband is. Can you help me out?"

She looked up at Dutch through her one good eye. "I told them he left for work about an hour ago. Why won't you believe me?" Her body trembled.

"He never showed up for work, and we're worried about him. He was supposed to meet with Mr. Velasquez this morning to talk about a new project at the mine, but he never showed. Now, think hard. Is there any place he would have gone? Maybe some secret place that only you two know about?"

Betty shook her head and tears flowed down her cheeks. "No. He went to work."

"It's okay, Betty," he said softly. "We'll just look around the house if you don't mind and see if we can find anything that might help us find him."

He stood up and walked over to the table. He leaned down and whispered, "Tear this place apart, but do it quietly. Laptop, phone, iPad, anything at all."

He walked to the refrigerator as the two guys left the kitchen, opened the door and pulled out a cold bottle of water. He twisted the cap, walked back to Betty, leaned down and put the bottle to her lips.

"A little cold water will make your mouth feel better."

He tipped the bottle and let Betty drink her fill. He stood up, placed the bottle on the table and looked around.

"You have a very nice house, Betty."

He looked out the kitchen window and the back door to make sure no one was watching. After twenty minutes, the guys came back.

"All we found was one phone. Flower case, so we figured it was hers."

He handed the phone to Dutch, who walked over to Betty and held up the phone.

"Betty, is this your phone? Love the case."

He held it so she could see it. "Do you know where your husband's laptop is?"

She shook her head. "He took his backpack with him. It's in there."

He stepped behind the chair. "You've been a big help, Betty, and I appreciate it."

The knife appeared out of nowhere and he slit Betty's throat from ear to ear. She struggled and gurgled and then fell silent. The two guys jumped back to avoid the spray and stared at the wound. He wiped the knife on her pink robe, leaving a long red stripe along the right shoulder and a large red puddle under the chair, and pointed towards the door.

He placed her phone in his pocket, looked around and followed the two guys out the door. They each climbed into their vehicles and left the small house on Springfield Street.

| 14 |

Chapter Fourteen

Buck pulled his Jeep into the parking lot of Abuela's Mexican Cantina in downtown Carbondale, parked and turned off the engine. He and Bax slid out of the seats and grabbed their backpacks. They stepped into the half-empty restaurant and spotted Paul sitting at a table for four in the back corner. The hostess, a medium-skinned woman with bright eyes and long hair pulled back in a French braid, welcomed them to the restaurant and told them to sit anywhere they liked.

Buck and Bax walked to the back corner and sat at Paul's table. He closed the lid on his laptop and slid it to the side.

Buck loved little local restaurants like this. He looked around at the comfortable chairs and all the bright festive art hanging on the walls. It gave you the feeling that you were eating in someone's kitchen, and the smells coming from the kitchen made his mouth water.

The waitress dropped off two more menus and took their drink order. Coke for Buck and a locally brewed Mexican style beer for Bax. They looked at the menus and when the waitress returned with their drinks, they ordered. Buck and Paul ordered the beef burrito platter, and Bax ordered the three-taco plate. They handed the waitress the menus, and she headed for the kitchen.

Paul looked from Bax to Buck. "Well, what do you think?"

"The video evidence is compelling," said Buck. "But I want to see what the geologists have to say and see what the science tells us before we call the governor. Did Franklin get the samples from the canyon to the state lab?"

"Yeah," said Paul. "They went by secure courier a couple of hours ago. Should be there by now. What are you hoping we find?"

"Something conclusive," said Buck. "Explosives residue would be great. Even a trace would give us a decent answer."

Bax took a sip of her beer. "That's delicious. Any luck with facial rec on the picture from the barrier camera?"

"Spoke to George and Mel a few minutes ago," said Paul. "The picture is grainy, but they thought they might be okay. Could take a while if the guy isn't in the system or on social media."

"What about the license plate?" asked Buck.

Paul waited to answer while the waitress set the plates on the table and then stepped away. "AI gave them one hundred twenty-seven possibilities. They're running them through the DMV to see if any are real plate combinations. Once that's done, they can narrow the search for a black Cadillac Escalade."

The conversation stopped as they dug into their dinners, and once finished, they pushed their plates aside. The waitress came by, picked up the plates and dropped off a couple of dessert menus, which led to another order from each of them. Before they could begin the next conversation, the waitress returned with their orders, and they stopped again to enjoy the food.

Buck finished his dessert, pushed the plate aside, leaned back in the chair and stretched, working out the kinks from the long drive over Cottonwood Pass and letting the meal and dessert settle. He leaned into the table.

"Anybody claiming responsibility for the rockslide?" he asked.

"The internet is buzzing. People complaining about the highway closing for past slides and people expressing concern for the environmental damage caused by the slide. Tons of conspiracy theories, from secret government tunnels crisscrossing the country to space-based laser weapons. It seems the crazies are out in force. Nothing worth anything, but George and Mel will continue to monitor, just in case."

"So, what's our plan for tomorrow?" asked Bax.

Buck thought for a minute. "Looks like we are stuck until we hear back from the geologists and the lab. Let's think about it overnight and talk about it at breakfast."

They each left money on the table and Buck nodded to the waitress, who walked over, picked up the cash and thanked them. They headed out into the cool evening, and Buck looked at the clouds forming overhead.

"Won't be long till we get some snow. Bet we get an overnight freeze."

They slid into their respective Jeeps, drove the three blocks to the B&B and headed for their rooms.

Buck's room was at the end of the short hall and had a view of the mountains to the west. It was comfortable with bright-colored blankets on the bed. He kicked off his shoes and sat on the desk chair. He pulled out his phone and hit the speed dial button.

"Evening, Buck," said Director Jackson. "How's it going?"

"Well, sir. We made some good progress today."

He told him about the videos from the tunnel and rest area cameras, the two semis and the black SUV.

"You think the semis could have been loaded with explosives?" asked the director.

"Well, I'm not ready to rule anything out yet, but the behavior of the black SUV and the missing passenger gives me pause. Once the geologists report back, we should be able to come up with an answer for the governor."

"Okay, Buck, get some sleep and let me know if you need anything."

Buck disconnected the call, closed his eyes and fell asleep in the chair.

| 15 |

Chapter Fifteen

Dr. Jeremy Ratzenberger and Todd Quinlin parked their SUV at the end of a long dirt track on the north side of Glenwood Canyon, outside the town of Dotsero. They grabbed their backpacks from the back and threw four long lengths of climbing rope over their shoulders. The path they were following was overgrown and near impossible to see unless you knew where to look, but with the closure of I-70 through the canyon, this was the only way to reach the No Name Fault.

After gaining elevation over the last two hours, they reached their destination about midday. They dropped their loads and Dr. Ratzenberger pulled a pair of binoculars out of his backpack and scanned the stratified wall in front of them. While he did that, Todd pulled a laser measuring device out of his backpack and took readings on specific landmarks along the fault line. He made notations and recorded the readings on his digital tablet.

"I don't see any slippage along the fault line," said Dr. Ratzenberger. "What do your readings show compared to the CDOT readings from when the highway was built?"

Todd set down the laser measurer and opened a file on his tablet. He opened a page to a list of seismic readings, ran his finger down the list and checked his notations.

"There's been some minor movement over the years, but nothing that would contribute to the damage we saw outside the tunnel. Most of the readings are negligible."

"Let's take a closer look," said the doctor.

They picked up their loads and continued the trek to the stratified wall's base, dropping their loads and pulling out their climbing harnesses. Todd hooked onto the climbing rope and approached the wall.

"On belay," he said.

"Belay on," said the doctor.

Todd reached up for his first handhold and started climbing the wall. Ten feet up, he pulled a small nut off his harness, slid it into a crack in the rock and pulled to make sure it was anchored. He slipped a carabiner onto the rope hanging from the nut, twisted the clip until it was tight and pulled to make sure it held. Satisfied, he clipped into the carabiner and continued climbing. He continued this same pattern every ten to fifteen feet for the next hour and a half until he reached the No Name fault line, where he anchored in.

He scanned the fault line for ten feet on either side of his position, pulled his phone, and took several high-resolution photos. He called down to the doctor and reversed the process, removing the nuts and cams as he lowered himself down the wall.

Once on the ground, he unstrapped his harness, recoiled the rope and handed the doctor his phone. Dr. Ratzenberger looked at the photos.

"Just like we thought. No movement. I don't think the slide was caused by an earthquake, but let's head over to the other side of the canyon. There's that large group of fault lines north of Cottonwood Pass Road. Let's check those to be sure."

They grabbed their gear and headed back to where they parked, loaded it and headed the SUV back towards Dotsero. After inching along Cottonwood Pass Road with all the westbound traffic, Todd took a right at a small farm road, crossed over the grate and continued north for another mile. He stopped in a small group of trees and parked. With dusk coming on, they set up camp in the trees, ate a meal of freeze-dried foods and crawled into their sleeping bags, sleeping cowboy style, out under the stars. They woke to frost on their sleeping bags, fired up a small backpacking stove and cooked breakfast.

Once again, they grabbed their gear and started a short one-mile trek over uneven ground until they reached the first of about a dozen unnamed fault lines that covered the area. They took measurements, compared them to historic readings and moved on. By midmorning, they had covered six of the lines and approached a crevice that had cracked open during an earthquake many eons ago.

Todd dropped his backpack and climbing ropes and walked up to the edge. Shading his eyes with his hands, he looked into the crevice and called over to the doctor. Dr. Ratzenberger stepped up to the edge. Todd pointed into the crevice.

"I think there's a person down there?"

The doctor looked at where he was pointing. "I think you're right. Hey, buddy, can you hear us? Hey, up here." He looked at Todd. "Grab your gear. He might be still alive."

"How the hell did he get down there? It's not like the crevice is hidden and you could fall into it by accident," asked Todd as he strapped on his harness. The doctor found a large boulder and tied off the rope so they had a decent anchor, and he threw the rope into the crevice.

The crevice wasn't deep, maybe thirty feet or so, but it was narrow and would be a tight fit for Todd, who clipped onto the rope and stepped over the lip. Using his feet, he worked his way down until he hit the bottom. He unclipped and stepped over to the body. He was shocked when he looked at the head wound.

He yelled up to the doctor. "Hey, Doc. This guy's been shot. He's dead."

He stepped away from the body, clipped back onto the rope, and climbed out of the crevice.

"Fuck. He was shot in the head," he said as he unclipped from the rope and removed his harness.

Dr. Ratzenberger pulled his phone out of his back pocket, looked up a number and dialed. This was not how he had hoped to finish the day.

| 16 |

Chapter Sixteen

Bax, Buck and Paul were sitting in the command center tent that was set up in Vogelaar Park, along with about a hundred other people, listening to the governor and his team talking about progress on widening Cottonwood Pass Road and making it a legitimate alternate route for the missing section of I-70. Buck was getting bored. Every time it sounded like progress was being made in the discussion, someone would oppose some part of the plan. Buck could see that the governor was getting frustrated. It had been two days since the rockslide had sealed off the canyon and he couldn't get people off dead center. Buck figured he would soon take things into his own hands and sidestep everyone.

Buck felt his phone vibrate, pulled it from his belt and looked at the number. He stood up and stepped out of the tent.

"Taylor."

"Agent Taylor, Jeremy Ratzenberger. Hope I didn't catch you at a bad moment."

"No, Doctor. Now's good. What have you got for me?"

"Well, sir. We have a problem."

"What kind of problem, Doctor?"

"We found a dead body in one of the fault lines. From the looks of it, it hasn't been dead long."

Buck had half an ear on what was happening in the tent, but at that, he turned and walked away.

"Doctor, did you just say you found a dead body?"

"Yes, Agent Taylor. We were investigating a series of small fault lines north of Cottonwood Pass Road and discovered a body at the bottom of a crevice. According to Todd, who climbed into the crevice, the body is a man, and he was shot in the head."

"Doctor, can you send me your coordinates?"

"Yes, sir. Sending them now," said the doctor. "What should we do?"

"Doctor, please stay right there and make sure no one goes near the body. I'm on my way."

Buck disconnected the call, returned to the tent and tapped Bax and Paul on the shoulder. They looked up, and he pointed with his chin towards the entrance. They stood up, grabbed their backpacks off the floor and headed for the tent flaps. Buck walked forward a few rows, tapped Garfield County Sheriff Paul Weaver on the arm and did the same thing. The sheriff spoke with the person sitting next to him, then stood up and followed Buck.

As Buck reached the tent flaps, he looked back and noticed that the governor, still talking, had his eyes on Buck. Buck stepped through the flaps and led Bax and the sheriff away from the tent.

"What's going on, Buck?" asked Sheriff Weaver.

"I just got a call from the USGS geologist I've got working in the field. They found a body at the bottom of one of the fault lines they were looking at off Cottonwood Pass Road. I sent you the coordinates. Bax and I are heading up there now."

"I've got a deputy sitting on the summit monitoring traffic. I'll have him head over and set up a perimeter. I'll follow you guys after I call the office."

The sheriff stepped away, pulling out his phone. Buck looked at Bax. "Why don't you head up there? I'll follow as soon as I call Sima and Franklin. I'm gonna see if the director can get them a chopper. It will be faster."

"You got it, Buck. I'll see you there."

"Paul, work with George and Mel and let's narrow down the list of black SUVs and open an investigation file."

Around the CBI office, Buck was known as a technological dinosaur. He was happiest when he had paper files and his little notebook, but the times were changing, and Buck tried to change with them.

CBI had gone digital a couple of years back, so instead of having a blue binder for each case, Buck just had to open a program on his laptop. The new case was automatically assigned a case number, and Buck would list everyone who needed access to the file and send them email invites. All evidence, lab reports, photos, etc., that were part of the case would be uploaded to the file, and anyone needing access just had to open the file. That was much better than the old system, where everything had been placed in the binder by hand, and Buck would spend half his time tracking down who had the binder.

Even for a tech dinosaur like Buck, this made his life so much easier, and he had ready access to anything he needed. Buck just had to click on a file and open the chronology page, which was the first page in the file. Nothing was ever entered into the file without a note entered in the chronology first. The chronology kept track of everything that happened in the investigation.

"No worries, Buck," said Paul. He turned and headed for his Jeep. Buck pulled out his phone and speed-dialed a number. The director answered right away.

"Hey, Buck. What's up?"

"Afternoon, sir. I just got a call from the geologist. They found a dead body at the bottom of one of the fault lines they were investigating. I need to mobilize the troops, but I have a favor to ask. Can you get a CANG chopper to pick up Franklin, his team and Sima and get them to the coordinates I am sending you? It will be faster. Traffic on Cottonwood Pass Road is a nightmare."

"No problem, Buck. The governor said whatever we need. You think this has something to do with the rockslide?"

"Don't know, sir, but it seems odd that we would find a body in a fault line we are looking at."

"Buck, I read your report last night. I get the feeling you are leaning towards this not being a natural disaster. Am I right?"

"Possibly, sir. This body may give us some answers."

"Okay, Buck. Call Franklin and Sima and tell them to head to the Grand Junction Airport. I'll get the chopper in the air."

"Thanks, sir."

Buck disconnected the call, called Franklin Williams and Dr. Sima Kalishe and gave them the information he had just given the director. They both indicated they would head right over to the airport. He thanked them and hung up. He turned to head for his Jeep and found Governor Kennedy standing in front of him. He reached out and shook Buck's hand.

"Buck, you look like something's going on. What's up?"

"Not sure yet, sir." He told the governor about the body in the crevice and that he had mobilized the team. The governor was quiet while Buck spoke.

"Coincidence, Buck, or something more nefarious?" asked the governor.

"We'll know soon enough, sir. It could be nothing, but someone shot in the head and dumped always gets my attention."

The governor looked around, then stepped closer to Buck. "What do you think so far, Buck? Was this natural or man-made?"

"Too early to say definitively, but with what we've uncovered so far, it looks less and less like a natural event."

"Okay, Buck. I'll let you get to it." They shook hands, and the governor headed back to the tent. Buck picked up his backpack and headed towards his Jeep. He threw his backpack onto the passenger seat, slid in and hit the gas. He hoped he wouldn't have to use the lights and siren, since there was little room to maneuver on the pass.

The traffic on Cottonwood Pass Road was flowing better today, and after an hour, Buck's GPS told him to take a left on a small dirt road. He turned and headed towards the flashing lights he could see in the distance. A CANG Blackhawk helicopter was sitting on a flat piece of ground a couple of yards from the emergency vehicles, its blades turning. Several white-clad figures were moving boxes of equipment from the chopper to where the vehicles were parked. Buck parked next to Bax's Jeep and slid out, grabbing his backpack.

The small group was standing near the crevice, and Bax was putting on her climbing harness. She'd spent many vacations rock and mountain climbing with her father and was an expert at both. She was talking to Sima and Franklin when Buck walked up.

"Sima, Franklin. You guys good?" he asked.

Dr. Sima Kalishe, dressed from head to toe in white Tyvek, was putting on her N95 mask when Buck walked up; she turned and shook his hand. Dr. Kalishe stood about five foot two. She had medium-dark skin and jet-black hair tied up in a bun, but her most striking feature was her incredible blue eyes.

Sima laughed. "I wish you would go work in some other part of the state. I haven't had a break in weeks, thanks to you."

Buck laughed. It had been a tough couple of months, first with the mass shooting at the drag club outside Grand Junction, where more than seventy people, both patrons and entertainers, perished, and then with the eleven bodies found buried under white roadside crosses on the Grand Mesa, the work of a serial killer of many years. Sima and her team had been busy.

Buck laughed. "Hey, look at it this way. This is only one body."

"Yeah," said Sima. "With you around, it's never just one body."

Everyone laughed, and Buck stepped over to Bax.

"What's the plan?" he asked.

Bax clipped her carabiner onto the rope that snaked down into the crevice, and she spun the lock. "I'm gonna go down and take a look. I'll take some pictures for Sima and Franklin. Not a lot of room to work down there. If Sima's good, Todd and I will hook up the body and pull it out. It will take too long to get search and rescue up here, so we'll take care of it."

"Okay. Be careful."

Buck stepped back to give her room, and she stepped off the top of the crevice and climbed to the bottom, where Todd was standing off to one side waiting. She pulled out her phone, switched to video and yelled up to the crowd at the top that she was filming. She moved towards the body. She examined the body and the shoulder bag from top to bottom and then sent the video to Buck's phone. She stood back and waited.

Buck's phone chimed. He pulled it from his belt and opened the text message with the attached video. Franklin and Sima stepped next to him and watched as he ran the video. He ran it several times until they both nodded. He walked over to the edge of the crevice.

"Okay, Bax. We're gonna send down a body bag and another rope."

While Buck was watching the video, the deputy—Gomez, according to the name tag on her uniform—had pulled her SUV around so it was facing the crevice and pulled out a long cable from the winch attached to the front bumper. Buck took the body bag from Franklin and attached it to the cable, and the deputy lowered the cable into the crevice.

"Got it," said Bax. "Give me another fifteen feet."

The deputy let out more cable till Bax yelled to stop. They waited a few minutes and then Bax yelled up to pull in the cable, which the deputy did. Bax and Todd climbed out of the crevice alongside the body bag to keep it from banging into the rough walls. At the top, Buck and Franklin grabbed the side handles, pulled it clear of the crevice and set it on the ground. Sima stepped over and unzipped the bag.

She took a liver temp and examined the body. She held up the two hands. "No defensive wounds." She put the hands down and moved the head from side to side. "One bullet hole behind the left ear." She pulled out the thermometer. "Based on rigor and liver temp, he's been dead at least twelve, but not more than twenty-four hours. I'll know more when we get him on the table. The rest of the scratches and bruising came from falling into the hole."

She zipped up the bag and Buck, Franklin, Sheriff Weaver and the deputy carried the bag to the helicopter and placed it on the floor. Dr. Kalishe and her assistant climbed into the chopper, and the rest stepped back as the rotors turned and the chopper lifted off.

Now out of her harness, Bax handed Franklin the shoulder bag, which he placed in a large evidence bag, sealed it and signed the flap. She looked at Buck.

"There's a laptop in the bag and he had a phone in his pocket." She held the phone up and handed it to Franklin. "Need to get those to Mel and George, and we'll need a warrant. I'll call Mel."

She handed Buck a leather trifold wallet, which he took after putting on a pair of black nitrile gloves. He opened the wallet and looked at the driver's license. He held it up so the sheriff could see. He pulled out his phone and took a picture of the license, attached it to an email and sent it to George with a note to do a full background check. He handed it to Franklin, and it went into another evidence bag.

"I'll call Eagle County and see if they can do the family notification," said Sheriff Weaver. "Let me know if you need anything else from me."

They shook hands, and he headed for his SUV after telling Deputy Gomez that she could head back to the top of the pass. Buck stepped over to Todd and Dr. Ratzenberger.

"Todd, thanks for your help today. I appreciate it."

"No problem," said Todd. "I'm gonna head back to the truck with our gear." He shook Buck's and Bax's hands and started loading up his gear. Buck looked at Dr. Ratzenberger.

"Quite the day, huh?"

"Yes. Not what I expected when we set out today."

"Doc. Any initial thoughts?" asked Buck.

"I can tell you conclusively that this was not an earthquake or any other geological phenomenon. There is no evidence in any of the fault lines that anything moved. I do not believe you are looking at a man-made incident, but I want to go back into the canyon and see which stratification level sheared off. Might tell us something."

Buck looked at Bax and then back to the doctor. "Without a doubt?"

"Yes, Agent Taylor. Without a doubt," he said. "I'll send you a full report when I get back to Denver, but I am certain of my findings, and Todd agrees. I don't know where that leaves you, Agent Taylor, but I hope you get to the bottom of this."

He walked away, stopped, turned and pulled something out of his pocket. He flipped it to Buck, who caught it and looked at the small crystalline rock. He looked at the doctor.

"That's a piece of neodymium, Agent Taylor. That's one of the seventeen rare earth metals. I found that yesterday morning while we were talking at the rockslide. That shouldn't be there. We need to look closer at the rockslide."

Dr. Ratzenberger and Todd grabbed their gear and headed towards their SUV. Buck turned and looked at Bax.

$$|\ \mathbf{17}\ |$$

Chapter Seventeen

Rodney stood in front of his boss's desk. His hands were shaking. "I'm telling you, boss, that Dutch guy is fucking nuts. He slit that woman's throat like it was nothing. Didn't even flinch."

"Yeah," said Boomer. "Son of a bitch wasn't even breathing heavy when he was done, he just wiped the bloody knife on her shoulder and walked away. Who does that kind of shit?"

Roger Burns looked up from his desk. The two guys standing in front of him were as hard as they come, and nothing had bothered them until today. Both men wore leather vests with patches all over, jeans and motorcycle boots. They had seen plenty of action, evidenced by noses that had been broken several times and an assortment of cuts and scrapes that had long since healed. They were no strangers to violence, but watching Dutch Heinrick slit that woman's throat without a second of hesitation got to them.

"Any word from the drivers?" asked Roger. "They should have checked in by now."

"No, sir," said Rodney. "You don't think they got caught in the explosion, do you?"

"They had enough time to get clear of the blast zone," said Roger. "Keep trying to get hold of them."

Rodney and Boomer left the office, and Roger leaned back in his chair and tented his fingers. He looked at the television hanging on the wall to the left of his desk. The national news had picked up the story of the rockslide, and he was looking at news helicopter pictures of the destruction.

Roger Burns was the owner of Roger Burns & Sons Demolition, Inc., one of the largest demolition contractors in the western United States. He had contracts with all the large mining operations, and his most prominent client was Velasquez Mining. He had been friends with Ramone and his father before him for more years than he could count, and that relationship had paid off in a big way, financially.

He glanced at the TV, propped his legs up on the desk and looked around his office. By most standards, his office was small for someone of his stature, but Roger liked it that way. He was never much for the limelight and didn't need to impress anyone by putting on airs. His office suited him just fine.

Roger was in his sixties but had the build of someone much younger. The muscles weren't from any gym but were developed over a long lifetime of hard work. His hair was gray, and his face had a lot of wrinkles on it, but each one came from a life experience, and he was proud of every one. His wife harped on him, saying that he needed a facelift, but he left that kind of crap to her. Roger was one tough son of a bitch, and he wanted people to know it.

He sat watching the news, thinking about the day Ramone and Gabriella Velasquez first came to him with the proposal. He thought Ramone was nuts. He knew Gabriella was nuts, but the proposal intrigued him—especially the part about the money. The prospect of making billions can steer a man's thinking, but now, as he watched the coverage and the talking heads discussing all the things that were impacted by the rockslide, he was having second thoughts about his involvement. Of course, there was the money.

The idea of blaming this on radical environmentalists and planting evidence sounded like fun. God knows how often environmentalists had gotten in the way of him doing his job. Ramone had told him that based on their geologist's reports, the road would be damaged, and the river would be blocked for a while, but the pictures showed a whole other story. He was glad that the news media was portraying this as an earthquake, but he knew Gabriella had all the evidence to the contrary, sitting, ready to go if needed.

His thoughts were interrupted by a knock at the door. "Come in."

The office door opened, and Keith Burns stepped into the office and closed the door. He stopped momentarily, looked at the destruction on the TV, walked over and stood in front of the desk.

Keith was his oldest son and the one who would inherit the company once Roger stepped down. He was of average height and weight, with dark wavy hair and a three-day stubble on his face. His piercing jade eyes switched focus and he looked at his father.

"Dad. We may have a problem," said Keith. "Our books and our inventory don't add up. We're missing between sixty thousand and one hundred thousand pounds of RDX that we have invoices for but were never shown in our inventory. The loading dock guys said they loaded two semi-trailers yesterday on your orders, but we don't show any trailers missing from our fleet. Any idea what's going on?"

He looked back at the TV and then at his father and waited for an answer. Roger shifted in his chair and looked out the window behind his desk.

"The RDX went to Velasquez, and the trailers were his."

"What do they need that much RDX for?"

"They're opening a new section of mine, and they didn't want to keep bothering us for more explosives since they had no idea what they were going to encounter. We were just acting as the middleman in this," said Roger.

"Who's doing the demolition for them? No one over there is qualified," asked Keith.

"Rodney and Boomer will handle the demo, just like always."

Keith could see the old man getting aggravated, but he had one more question and hoped he wouldn't get his head bitten off.

"Dad, did we get paid for the RDX?" He waited for the explosion he knew was coming.

Roger stood up and walked around the desk, clenching his fists as he moved. "What are you suggesting, boy? You think I did something shady, is that it? Let me tell you this."

He stopped to catch his breath. "I've been running this company for over forty years, and you've got the nerve to walk into my office and accuse me of doing something shady. Huh. You think your old man is a crook? You remember who paid for you to go to that fancy-ass school back east and who took care of you and your brother and sister after your mom died, and you dare to question anything I do in my own company."

"Dad, I wasn't accusing you . . ."

"Get the fuck out of my office and go do your damn job while you still have one, because if you ever question me again about anything that goes on around here, you'll find your ass out in the street so fast your head will spin."

Keith opened his mouth, but Roger cut him off. "Get the fuck out, and I don't want to hear about this again. You got it?"

Keith turned and raced for the door. He hated it when his old man got like this, but at least he wasn't running away with a broken nose. He opened the door, stepped through and pulled the door closed. Sharon, his dad's secretary, stopped clicking computer keys, looked at him and shook her head. She went back to typing.

Keith headed down the hall to his own office and closed the door. He sat in his desk chair and put his head in his hands. He wasn't sure why, but he had a bad feeling about this.

| 18 |

Chapter Eighteen

Buck, Bax and Franklin stayed at the crevice after everyone left to look around and ensure they hadn't missed anything. It might have also been that no one wanted to face the traffic on Cottonwood Pass Road. They walked the area, and Bax even got back into her harness and climbed back into the crevice again to look around.

The bullet casing wasn't located in the area, which led them to several conclusions. One was that the killer was a professional and had policed his brass. The second was that the victim was killed elsewhere and dumped. The only problem with that theory was the mile-long walk from the nearest parking location to the dump site. The third option was that the killer used a revolver. Now they needed to figure out which one it was.

They were heading for their Jeeps when Buck's phone rang. He looked at the number and answered.

"Hey, Al. Been a while."

"Hiya, Buck. Yeah, it has been," said Eagle County Sheriff Al Hartman.

"What's up?" asked Buck. Bax and Franklin moved closer.

"We made the notification to the Woodman family a little bit ago. His wife didn't take it well, which was to be expected, but that's only part of the reason I'm calling."

Buck waited. He'd known Al Hartman a long time and never knew him to be at a loss for words. He waited.

"Listen, we got a call out earlier today for a woman who was found bound and had her throat slit in her home in Gypsum. None of us believe in coincidence, but I thought you might find this interesting. The woman who was killed was married to a geologist who works at Velasquez Mining. The geologist is missing. Here's the odd part. Your victim's wife told my deputy that her husband also worked as a geologist for Velasquez Mining. I just got off the phone with her and she confirmed that both men worked together."

"Al, we're not that far away. Can you text me the address, and can someone meet us at your victim's house?"

"That won't be a problem. I'm standing on the front lawn and my detectives and forensic folk are working inside. I'll see you when you get here."

Buck disconnected the call and his phone chimed with an incoming text message. He checked the message.

"That's interesting. Let's head over there and take a look. Then you can run Franklin back to Grand Junction and see if you can help Mel and George with our victim's laptop and phone."

They put their gear in the backs of their Jeeps, and Franklin slid into the passenger seat beside Bax. She started the Jeep and pulled out of the parking area. Buck put his backpack onto the passenger seat, slid in and followed her down the trail. They pulled onto Cottonwood Pass Road and headed east towards Gypsum, Bax leading the way. The traffic had lightened up with the lateness of the day, and they made it to Gypsum a lot faster than they expected. Following her GPS, Bax turned onto Springfield Road and parked behind several Eagle County emergency vehicles. Buck pulled in behind her.

Sheriff Al Hartman was standing on the sidewalk talking to two women. He spotted Buck, shook the women's hands, excused himself and headed towards Buck, Bax and Franklin. They shook hands.

Al Hartman had been the Eagle County sheriff for going on seventeen years. He was six foot two and weighed two-forty. His gray hair was thinning, and he sported a gray mustache. He wore jeans and a flannel shirt. His badge was pinned to the left pocket of the shirt.

"Good to see you guys. What a crazy week so far, huh? First this landslide, now a couple of murders. I might be getting too old for this shit." He laughed.

Buck laughed with him. "Yeah, tell me about it. So, what have you got?"

The sheriff stepped back and lifted the crime scene tape surrounding the front lawn. He strode towards the front door.

"Got the call from a neighbor lady. Wanted us to do a welfare check on Mrs. Betty Mortensen. The one neighbor spotted some large biker types and another man leaving her house earlier today. When they came over to check on her, the door was locked and there was no answer. Those were the women I was talking to when you walked up. Our deputy responded, forced his way into the house and found Mrs. Mortensen in the middle of the kitchen, bound to one of the chairs and sitting in a pool of blood. Someone beat her up and then slit her throat. Damn shame."

They signed in with the deputy at the front door and stepped into the house. The coppery smell of blood was unmistakable. The sheriff led them into the kitchen.

"The pathologist released the body, so we sent it over to the morgue," said the sheriff.

He stood back and let Buck take in the scene. He was well aware that Buck liked to look at a crime scene first before getting the details from the investigating officers.

Buck walked around the kitchen, looking at the scene from different vantage points. While Buck was looking at the scene, Franklin looked at the evidence. He leaned over and looked at the floor near the body. Buck stepped next to him. He stood up.

"Two people were standing in front of the victim when her throat was slit." He kneeled and pointed towards the blood splatter on the floor. "The arterial spray covered the area, but you can see four spots that weren't spattered. Here and here. Two people were standing in front of her when she was cut. That means the killer was behind her."

Buck looked at the spatter mark. "Makes sense." He stepped over to the sheriff.

"Al, have you put out the descriptions of the three men yet?" he asked.

"Yeah. Went out about an hour ago. Also put out a BOLO on the truck and the SUV. The truck should be easy to find.

Older yellow GMC with jacked-up suspension. The neighbors didn't catch the plate. The SUV was a black Cadillac Escalade. Dark tinted windows. I've got my people checking Gypsum and Dotsero."

"Good, let's keep in mind that we might have two pairs of shoes with blood spatter on them," said Buck.

They all headed for the front door when Buck stopped. "Did you find a laptop or phone for the missing husband?"

"No, but the neighbor remembered the husband leaving this morning with a backpack over his shoulder. Most likely heading for work. Speaking of which, we called the Velasquez Mining Company earlier. The husband never showed up for work today."

"Looks like we either have another victim or a runner," said Bax.

"Yeah," said Buck. "Al, can you put out a BOLO for the husband's vehicle and can you lead us to our victim's wife? I'd like to talk to her."

"No problem, I've got a deputy watching the house. The wife took the news about her husband hard, but she was able to answer some of our questions."

They walked across the lawn and passed under the crime scene tape. Sheriff Hartman headed for his SUV, as did Buck, Bax and Franklin. They followed as the sheriff led them back to Gypsum Creek Road, turned left and headed towards town. At Vicksburg Lane, he turned left then right onto Second Street, turned right into a cul-de-sac and stopped at the house on the left. Buck pulled in behind him. They slid out, walked up the driveway to the front door and rang the bell. A gray-haired woman wearing a floral apron answered the door. Her blue eyes were bloodshot, and they could see dried streaks under her eyes.

"Sheriff," she said.

"Marge, these folks are from CBI. They'd like to talk to Janice for a minute, if she's up to it."

"Let them in, Mom. It's okay," said a voice from behind her. She stepped aside and invited them in with a wave of her hand.

Several people were sitting and standing in the living room, surrounding a young woman with blond hair and blue eyes. She was a younger version of the woman who answered the door. The noise level dropped as everyone looked at the visitors. Bax approached the young woman and kneeled in front of the chair.

"Janice, we'd like to offer our condolences for your loss. My name is Ashley, and my partners and I work for CBI. We know this is a hard time, but we have a few questions that would help our investigation. If you feel up to it."

"Can't this wait, Sheriff? She just lost her husband; have a heart."

A tall, striking woman stepped through the door leading to the kitchen. She wore a short skirt and loose blouse that accented her figure, and her sunglasses were perched on her red hair.

Buck stepped forward and stood in front of the woman with his hand extended. "Buck Taylor, ma'am, and you would be?"

The woman shook his hand, and he noticed her firm grip and that she never took her eyes off him.

"Gabriella Velasquez, Detective Taylor. Timothy Woodman worked for my company. Can't this wait? Janice is in pain."

"I apologize, ma'am. Every minute counts in a murder investigation, and we will be respectful of Mrs. Woodman and her time."

"It's okay, Ms. Velasquez. I will talk to these folks," said Janice.

She stood and directed them to follow her through the kitchen and onto the back patio. She took a seat at the round glass picnic table and waved her hand towards the other chairs. Bax closed the patio door, walked over and sat next to her. The sheriff and Franklin stood by the door. Buck pulled out the chair opposite her and sat, sliding his business card across the table. She picked it up and stuck it in her shirt pocket.

"Ma'am," said Buck. "What did your husband do for Velasquez Mining?"

"He was a geologist. I don't know what that entailed. Tim seldom discussed his job with me other than to say that he spent a lot of time looking at reports about rocks."

"When he left the house yesterday, was there anything unusual or different about his routine? Was he nervous, scared, distracted, anything that seemed odd?"

"No, nothing. I don't understand this. Tim was happy in his work."

Tears flowed down her face, and she used a handkerchief to wipe her eyes. "Tim loved his job. Who would have done such a thing?"

Bax reached out and placed her hand on top of Janice's. "That's what we're trying to figure out. Have you noticed anything odd in the neighborhood, strange cars, odd people, maybe nuisance phone calls? Anything like that?"

"No, nothing," said Janice.

"Mrs. Woodman," said Buck. "Did your husband know a man named Jack Mortensen?"

Janice stopped and stared at him. "Jack was his best friend. They've known each other since college. They work together and have for years." She started to shake. "You can't believe that Jack . . ."

"No, ma'am, we don't believe anything yet." Buck hesitated. He looked at Bax, and she nodded.

"Mrs. Woodman, this afternoon Betty Mortensen was found murdered in her home, and her husband is missing. We are trying to locate him."

Janice stared at Bax in disbelief. "Betty. Betty is dead? How can that be? I just spoke to her this morning and she was fine." Tears flowed like water. The patio door opened, and Gabriella Velasquez stepped onto the patio, walked over and wrapped her arms around Janice. She looked at Buck.

"I think that's enough. Can't you see what this is doing to her?"

"Ms. Velasquez, we appreciate you looking out for Janice, but we have two murders we are trying to solve."

"Two murders? What two murders?" asked Gabriella.

"The wife of another of your employees was found beaten and murdered this afternoon, not far from here. We are trying to figure out if the two crimes are related. Her husband is also missing."

Gabriella stood up and stared at Buck. "Who?" she asked.

"Betty Mortensen," said Buck. "Her husband is Jack Mortensen, and we were told that he worked with Tim Woodman at your company. We are trying to find him, but he seems to have disappeared."

Gabriella's hand went to her mouth, and she stood there stunned. Buck watched her. He was looking for little micro-expressions and felt she wasn't being honest, but he wasn't sure about what. Janice jumped up and ran into the house.

"Since both these people are related to your company, Ms. Velasquez," said Buck, "we'll need to speak to you and others at your company as soon as possible."

"I need to tell my brother," said Gabriella. She stepped past Buck and ran to the house. The group followed the sheriff around the side of the house and exited the yard through a gate in the fence. They walked around the front of the house and stopped at the sheriff's SUV as a black Escalade tore out of the cul-de-sac with Gabriella at the wheel.

"That was interesting," said Bax. "I got the impression Gabriella knew something about Mortensen."

"Yeah," said Buck. "We need to talk with her. It's getting late. Let's head back to Glenwood Springs, and then you can get Franklin back to Grand Junction."

"Al, we'll keep you posted. You need anything, you let me know," said Buck.

They shook hands with the sheriff, slid into their vehicles and left the cul-de-sac. Buck glanced towards the house as he pulled forward and spotted Janice Woodman standing at the front door. Buck noticed she wasn't crying. She looked . . . mad. He drove out of the cul-de-sac and headed back to Glenwood Springs.

| 19 |

Chapter Nineteen

Gabriella parked next to the massive ten-foot-tall doors with a relief carving showing mountains, elk and bears. The doors alone cost more than most people's houses. The mansion was enormous and had been designed by the same architect who designed the office building. It was a monument to wealth and prosperity, made of glass and steel, with massive rock walls that seemed to rise out of the surrounding landscape to blend in to the red and tan rocks of the high desert. From the back, Ramone could monitor his herds of cattle and horses, and from the front, he had a beautiful view of the snowcapped mountains and ski slopes in the Eagle Valley. It was lavish, and with the lights on at night, the glow could be seen for miles. She slid out of her Escalade, raced up the stairs, pushed open the doors and found herself face-to-face with her younger sister.

"Tina." She stopped short. "What are you doing here?" she asked, composing herself. "I thought you went back to Denver?"

"I did, but when the boys heard about the huge landslide, they wanted to come see it. Peter took the day off from work so we could all come, but we couldn't get near it. What a crazy thing to have happened."

Two teenage boys ran past the front door on their way to play video games. They yelled as they went by, "Hey, Aunt Gabby." They disappeared down the stairs to the right of the front door that led to the huge media room in the basement.

Gabriella yelled back to them, but they were already gone from sight. She looked at Tina. "Where's Ramone?"

"In his study with Peter. Gab, what's up? You look upset. Has something happened? Are you all right?"

"I'm fine. There is just some work stuff I need to discuss with Ramone. Are you staying for dinner?"

"Yeah," said Tina. "We thought we would head back in the morning."

"That's great. We can talk more later." Gabriella headed for Ramone's study. She stopped at the eight-foot-tall mahogany doors and composed herself. She knocked and pushed open the door without waiting.

The room was huge, with incredible views from all sides. The rough-hewn beams and panel walls had a rich honey color, and the pine floors, taken from an old warehouse that used to belong to the family, and the sun setting through the west-facing windows made the room feel warm and cozy. There was a fire burning in the gigantic Rumford fireplace that took up a huge part of the wall along with the book-shelves that covered the wall to either side, the stone in the fireplace surround taken from the site during the excavation. It was a man's room, from the massive leather couches and chairs to the incredible custom-made brass-and-glass light fixtures, and Ramone felt right at home in its splendor and opulence.

Ramone was standing next to his desk holding a drink of amber liquid in a cut glass crystal glass. Her brother-in-law Peter was standing next to him looking at the drone footage they had taken from the canyon, now displayed on the big-screen television over the fireplace. Peter set his glass on the burled wood desk.

"That's incredible. And you never felt a thing from the earthquake?" he asked. He turned as Gabriella entered the room.

"Hi, Gab," he said. "Ramone was just showing me the drone videos you guys took. I can't believe with all that damage you guys didn't feel it or hear it. Amazing."

"Yeah," she said. "Amazing. Peter, can you give us a minute? I need to talk to Ramone about something."

"No problem. I was heading for the basement to play video games with the boys."

He swallowed the last of his drink and walked past her and out the door. She turned, closed the door, walked to the bar and poured herself a drink. She faced Ramone.

"What the fuck have you done?" she asked. Her voice was full of accusation.

"What are you talking about?" asked Ramone.

"Did you order him to do it?"

"Do what?" he asked.

"That fucking Dutch. Did you? Did you tell him to kill her?"

Ramone set his drink on the desk. "Kill who?"

"Don't act all coy with me. Did you tell him to do it?"

"Gabby. What the fuck are you talking about? Kill who?"

"Mortensen's wife. Betty Mortensen was found this afternoon, beaten and murdered in her house. I found out from the family that the sheriff was looking for two biker types in a yellow pickup truck and a guy in a black Escalade. What the fuck did you do?"

Ramone turned his back to her so he could gather his thoughts. He turned around. "Mortensen didn't show up for work today. I told Dutch to talk to his wife and find out where he was. That's all. She's dead?"

"Yeah, and with finding the body of Woodman, that fucking psycho has put us right in their crosshairs."

"Relax," he said, realizing his mistake as soon as he said it.

"Relax my ass, you stupid son of a bitch. This could all lead right back to us."

"Look, Gab. Nobody can prove that we had anything to do with the rockslide. It was an earthquake. The governor held a press conference an hour ago and reiterated that. We are in the clear."

"You had better fucking hope so. What are you going to do about Dutch?" she asked.

"I'll talk to him. He must have had a good reason to kill her. I'll talk to the sheriff about the investigation into Woodman and Mrs. Mortensen . . ."

"He won't be able to help you, asshole. CBI is involved, and those people don't give up."

Ramone sat in his chair. "Fuck."

"What about Burns? Can we count on him to stay quiet?"

"I'll talk to him."

"That's great," said Gabriella. "But what about those two morons who work for him? Their bright yellow truck was seen in front of the Mortensen house just before she was discovered dead in her kitchen."

Ramone took a sip of his drink. "I'll deal with them."

Gabriella laughed. "No, you're gonna get that psycho fuck to do it for you, just like always. Sometimes you are pathetic, Ramone."

She finished her drink, put the glass on the desk and walked out of the study, slamming the door behind her. Ramone sat for a moment. Gabriella rarely spoke to him that way, but she was pissed, and he was concerned. He would have to deal with Dutch, which might be a problem. They were as close as brothers, but he may have gone too far, and they still hadn't found Mortensen or his laptop.

He walked over to the bar and poured himself another drink. He needed to think.

| 20 |

Chapter Twenty

Buck parked his Jeep at the B&B they were using as their base in Carbondale, slid out of the seat and grabbed his backpack. He walked around the back of the house, across the yard, and stood looking out over the Roaring Fork River. It had been a couple of years since he had fished the Roaring Fork, and since the river flowed through the rental's backyard, he figured he owed it to himself to try it.

He headed back to the house and found Paul sitting in the common room.

"You look beat," said Paul. "You want to go grab some dinner before you crash?"

Buck dropped his backpack on the floor in the corner by the fireplace and thought about the fact that he hadn't eaten since breakfast, and that was a long time ago.

"Yeah, let's go," he said, and Paul stood up and they headed for the door.

There was a small steakhouse just down the highway, so they decided to walk. The night was cooling off, and Buck looked at the clouds. A storm was brewing, he thought; he had no idea at the time how right he was.

Paul pulled open the door to the steakhouse and they entered a fragrance extravaganza. The hostess showed them to a small table near the window overlooking the Roaring Fork and they ordered drinks. A house draft beer for Paul and a Coke for Buck. They looked at the menu, and when the waitress returned with their drinks they ordered dinner, then sat back and enjoyed the ambiance.

The little restaurant looked like a Western barn, with wood everywhere. It was crowded for the middle of the week, and the crowd was a mix of locals and people who had come to see the destruction in the canyon. He spotted several TV personalities he recognized; everyone seemed to be looking at their phones. The story was now national news, and everyone was looking for a scoop. He was thankful that, for once, no one recognized him.

The bar was a small counter in the corner with three draft beer taps and a small assortment of bottles behind the bar. The bartender was flipping through several news channels in between pouring drinks. The sound was off, and a pretty young woman wearing a long denim skirt and Western shirt was strumming a guitar in the corner next to the bar. Her long blond hair was tied in a ponytail, and she had beautiful jade-colored eyes. Her voice was like pure honey, and Buck sat watching her. His son David, besides being a cop, played in a country rock band, and he had a nice voice, which must have come from his mother because Buck couldn't carry a tune in a bucket. This woman's voice was mesmerizing, and before Buck realized it, his steak and baked potato were sitting in front of him. He turned and faced Paul.

"You guys had a busy day," said Paul. "Two murders, huh? You think they're tied to the rockslide?"

Buck swallowed a piece of steak. "Yeah. Too much of a coincidence not to be. Call George and Mel after dinner and let's get some background on Velasquez Mining, the owners and both geologists. I met one of the owners earlier today at the male victim's house. She spent time hovering. She might have been looking out for her employee, but that's not the vibe I got from her. She also drives a black Escalade."

"Why would a mining company be involved in causing a rockslide and destroying a major highway? I don't see any monetary value. What's to gain?" asked Paul.

"No idea," said Buck. "Let's see if we can find out. Any luck with the DMV search?"

"Slow going, but with this new information on the mining company, maybe we can speed up the process."

They finished their meals and pushed their plates to the side. Buck leaned back in the chair. He watched the young singer for a few minutes, then his phone rang. He looked at the number and answered.

"Hey, Max. What's up?"

"Buck Taylor, how's my favorite cop?" asked Max Clinton.

"Doin' good, Max." He looked at his watch. "What's got you up so late?"

"Just got off the phone with the Alcohol, Tobacco, Firearms and Explosives lab in Washington. I sent them the samples Franklin had delivered to confirm our findings before I called you. What do you know about RDX?"

Paul pulled out his phone, opened the Chrome app and searched for RDX. He laid his phone on the table so Buck could see it.

Max continued. "RDX is a synthetic explosive that was first patented in the 1890s in Germany. It was used by the U.S., the UK and Germany during World War Two. It is a major component in plastic explosives and is significantly more powerful than TNT. It was used in depth charges, torpedoes and dam buster bombs. It is still commonly used today and is often combined with TNT and aluminum powder. That product is commonly called Torpex and is about fifty to sixty percent more powerful than TNT alone. This is a monstrous product."

"So, this was a human-caused explosion?" asked Buck.

"We found minute concentrations in the dust from the tunnel. That's why we asked the ATF to confirm our findings. Based on their confirmation, we believe it was. The ATF lab ran some simulations and estimated that there would have to be north of a hundred thousand pounds of Torpex used. It would have been a massive explosion. Enough to bring down a mountain."

"Max, obviously you can't buy this product off the internet, but where do you get it?" asked Paul.

"It's military, but it is available in several forms commercially. Terrorist organizations are always on the lookout for this stuff. It's not easy to get, but not difficult if you have the connections. And before you ask, the ATF is looking at any large shipments of RDX either within the U.S. or coming in from Britain, Germany or Canada. The problem is that it could have come in as small quantities for legitimate purposes."

"Shit, Max. The governor is not going to be pleased, and our job just got a lot bigger and more complicated."

"Buck, have you thought about why this happened? Who benefits from either the landslide or the highway closure? There has to be a damn good reason someone would do this," said Max.

"Funny you should ask. Paul and I were sitting here wondering about the same thing, and we couldn't come up with an answer that made sense."

"Okay, Buck. If you need anything else, let me know."

"Hey, Max. Before you go. Franklin and Sima should be sending you some samples from a murder victim, and Eagle County should be sending you their samples from another victim. Can you keep an eye out and let me know what you find?"

"These two victims related to the landslide?" asked Max.

"They might be," said Buck. "Too coincidental not to be."

"Okay, Buck. You take care and stay safe." She ended the call the way she always did. "You're a good man, Buck Taylor. God will watch over you."

She disconnected the call, and Buck looked across the table at Paul. "This just got a hell of a lot more interesting."

"Fuck, Buck," said Paul. "Our workload just increased exponentially. Now we also have to think about terrorism, along with anything else we might come up with."

"Yeah, let's head back to the house and get some sleep. We are gonna be busy tomorrow."

Buck called for the check, and they left money on the table and a nice tip for the waitress since they took so much time at her table. She picked up the cash, counted it, smiled and waved as they left. She didn't look disappointed.

They walked back to the B&B, and Paul went inside while Buck stopped at his Jeep and grabbed his fly rod and waders. He slipped them on and spent the next couple of hours fly-fishing along the Roaring Fork River. He caught and released several trout of varying sizes and then decided to call it a night. He knew he should call the director and the governor, but he didn't want to ruin their night. He climbed out of the river, pulled off his waders and hung them in the Jeep to dry. He disassembled his fly rod and packed it away. He felt refreshed, and that would help him tomorrow when the real work started.

Chapter Twenty-One

Buck woke up before the sun came through the window of his room. He grabbed a quick shower, dressed and met Paul in the common room. Buck grabbed a Coke out of the refrigerator in the kitchen and took a long drink. He put the can on the counter, pulled out his phone and tapped the first number in his speed dial list.

"Hey, Buck," said Director Jackson on the second ring.

"Mornin', sir. We got back the lab results of the tunnel's debris samples late last night. Samples were positive for RDX, TNT and aluminum powder."

"Torpex," said the director.

"You're familiar with the product, sir?" asked Buck.

"Yeah," said the director. "My grandfather worked on a destroyer during World War Two. The Navy used Torpex in the depth charges they used on enemy subs. He used to rave about how effective it was. Torpex is obsolete for the most part. How did it get into Glenwood Canyon?"

"That's a good question, sir. Max has the ATF tracking shipments of RDX, but if someone was stockpiling the RDX over a long time, we're gonna have trouble tracking it. The TNT is a dead end as is the aluminum powder. Those products are prevalent in all kinds of demolition. We'll check local demo companies and see if anything shakes loose."

"You okay with the ATF being involved? That means our friends at the FBI and Homeland will not be far behind."

"We had no choice, sir. Max needed verification of the explosives, and she had to go to the ATF. We just need to move fast. Do you want to call the governor, or do you want me to do it?"

"He told me you spoke with him yesterday morning, so go ahead and call him. We need to hit this hard, Buck. The checkbook is open on this. Whatever you need, you ask, and I'll make it happen. Keep me posted."

Buck disconnected the call and looked at Paul.

"Bax called while you were on the line," said Paul. "She needs to talk to you."

Buck dialed her number and waited.

"Hi, Buck. George needs to talk to you. Hold on a sec."

George came on the line. "Hiya, Buck. The encryption on the laptop you guys retrieved from the crevice is top-notch. We screwed with it all night and have gotten nowhere. I may need some help."

Buck knew what George meant. A couple of months back, the team had been involved in an investigation into a dead state brand inspector and a bunch of dead cows. The investigation also uncovered murder, human trafficking and baby farming. It was determined that the cows were killed by airborne botulinum toxin, and the general in charge of a secret lab that had been built in the Colorado mountains to replace Plum Island in New York was concerned that this lab might have been the cause of the deadly toxin. When the investigation stalled, the general gave Buck a sophisticated encryption-breaking software to get into some government files. He let Buck keep the software with the promise to use it wisely.

"Do what you need to do," said Buck. "I'm about to call the governor and tell him this was a terrorist act and not a natural occurrence. We need to get to the bottom of this, and fast."

"You got it, Buck. Hold on. Here's Bax."

"Buck. I uploaded a bunch of background on the mining company, the owners and the two geologists. Take a look next time you're in the investigation file. I'm also narrowing down the AI-generated license plate list. What convinced you of the terrorism aspect of this case?"

Buck told her about the late-night call from Max and the confirmation of RDX.

"Shit," said Bax. "That changes things. We'll keep plugging along and see what we can find on the laptop and phone. Talk later."

Buck disconnected the call and looked at his phone. He dialed the next number and waited. The phone was picked up after the first ring.

"Buck," said Governor Kennedy.

"Morning, sir," said Buck. "Afraid I have some bad news for you."

"This wasn't a natural disaster, was it?" asked the governor.

"No, sir. From everything we looked at and the lab results we got back, it looks like this was a man-made disaster."

There was silence on the other end of the phone. Buck waited.

"Fuck," said the governor. "Anyone claiming responsibility?"

"No, sir. Nothing has come to our attention."

"I guess I need to call a press conference. Anything you'd care to share with me?"

"Not at this time, Governor."

"Can you at least confirm that the trooper is dead?"

"No, sir. But I think it's unlikely he survived the blast."

"Buck, any thoughts on what the terrorists were after? Doesn't make any sense."

"No, sir. We've been trying to come up with a motive, but there doesn't seem to be any reason to blow up a highway, cause a landslide that blocks a river and endanger the lives of thousands of people downstream. We'll keep looking, sir. You can count on that."

"Buck, you find the sons of bitches who did this. Anything you need, you reach out."

"Thank you, Governor. We'll do our best."

Buck disconnected the call and looked at Paul.

"Let's go through the deep dives on the mining company and the engineers. See if anything jumps out at us."

Buck was about to open his laptop when his phone chimed. He looked at the number and answered.

"Hey, Gabe. What's up?"

"Mornin', Buck," said Chief Molina. "Hope it's not too early?"

"No. You're good, Gabe. What's goin' on?"

"Saw that APB on a jacked-up yellow pickup truck and a couple of biker-looking dudes. One of my officers thinks he spotted it outside a restaurant at the edge of town. Thought you might be interested."

Buck stood up. "Shit, yeah, I'm interested. Is it still there?"

"I have the officer sitting on it to make sure it doesn't move. What do you want me to do?"

"Hold tight, we're on our way. Text me the address. And Gabe, if it moves, tell your officers to make a traffic stop, but don't approach."

"You want to tell me what's going on, Buck?"

"Yeah, as soon as we get there."

Buck hung up and followed Paul, who had packed up his laptop and headed for his Jeep. They took a minute to grab their ballistic vests out of the back hatch and put them on, then they slid into their Jeeps and tore out of the parking lot.

They needed a break, and Buck hoped that they may have just gotten it.

Chapter Twenty-Two

Rodney pulled his truck to the side of the road outside Boomer's house and beeped the horn. If he could get Boomer's ass in gear, they would have time to stop and get breakfast before heading to the mine. Today was one of the days they always looked forward to. Today they would set the charges to expose a new section of the mine. They both loved this part of the job. There was a great deal of precision needed for opening a new tunnel. Too much explosives and they could bring the whole thing down on their heads and destroy the tunnel; too little and they would have to go back and start all over again. That would mean lost time and lost revenue. They never worried about starting over. They knew their stuff and had been taught by the best.

Rodney Toobin loved blowing things up as a kid, growing up outside Cleveland, Ohio. He was a scrawny kid whose parents had little money to spend on the finer things in life, like clothes or shoes that fit. To escape his home life, Rodney spent his time in the small public library next to the elementary school reading books about World War II and

Korea, and he loved the parts about blowing up bridges and tunnels. When he got to high school, his favorite class was chemistry, and he would spend every hour he could playing around in the chem lab. With the encouragement of his chemistry teacher, a former Army Explosive Ordnance Disposal officer, after graduation, Rodney found himself in the army, blowing up bridges and buildings during the first Iraq invasion. That was where he met Boomer.

Henry Walton hated his name. Henry was the name of his father and grandfather, and after leaving school, he wanted nothing to do with either of them. His mother, a kind housewife, lived with the abuse, but she encouraged her son to leave as soon as he graduated from high school. The morning after graduation, Henry sat in the army recruitment office in Modesto, California, signing his name on the dotted line. The aptitude test he had taken that morning showed that he had a good mind for chemistry, so they offered him a position in EOD. He thought it sounded like fun, and what could be wrong with blowing shit up for a living? He gave himself the nickname Boomer in boot camp, and no one ever questioned him about it.

Boomer and Rodney met when they were assigned to the same unit in Iraq. Their primary duty was bomb disposal. Improvised explosive devices were everywhere in Iraq, armed and buried as Saddam's troops fled their areas of occupation. They ranged from the simplest to the most complex, and Boomer and Rodney soon became two of the best disposal experts on the base. When they weren't taking bombs apart, they were blowing things up. Destroying tanks, blowing open barricades, blowing down statues of Saddam and his family. They did it all.

After their time in the service, they were looking for a new challenge, and they saw an ad for mine blasters in a place called Dotsero, Colorado. Since neither one of them had been to Colorado, they thought they would give it a try. They applied for the open positions and were hired by Roger Burns. Roger Burns had forgotten more about blasting than most people in his industry ever knew. He was a legend; Boomer and Rodney felt lucky to have found him, and he felt the same. Ten years later, they were still blowing things up and enjoying their jobs.

Boomer came out of his house carrying his lunch pail. He stopped to pet his dog on the head and rubbed his ears. The mine they were working at today was north of the small town of New Castle, west of Glenwood Springs. The mine, another Velasquez Mining project, was a deep coal mine, and today they would work 800 feet below the surface.

Rodney pushed the button and rolled down the side window. "Hey, fuck. Let's get a move on. We have to go over Cottonwood Pass, and I want to beat the traffic so we can get breakfast."

Boomer's response was a raised middle finger. He closed the front yard gate and climbed into the truck.

"Well, what the hell are you waiting for? Let's go," he said with a hearty laugh.

Rodney pulled away from the curb and headed for Gypsum. He knew a couple of back roads that would get them to Cottonwood Pass Road without having to go through Gypsum, avoiding some of the traffic, but this morning the traffic was light, and they made good time getting into Glenwood Springs with plenty of time for breakfast.

Rodney pulled into the parking lot and parked in front of the Storm King Cafe, a small restaurant that served man-sized breakfasts. They slid out and went inside.

The small cafe was named after Storm King Mountain, north of Glenwood Springs, and part of the tragic history of the area. A fire started by lightning on July 2, 1994, smoldered for a couple of days until authorities sent in firefighters to attack the fire while it was still small and manageable. The terrain and hot weather created a dangerous situation.

The assault on the fire began in earnest on July 5, as firefighters struggled over the rugged terrain and built fire lines to protect a nearby community. The following day, a hotshot team from Pineville, Oregon, joined the firefighters, several smoke jumpers and a helitack team on the mountain.

Later in the day, a dry cold front brought increasing winds, which helped the fire grow. Embers jumped the fire lines and ignited the rough, dry terrain below the firefighters. Aided by the strong winds, the fire raced up the mountain towards the firefighters. The approaching flames overtook the firefighters, resulting in the loss of twelve firefighters and two members of the helitack team in one of the worst tragedies to ever befall the firefighting community.

Rodney and Boomer finished breakfast and were looking at pictures and newspaper clippings of the fire that hung on the wall behind the register as they waited to pay. They pushed through the door and climbed into the truck. As Rodney backed up into the drive aisle, a Glenwood Springs

Police SUV appeared behind him. The blue-and-red lights came on, and the officer whooped his siren to get their attention. Rodney stopped and looked at Boomer.

Two more police SUVs and a pair of Jeep Cherokees, one black and one gray, with emergency lights on, stopped in front of them, blocking their way. Cops slid out of the SUVs, and guns were leveled at the yellow truck. Rodney put the truck in park and stared out the front window. He wondered what was going on.

| **23** |

Chapter Twenty-Three

Buck and Paul parked their Jeeps behind Chief Molina's SUV and slid out. Buck walked up to the chief, who was standing outside his vehicle talking with an older officer. They shook hands.

"What have we got?" asked Buck.

"Your two suspects are still having breakfast. Been in there awhile, so they should be getting close to being done. The APB on the truck mentioned it was wanted in connection with a homicide in Gypsum. You want to tell me what we might be walking into?"

"You need to keep this under your hat for now," said Buck. The chief nodded. "We have two dead bodies, one a geologist and one the wife of a geologist, that were found between here and Gypsum. We also have a missing geologist. There is a possibility that these murders are connected to the rockslide in the canyon."

"The slide was man-made?" asked the chief.

"Yeah, we think so—lab results on dust samples we took from the tunnel show explosive residue. Not much, but it changed the way we were thinking. The two bodies only added to that."

"Fuck, Buck. You've got to be kidding. Who would do such a thing and why?" asked the chief.

"All good questions, Gabe." Buck pointed at the truck. "That truck and its occupants were seen leaving one of the murder scenes. The wife of the geologist."

The chief was about to say something when the officer said over his shoulder, "Chief, two guys coming out of the cafe and getting in the truck."

Chief Molina looked at Buck.

"Officer, pull in behind them when they back out. Let them know you're there but stay with your vehicle. Do not approach. Chief, who else have we got?"

"I've got two cars on the other side of the highway facing the parking lot."

Buck was impressed. The chief had positioned his units to block off both ways out of the parking lot. The truck would have nowhere to go, but Buck always expected that anything could happen during a stop like this. He didn't know how right he was. They headed for their vehicles.

The officer pulled forward and turned into the parking lot. He stopped behind the truck as it backed into the drive aisle, hit his lights and whooped his siren. He slid out of his patrol vehicle and positioned himself near the back with his shotgun. He leaned on the trunk and waited.

Two more Glenwood Springs PD SUVs entered the drive aisle from the other side and blocked the exit. The chief, Buck and Paul pulled in behind them and exited their vehicles with weapons drawn.

Buck pulled his microphone off the clip on the dash, turned his radio to PA and pushed the button. He hesitated for a moment as he saw someone inside the cafe approach the front door and appear to lock it. Smart move.

"Driver of the yellow truck. Turn off the engine and place your hands on the top of the steering wheel where we can see them." Buck's voice was calm and authoritative. "Passenger, roll down your window and put your hands out. Do it now."

Buck could see the driver and passenger talking. The passenger, hands out of view, appeared agitated. It looked like the driver was trying to calm him down. Buck had a bad feeling about this.

"Driver, hands where we can see them; passenger, hands out the window. Do it now," he repeated.

Buck was patient. He had learned a long time ago never to make threats you weren't prepared to back up. He never said things like "You have one minute to . . ." or "If you don't do this, we will . . ." He always laughed at the cop shows on TV where there were always threats being made and time-lines to meet. He could wait.

Buck had made patience into an art form. There had been a story circulating the CBI offices for years about Buck getting a murderer to confess just by sitting at the table opposite him and not saying a word for four or five hours. Of course, the time got longer or shorter depending on who told the story, but it was always told as a sign of respect.

Paul had made his way along the back side of a row of cars until he was perpendicular to the driver's door. He looked at his sight lines and realized that a missed shot would go through the front window of the cafe. He wouldn't let that happen. He moved back towards Buck and the chief.

Buck keyed the mic. "There's no way out of here. We've got you boxed in. Let's talk about a solution to this problem so that no one gets hurt."

The driver turned off the engine and placed both hands on the top of the steering wheel. Buck waited. The passenger window rolled down, and the passenger put both hands out the window.

"Fuck," said the chief. "Is that what I think it is?"

"Shit," came the responses from several of his officers.

Buck looked at the brown tube in the passenger's right hand. "TNT," said Buck. He turned to Chief Molina. "Call Dispatch and have them call the cafe. Tell them to get everyone out through the back door as quickly as possible."

"I need to call SWAT. It's gonna take time," the chief said as he keyed the mic on his shoulder.

"We don't have time for SWAT," said Buck, watching the truck. "We need to end this now."

The chief relayed the message to his dispatcher. Buck turned and looked at Paul. "Get your rifle and set up somewhere behind the truck. Scope the passenger. Two fingers, green light."

The driver appeared to be talking to the passenger. It seemed like they were engaged in an animated conversation.

Paul ran to his Jeep, pulled his rifle out of the gun safe that was mounted in the floor and, staying low, ran behind the cars and found a vantage point on the opposite side of the parking lot. He assembled the rifle, attached the scope and sighted in on the back window of the truck. He put the crosshairs on the passenger.

"Passenger," said Buck. "What is your intention?"

"We're getting out of here," yelled the passenger through the window. "If you don't back off all these cops, I will light this and blow us all up. And don't think I won't."

"Driver. Are you going along with this plan?"

The driver shook his head and said something to the passenger. The passenger reached his left hand into the truck and came back out with a lighter.

"Passenger, no one has gotten hurt so far. Why don't we keep it that way?" While he was talking, Buck raised two fingers in the air in the shape of a V.

The passenger flicked the lighter, and a yellow flame ignited from the top.

"I have enough TNT," said the passenger, "to destroy most of this parking lot. Don't push me! Get those fucking cars moved or I swear . . ."

He never finished the sentence, as the truck's back window exploded and a red mist and gray matter covered the front windshield. The driver threw open the door and fell to the ground.

"Don't shoot. I'm unarmed. I surrender." He started crawling away from the truck. The chief and two of his officers ran forward and held their weapons on him. The chief cuffed him and then frisked him before letting him stand up. He looked in the truck.

"Fuck, man. You shot him. I could have talked him down."

"He made his choice," said Buck as he approached the truck. "I would have waited all day, but your buddy pushed the issue. Is there any more dynamite in the truck?"

"I don't know," said the driver. "He pulled that out of his backpack. I didn't know he had it. Scared the shit out of me."

Buck looked through the door and saw the backpack on the floor.

"Chief, please lock him up until the sheriff can send an investigator. I'll be along in a minute to question him. Make him as comfortable as possible."

Sirens could be heard in the distance, and moments later, a paramedic unit arrived at the parking lot. The paramedics exited their vehicle and sprinted towards the truck. They stopped running when they saw the red splatter all over the windshield. One paramedic reached through the window and pressed his fingers on the passenger's neck, even though it was obvious he was dead. He shook his head and walked back to the ambulance to get the gurney and a body bag.

Having disassembled his rifle, Paul walked up and placed it back in the gun safe. "Do you think he would have done it?" asked Paul.

"Couldn't take the risk," said Buck. Paul looked to where Buck was looking. The storefront two doors down had a large sign hanging over the door that read drop-in daycare. He called the director, explained the situation and asked him to call the district attorney who covered Garfield County and have him send out a shooting investigation team and the state patrol bomb squad. He needed to make sure there were no other explosives in the truck. He called Sheriff

Weaver and asked him to send his forensic unit to oversee the shooting investigation.

The chief directed one of his officers to hang some crime scene tape around the truck and to stay until the forensic unit and the bomb squad arrived, and then he left to follow his other deputy and the prisoner back to the police station.

Buck walked over and patted Paul on the shoulder. "You okay?"

"I'm good," said Paul. "You want me to wait for the shooting team and forensics?"

"Yeah, and then head back to Grand Junction and work with George and Mel. You'll be on desk duty until the shooting team is done. I'll call Bax to head back out here."

He walked back to his Jeep while he phoned Bax. He slid into the seat and disconnected the call. Today did not go as he had planned. He pulled out of the parking lot and headed to police headquarters. He had a statement to make and an interview to start.

| **24** |

Chapter Twenty-Four

Gabriella flew into Ramone's bedroom. "We've got a problem," she said. "Get your ass out of bed." She walked out of the room and slammed the door.

Ramone, hungover from the night before, hated when his sister played the drama queen. He wondered what the problem was now. He slid out of bed, put on his sweatpants and a robe and walked out of his room. He found Gabriella leaning against the counter in the kitchen, drinking coffee. She set the cup on the counter and glared at him. Ramone walked over, poured himself a cup and sat at the table.

He looked at Gabriella. "Knock off the angry woman look, Gab. I'm not in the mood." He sipped his coffee. "So, what's got you so riled up this morning?"

"Did you talk to that moron, Dutch, yesterday like I asked you to do?"

"No, I was going to talk to him today. What's this all about?"

"I just got off the phone with a friend in Glenwood Springs. Those two imbeciles from Burns Demolition got into it with the cops this morning. One of them is dead. My friend says he threatened to blow everyone up." She stared at him.

Ramone held back a laugh. He doubted his sister had any real friends. "They can't hurt us," he said. "They can't point to us. Dutch was the shot-caller on this project. We weren't involved, and as long as you remember that, we are okay."

The kitchen door opened, and Tina walked in. She stopped at the door and looked from her brother to her sister. "Seems a little tense in here. Is everything okay?" she asked. She walked to the counter and poured two cups of coffee.

Ramone smiled at her. "Everything is fine, little one. It's just a personnel matter at one of the mines. Nothing for you to be concerned about."

Tina looked at him, not quite believing him, but she knew better than to cross him. She was not an active part of the business and liked it that way. She had her own life and her own family to worry about. She picked up the cups, nodded and walked out of the kitchen.

Gabriella opened her mouth to speak, and Ramone waved his hand. "Enough," he said. "I told you I would deal with it, and I will. End of discussion."

"You're just like our father," she said as she picked up her cup and walked to the door. "And there are times I hate you for it." She left the kitchen, and Ramone sipped his coffee.

He set the cup down and pulled his phone out of his pocket. He dialed a number from memory.

"Yes, sir," said the voice on the other end.

"Dutch, I am thinking about reopening the old Lodestone Mine. Meet me there at noon. I want to make sure there are no squatters hiding in it."

"No problem, boss. See you there." The line went dead, and Ramone poured another cup of coffee and sat back. He rang the bell on the table, and when one of the cooks—he could never remember her name—came in, he ordered a big breakfast of scrambled eggs, bacon, sausage and French toast. He had a lot to think about and thought better on a full stomach.

Upstairs, in her bedroom, Gabriella was fuming. She hated being dismissed. She hated it when her father did it and even more when Ramone did it. She was smarter than all of them. She could run this company just fine without them, and she was never happier than the day her father had his heart attack and never recovered. She didn't shed one tear at his funeral, and she was furious when her father's will was read and she found out he gave 70 percent of the company to Ramone. She should have gotten it all instead of just a tiny piece.

She paced back and forth in front of the window. This entire plan was hers—the explosion, the rockslide, the new rare earth mine, all of it—but Ramone treated her like it was his idea. His only contribution was Dutch, and she knew they wouldn't be in this mess if she had handled everything. She needed a plan.

Gabriella stripped out of her robe and walked into the bathroom. She looked at herself in the full-length mirror and liked what she saw. She stepped into the steam shower and for the next twenty minutes just relaxed and let the hot water take her away. When she shut off the shower and stepped out, her mind was clear, and she was ready for the day. She toweled off and dressed in jeans, boots and a flannel shirt. She knew what she had to do, and she was ready. All she needed now were the tools to make it happen.

| **25** |

Chapter Twenty-Five

Buck finished his interview with the young woman from the DA's office. Janine Garvey was five foot six and had the physique of someone who loved the outdoors. Her brown hair was shoulder length, and she kept it loose so it framed her face. If you met her on the street, you would have thought she was a college student, but Buck had seen her in court, and he knew she was a tough, no-nonsense prosecutor who loved her job. He had seen her take on older defense attorneys with years more of experience and tear them up. She was well respected, and she took the shooting investigation seriously.

For the hour she interviewed Buck, she asked pointed and direct questions and pushed for answers if she thought Buck was evasive. When she asked Buck why he hadn't called for the evacuation of the daycare center like he did with the cafe, he had to look deep into his soul to find the answer. The truth was, he was so involved in watching the guy with the bomb that he never noticed the daycare center.

Navy pilots landing on aircraft carriers call it target fixation. This happens when you are so focused on the target you don't notice what's happening around you. The mountains are littered with plane wrecks from pilots so focused on their instruments that they never saw the mountain in front of them. His conversation with Janine and those moments of soul-searching left him wondering if he was getting too old for this job. There was no excuse for not seeing the daycare center.

He walked out of the interview room, and Bax was sitting in the chief's office, waiting for him. She walked to the door as he approached. He glanced over as Paul stepped out of the second interview room and walked over.

"You good?" he asked.

"Yeah. All good. I answered all their questions, and now it's up to the science."

"It was a good shoot, Paul," said Chief Molina. "State patrol bomb squad found four more sticks of TNT in the backpack. Would have made a hell of a mess."

Paul nodded and picked up his backpack from an empty desk. "I'll head back to Grand Junction and run background on him." He pointed to the interrogation room. "And his partner. Got the names from the coroner."

He stepped away and headed out of the building. Bax looked at Buck. "He okay?"

"Yeah. Paul does a lot of soul-searching after something like this. He'll be fine once he gets home and hugs his wife and kids."

He spotted Janine coming out of the interview room and waved her over.

"What's up, Buck?" she asked.

"Can your partner handle the rest of the interviews for the shooting? I'd like you to sit in on the interview with the guy who was driving the truck."

"No problem, Buck. You want to give me some background on what this was all about?"

They stepped into the chief's small office and closed the door. Buck told her about the cause of the rockslide, the dead geologist, the dead wife and the missing geologist. She sat on the edge of the desk and listened, her mouth agape.

"Is this why the governor is holding a press conference this afternoon?"

"Yeah," said Buck. "I only told him our final thoughts this morning."

"Shit, Buck. Who the hell would have the resources to carry something like this off?"

Buck smiled. "That's what I hope this interview will tell us."

She nodded, set her shoulder bag on the floor and pulled out a notebook and a small digital recorder.

"Okay, Buck. Let's see if we can answer some questions."

They opened the door and walked towards the interview room. Bax and the chief followed and stopped at the one-way window, and the chief turned on the cameras and the recording equipment. Buck handed his pistol to Bax, and he and Janine stepped into the interview room.

Buck had been in many interview rooms during his long time in law enforcement, and this room was not as intimidating as some. The walls were painted a light pastel blue, the chairs were padded and instead of a cold stainless steel table, this table was wood. The room had been designed to make people more comfortable, except for the handcuff bolt that was anchored to the table.

Rodney Toobin was talking to his attorney when they walked in. Buck introduced Janine and himself, and they took seats on the opposite side of the table. The lawyer turned on his recording device, as did Janine.

"Robert Crawley," said the lawyer. "I'll be representing Mr. Toobin. Ms. Garvey. Nice to see you again."

Janine nodded. "Shall we begin?" Everyone nodded and said yes for the tape. She picked up a small laminated card that had been sitting on her notebook. "Mr. Toobin, I am going to read you your rights." She read the Miranda warning from the card and then set it aside. "Do you understand your rights, Mr. Toobin?" Rodney nodded. "Please answer for the tape, sir," she said. Rodney answered with a soft yes, and she looked at Buck.

"Rodney," he said. "May I call you Rodney?"

Rodney nodded, looked at Janine and said, "Yes."

"Rodney. Were you aware that . . ." He looked at the paper Bax had handed him when he handed her his pistol. "That Henry had an explosive device with him this morning?"

"No."

"Do you know why he might have had the explosives with him?"

"No."

"Rodney, do you know where Henry got the explosives?"

Rodney looked at the lawyer, who nodded.

"Probably from the shop, but it's against the rules."

"What shop would that be?"

"We work for Roger Burns and Sons Demolition, Inc."

"And what do you do for them?" asked Buck.

"We're blasters."

"Rodney, what do you do as a blaster?"

Rodney smiled. Buck sensed he was proud of his job. "We use explosives for a lot of things. We take down old buildings, and we blast mountains for construction crews. Lately, we've been doing a lot of blasting in various mines."

Buck asked Rodney about his background and how he and Henry came to be blasters, and Rodney told him about their time in the army and the work they had been doing over the past ten years after leaving the military. Buck and Janine sat back and listened.

"Rodney, why do you think Henry reacted the way he did this morning?"

"No idea. I didn't know he had the explosives in his backpack. It was a stupid thing to do."

There was a tap on the window behind Buck, and he excused himself and walked over to the door. Bax handed him another piece of paper, and he closed the door and sat down. He read the paper and handed it to Janine. She read it and set it on the table. Rodney looked nervous.

"Rodney, do you know why you were stopped this morning?"

"No, sir. We were just eatin' breakfast. Weren't botherin' nobody."

"Rodney, we have several witnesses who spotted your truck yesterday at a house in Gypsum. Was your truck on Springfield Street yesterday morning?"

"No, sir." Rodney started to sweat and looked at his attorney.

"Agent Taylor," said the attorney. "What's this all about?"

"Your truck is pretty distinctive, wouldn't you say?"

"It's just a truck," said Rodney.

"Rodney, a woman was murdered yesterday morning on Springfield Street. Beaten and murdered."

The lawyer jumped up. "Ms. Garvey. What's going on here?"

"Mr. Crawley," said Janine. "Your client and his partner were seen leaving a house that belonged to Jack Mortensen. Mr. Mortensen is missing, and his wife was murdered."

"Then why aren't you looking for the husband?" asked the attorney. "You know what they say."

Janine interrupted. "Yes, I do know what they say about husbands killing wives, but that doesn't explain why there is blood spatter matching the victim on your client's work boots." She slid the paper across the table, and the attorney picked it up and read it. He put it down and grabbed Rodney's arm to pull him closer. The conversation looked a little heated to Buck, and he was ready to intervene when Rodney turned back around in his seat. His face was ashen.

"Ms. Garvey, I'd like some time to consult with my client. We were not prepared for this matter."

Janine stood up and picked up her notebook. Buck followed her lead. "One hour, Mr. Crawley. We'll be back."

She pushed open the door, and she and Buck walked out. Bax was waiting on the other side and handed him his pistol, which he placed in his holster.

"That set them back on their heels," said Janine. "Let's see what they have to say when we go back in there." She walked away and left Bax standing with Buck and Chief Molina.

"Nice work on the blood spatter. Who do we have to thank?" asked Buck.

"The sheriff's forensic team. They were able to match the blood type at the hospital and got it back to us right away. They did say the blood is degraded from dust and dirt and the DNA might be tough, but the blood type matches Mrs. Mortensen. They sent it to the State Crime Lab to see if Max's team can do anything more with it."

"Good work, Bax."

"Something else," said Bax. "I'm down to two SUVs from our list. I have Aurora PD checking on one registered to a man there, and the other is a fleet vehicle registered to Velasquez Mining."

Buck walked to the small kitchen, pulled out a Coke can, popped the top and took a long sip.

"Velasquez, huh," said Buck. "The mine headquarters is in Garfield County, correct?"

"Yeah," said Bax.

"I'm gonna be tied up here for a while yet. Call Sheriff Weaver and see if he can spare a deputy to go with you and have a chat with the folks at the mining company. Try to talk to the owners. When we met her at the Woodman home yesterday, something didn't sit right. See what they can tell you about the SUV."

"No worries, Buck." She walked away, grabbed her backpack from the chief's office and pulled out her phone as she left the office.

"You think Velasquez Mining had something to do with the rockslide and the murders?" asked Chief Molina. "They employ a lot of people from around here and have been generous to the towns in the area for a lot of years."

"Not sure, Gabe. But we will find out."

Chapter Twenty-Six

Dutch parked his SUV next to an old rusty mine car lying on its side in the dirt. A relic from a time long ago when hardy men using picks and shovels dug for coal and shiny minerals in dirty, dark and dangerous mines. Personal protection had no place in the old mines, and safety was a concept that would take years to take hold, if it ever really did. The miners' lives were less important than the shiny baubles they brought forth.

This mine was no exception. The old, cracked timbers that supported the mountain above the mine were often no match for the weight of the mountain. Over the years, too many men had lost their lives in this mine and others in the area, but the rest of the men still showed up for work every day. They were hard men who worked hard, drank hard and lived in the moment, and some paid the ultimate price.

The last cave-in at this mine had been the death knell. Twenty-seven men were crushed under the weight of the mountain and the mine was shuttered, abandoned to the elements, which, from the looks of it, had reclaimed a lot of it.

Dutch wondered why Ramone was thinking of reopening this mine. The mine was cursed and had been from the day the first shovel went into the ground. Since records were poorly kept in the early days, no one knew for certain how many men perished in this dark, forbidding place, but the ghosts would be inside waiting for the unsuspecting miners of today. Sure, Ramone could bring in the experts and make it safer, but there would always be the stories, and the first incident would revive the tales about ghosts and demons from deep in the ground protecting what was theirs.

Dutch shivered and slid out of the SUV. Sometimes he made himself nervous. He shook off the bad vibes, made sure his gun was nestled in his holster and walked towards the entrance. He shined his light into the vast cavity, the light disappearing in the darkness. This was a fool's errand, he thought as he stepped closer to the opening.

The rusted iron gate that was supposed to block the entrance after the mine was closed had been torn open—by vandals or demons, who knew?

He put on the hard hat he had grabbed from the passenger seat and stepped past the broken gate. He was about to enter the lair of the beast. He stopped at the entrance to listen, but all he heard was the eerie whistle of the wind blowing through the tunnels. The wind was foul smelling, like it was coming straight out of the vile mouth of a demon.

"Fuck, Dutch. Get a grip," he said to no one. "You're freaking yourself out."

Touching the pistol on his hip, he ventured farther into the mine. He wanted an opportunity to scope it out before putting Ramone in danger. Twenty feet into the mine, he spotted the first signs of human habitation. A torn blanket lay balled up and stuffed in a crevice, and there were the remains of a small campfire, cold to the touch, with burned pieces of food wrappers. Dutch didn't see any evidence of anyone having been in the mine in a while.

He turned towards the entrance when he heard car tires crunching on the gravel. He heard a door close, and a light appeared at the entrance.

"Dutch, you in there?"

"About twenty feet in, Ramone."

Ramone entered the tunnel and stopped as dirt sprinkled down from the roof. He heard timbers cracking and wondered if this was a good idea, but he knew what had to be done.

He stepped up to Dutch and looked at where he was pointing. "That looks like it's been here awhile," said Ramone. "See anyone around?"

"No," said Dutch. "This is as far as I got. Want to go in farther?"

"No, but I wanted to talk to you," said Ramone. "The cops are all over the murders of Woodman and Betty Mortensen. They have a couple of eyewitnesses that saw you at the scene. Worse than that, those two idiots from the demo company got into it with the cops this morning, and one is dead, and the other is in custody."

Dutch had a funny feeling in the pit of his stomach. The incarceration of one of the blasters was a problem, but he sensed something in Ramone he had never sensed before, and he didn't like what he was feeling or thinking. He stepped deeper into the tunnel.

"How did they get onto Rodney and Boomer?" he asked.

"Their truck was spotted at the Mortensen home and then spotted this morning in Glenwood. One of them threatened to blow up the cops, and the cops found dynamite in the truck. If the guy in jail talks, we are all sunk. They know everything."

"How did they find Woodman so quickly? He was down in a crevice," asked Dutch.

"I don't know, but we are not happy about it. They work for us. This is going to land right on our doorstep."

"What do you want me to do?" asked Dutch.

He raised his flashlight and the beam fell on Ramone, who had backed up a couple of paces and was now holding a pistol in his right hand. The pistol was pointed at Dutch.

"Come on, Ramone. You can't be serious. We've been friends a long time. Put that thing away, and let's figure a way out of this."

"Sorry, Dutch. Take your pistol out of your holster and throw it towards the wall."

"Ramone, this isn't you. This is your sister. She's pulling your strings again. Come on, man."

"Don't bring my sister into this. Now, gun. On the ground."

Dutch pulled his pistol from his holster and threw it towards the wall. As he did it, Ramone made the biggest mistake of his life. He followed the pistol with his eyes. Only for a split second, but it was enough. Dutch pulled his knife from the sheath at his back and threw it with point-blank accuracy. The knife hit Ramone in the chest, and Ramone pulled the trigger. The bullet hit Dutch in the side, and he flipped the switch on his flashlight and disappeared into the dark.

Ramone dropped the pistol, reached up with his right hand and touched the knife. Blood was streaming down his shirt and pooling on the floor around his feet. He stared in disbelief, and then he dropped to his knees in the blood puddle that was already being sucked into the earth. Dust and dirt were falling from the ceiling, and timbers continued to crack.

Dutch watched from the dark as Ramone fell over onto the dirt. He heard the cave moan, and he wondered if his friend's blood was now feeding the demons. He felt his side, and his hand came away wet. He found his pistol on the dusty floor and returned it to his holster. He picked up his flashlight and walked up to Ramone, who was lying motionless on the dirty floor. He wiped a tear from his eye, pulled the knife from Ramone's chest and stepped towards the entrance.

The bullet slammed into his right thigh, and he fell to the ground. He reached for his pistol.

"Don't," said the shadow standing at the entrance. More dirt and dust fell from the tunnel roof.

Gabriella walked a few feet into the tunnel. She had grown up in mines and was not bothered by the dirt and creaking timbers, but she knew Dutch hated being underground. He always had. That's why this was such a fitting end.

"Did you kill him?" she asked. She spotted the knife in his hand, still dripping with her brother's blood. "Drop the knife."

Dutch let the knife fall from his hand. He was having trouble focusing and knew he was losing a lot of blood. He had to do something quickly, or he was going to die in this tunnel.

"He tried to kill me. I had no choice." His right hand grabbed the gun at his belt, but Gabriella wasn't fooled as her late brother had been. She fired twice, both bullets finding their mark, and she watched as Dutch slumped backward onto the ground. She walked over, looked into his eyes and fired the next shot into his head. She walked down the tunnel to check on Ramone, found no pulse and returned to the entrance.

Once outside, she picked up the block of plastic explosives she had gotten from Roger Burns, set it down inside the entrance and set the timer. She set it for ten minutes and walked over to the two SUVs sitting next to each other. She placed a block of plastic explosives inside each vehicle and checked her watch. She set the timers and headed down the hill to where she had hidden her car behind a rock outcropping. She sat in her SUV and waited, keeping an eye on her watch. Her timing was off; the tunnel entrance blew fifteen seconds before the SUVs.

She could hear the tunnel collapsing and she saw the thick black smoke from the SUVs as the fire turned what was left of them into cinders. She smiled, put the Escalade in gear and headed back down the mountain. She had work to do now that she owned the entire company.

Chapter Twenty-Seven

Buck grabbed an empty desk, opened his laptop and opened the investigation file. He pulled up the background checks on Velasquez Mining, Ramone and Gabriella Velasquez and the two geologists. For the next forty-five minutes, he read and reread the reports.

Ramone and Gabriella Velasquez had no internet footprints and there was little public information about them. Both attended Ivy League schools and were notable for their charity contributions, but there was very little else.

The two geologists were active on social media, but nothing that was informative. All these folks were squeaky clean, and that frustrated Buck. He pulled out his phone and dialed Paul.

"Hey, Buck," said Paul.

"Paul. Did you review the backgrounds of the mining company and the two geologists?"

"Yeah. Hard to believe in this day and age that there was so little information on all of them."

"That's what I was thinking. Are there any other stones we can turn over?" asked Buck.

Paul was quiet for a minute. "Let me do some digging. I'm gonna try some old-school stuff and see if any of it pays off."

Buck had no idea what Paul meant by "old school," but he trusted Paul with his life, so he didn't question it.

"Hold on, Buck. George needs you."

"Hey, Buck," said George. "We ran background on the dead guy and the guy you arrested. These guys don't have a speeding ticket, let alone anything significant in their backgrounds. It's weird. Everyone connected to this case is clean. What are we missing?"

"I was thinking the same thing, George. Are we missing a player? People like this don't suddenly become ecoterrorists. It's frustrating as hell."

"Yeah, tell me about it."

"George, any luck with Woodman's phone or laptop?"

"We got into both," said George. "Nothing interesting in the phone. A bunch of calls to Mortensen and to his wife. A few to the office, and several to Ramone. Oh yeah. In the week before the landslide, he spoke to Gabriella Velasquez twelve times. Several after business hours."

"Can we get transcripts of the calls?" asked Buck.

"I requested a warrant, but even when I get it, the phone companies are notoriously slow. I'll keep working it."

"What about the laptop?"

"It's odd, Buck. He had some heavy-duty encryption software running, yet nothing we looked at seems to have needed that kind of protection. It was all lab reports and meeting notes. Nothing earth-shattering. Sorry for the pun."

Buck laughed. "You think he's hiding something in there we haven't found?"

"Mel is running some checks. She's wondering if something on there got moved to a thumb drive or external hard drive."

Buck moved and felt the rock in his pocket that Jeremy Ratzenberger had thrown to him. He pulled it out and stared at it.

"Hey, George. Scan the laptop for any information about rare earth metals and see if anything pops up."

"You got something in the back of your mind?" asked George.

"Just something someone told me about. It's a long shot, but see what clicks."

"You got it, Buck. Talk soon."

George disconnected the call.

"Buck," said Janine Garvey. "The lawyer is ready for us."

Buck hooked his phone back onto his belt and closed his laptop. He followed Janine to the interview and handed Chief Molina his pistol. They stepped into the room and took their seats.

"Folks," said Robert Crawley. "My client has something he wants to say. Rodney, go ahead."

"We didn't kill that woman, the wife of that geologist. We roughed her up, but we didn't kill her."

"Okay, Rodney. You want to tell us about it?" asked Buck.

Rodney sat upright in the seat. "Not with him in the room." He pointed at Robert Crawley, who turned, looking stunned.

"Rodney," said Crawley. "This is not what we talked about."

"You're right." He looked at Janine. "I don't want him as my lawyer anymore."

Janine, without changing her expression to show her surprise, said, "Rodney. That's your right, but can you tell me why?"

"Rodney," said Crawley. "What are you doing?"

Rodney looked at Crawley. "I don't want you here. You're fired."

Crawley looked around the table, then back to Rodney. "You can't fire me. I'm here to help you."

Rodney pulled back and crossed his arms over his chest. "I'm done talking with him in the room."

Crawley opened his mouth, but Janine stopped him. "You heard the man, Mr. Crawley. Mr. Toobin has made it clear that you no longer represent him. Please gather your things and leave."

Crawley's face turned red. "This is an outrage."

Buck stood up and walked to the door and pushed it open. "Mr. Crawley, this way, if you please."

Crawley picked up his notepad and recorder and placed them in his briefcase, stood up and snapped his sleeves. He adjusted his tie, picked up the briefcase and walked through the door. Buck pulled the door closed.

Buck sat back down and looked at Rodney. "Well, Rodney. That was unexpected. What do we do now?"

Rodney looked at Janine. "Sorry, ma'am, but that guy wasn't here to protect my best interests. He was . . ."

Janine leaned forward. "Mr. Toobin, before you say another word, I must caution you that you are still under oath. I am going to call the public defender's office and have them send over a lawyer to represent you. Will that be okay?"

Rodney nodded, and she tapped Buck on the arm and indicated for him to follow her. They both stood and walked to the door. Buck stopped and turned.

"Rodney, you've been here awhile. Can I get you something to eat or drink, or do you need to use the restroom?"

"I sure could use a sandwich and a soft drink if it's not too much trouble."

Buck nodded and pushed through the door. Janine was standing next to Chief Molina.

"I'll send one of my officers to get him a sandwich and drink. What the hell do you think that was all about?"

Buck thought for a minute. "I'd like to know who hired Crawley."

"You think there's something hinky going on?" asked Janine.

"Just a feeling," said Buck.

Janine pulled her phone from her pocket. "I need to make a couple of calls." She stepped away.

Chief Molina looked at Buck. "You think someone was trying to make him the fall guy?"

"I'll bet our friend in there got the same feeling after talking to Crawley. I have a feeling there was a plan in place that Rodney disagreed with."

"That's not gonna make someone happy," said the chief.

"No, it's not. Do two things for me. Let Janine know I'm going over to talk to his boss at the demolition company, and keep an eye on Rodney."

"You think someone would try something while he's in police custody?"

"I don't want to take that chance, Gabe. Just a precaution."

Chief Molina nodded, and Buck walked over, placed his laptop in his backpack and headed for the door.

Chapter Twenty-Eight

Bax parked her Jeep next to the Garfield County Sheriff's Department SUV, grabbed her backpack and slid out. She looked at the stone, glass and steel building in front of her and whistled. The deputy slid out of his SUV and walked towards her.

"Agent Baxter," he said, holding out his hand. "Isaac Reed."

"Sergeant Reed. Nice to meet you. Please call me Bax." She shook his hand.

Sergeant Reed was a tall, thin Black man who had spent twenty years with the sheriff's department. He stood ram-rod straight. His uniform had sharp creases.

"Sheriff didn't give me much to go on. Mind tellin' me what we're doing here? I assume this has to do with the rockslide. I heard the governor's press conference. An explosion did all that damage. Incredible."

"Yeah. The perfect word for it. Incredible," said Bax. "We are here to find out about two geologists who worked for this company. One is dead, one is missing, and the missing man's wife is also dead."

"And you think they're related to the bombing?"

"That we don't know yet, but their deaths are suspicious."

"Then we best go talk to these folks," said Reed.

Bax and Sergeant Reed walked across the parking lot and approached the door, which slid open as they approached. They entered a lobby that could have been in a modern luxury hotel. The harsh windows and steel construction were softened by bright-colored, plush furniture. Huge pieces of art, most abstract, hung on the walls, and soft music played in the background.

Bax stepped up to the front counter, where a young man and woman wearing dark suits stood as they neared.

"May we help you?" asked the young woman.

Bax held up her badge and ID. "Ashley Baxter. We'd like to see Ramone Velasquez, please."

"Do you have an appointment?" asked the young man, clicking keys on the keyboard and looking at the monitor.

"No, we are here as part of a murder investigation and need to speak to him."

"I'm sorry, but Mr. Velasquez is not in the building, and I have no way of knowing when he will be returning."

Bax looked at the young man—Stewart, according to his name tag. She leaned in to the counter.

"Stewart, would you please check and see if Gabriella Velasquez is in the building?"

Stewart clicked a few more keys. "Yes, ma'am. She is in the building. If you'll have a seat, someone will come get you."

Bax thanked him, and they walked over to a couple of comfy chairs and sat. Bax rubbed the arm of the chair. "Nice," she said. Reed nodded, his eyes in constant motion, looking around the lobby.

A few minutes later, a young woman exited the elevator and passed through the security gate.

"Agent Baxter, Sergeant Reed, if you'll follow me," she said.

They stood and followed her as she swiped the laminated card around her neck across the scanner and the gate light turned green. She stepped through and held the gate for them. They followed her into the elevator, and she pressed the number three. The door closed. Soft music filled the car as they rose to the third floor. When the door opened, they followed the young woman along an open walkway until she reached a door at the end of the hall. She tapped on the door and pushed the door open.

"Agent Baxter and Sergeant Reed," she said and stepped aside.

"Please come in," said Gabriella Velasquez. "Please have a seat." She waited as they approached, shook hands with each of them and then sat down. Bax looked around the office.

The office was a lot more feminine than she expected. When she had met Gabriella at the Woodman house, she got the impression she was a hard, cold, all-business woman. The office was just the opposite. It was bright and warm, with soft furniture and dozens of plants on a credenza along the windows.

Gabriella noticed Bax looking at a large picture on the wall behind the desk. "My family," she said. "My brother, Ramone, my sister, Tina, and her husband and children."

"Nice-looking family," said Bax.

Gabriella turned back to face her. "How can I help the police today? I assume this is about the terrible deaths of Tim Woodman and Betty Mortensen. Such tragedies; their deaths have affected us a great deal. They were well liked around here." She pulled a tissue from the box on her desk and dabbed her eyes. "How can I help?"

"We're trying to get some background on them. Neither seemed to have much of a social media presence, and we know very little about them. We were hoping you might be able to enlighten us."

Gabriella clicked the keyboard and sat back. "Tim has been with us for almost fifteen years. He started with us right out of college. He worked his way to being our chief geologist. His performance reports are all exemplary."

"Did you socialize with him outside of work?" asked Bax.

"No. I'm afraid we traveled in different circles," she said.

"What about Jack Mortensen?"

She clicked more keys. "Dr. Mortensen was Tim's assistant." She hesitated for a moment. "There have been some disciplinary problems over the past few months, nothing terrible. He would show up late for work or call in sick. I hate to speculate, but I think he might have had a drinking problem. It's a shame. He has been a good and loyal employee for over ten years. We were all surprised when he didn't show up to work, but then, with the death of his wife and him being missing, we're not sure what to think."

"Ms. Velasquez, do you know if anything is missing from their offices?"

"Why, yes. Both their laptops are missing, as are their company phones. I have had our IT department and security disable the phones and the laptops, and we have gone through their files and haven't found anything amiss. Why do you ask? Do you think they were involved in that landslide in the canyon? The governor seemed shaken at his press conference that this might be the work of ecoterrorists. How awful, but I can assure you. Both men are pillars of the community, valued and respected."

"Ma'am, you have several Cadillac Escalades registered to your company. Can you tell me who drives these?" She handed a list to Gabriella, who read down it. "This first one is mine. Ramone drives the second one; the third is part of our fleet and is usually driven by our chief of security, Dutch Heinrick. Why do you ask?"

"Just came up during our background checks on the victims. I would like to speak with your brother and Mr. Heinrick if that's possible."

"I'm sorry, Agent Baxter. They are both on a tour of our mines. With the possibility of ecoterrorists being involved in the canyon rockslide, we thought upgrading some of our security procedures might be prudent. Just routine, I assure you. But I don't know when they will be back."

The laptop on her desk chimed, and she clicked a button. "Is that all, Agent Baxter? I have a meeting to get to and I don't want to be late." She stood and walked around the desk. Bax and Reed stood, shook hands with her and walked to the door. Bax stopped.

"One last question. Is there anything coming out of your mines that might lead ecoterrorists to want to shut you down?"

Gabriella laughed. "I can assure you, Agent Baxter, what we mine is common and found in mines worldwide. Nothing we produce would interest anyone nefarious."

Bax nodded and thanked her for her time, and she and Reed were escorted back to the elevator by the same young woman. Once on the ground floor, she led them through the security gate and bid them a good day. They walked through the automatic door and headed for their vehicles. As they approached Reed's SUV, he stopped and called to her. He pulled the mic off the tab on his shoulder. "Ten-four, Dispatch. We'll check it out."

"What's up?" asked Bax.

"Dispatch took a call a few minutes ago from a civilian who spotted black smoke near an old mine nearby. I'm the closest unit. Because of the drought, I need to check it out. You're welcome to tag along."

Bax nodded, and they slid into their vehicles and pulled out of the parking lot.

| **29** |

Chapter Twenty-Nine

Gabriella stood on the balcony overlooking the lobby and watched the two cops enter their cars and race off towards the old mine. She hoped the plastic explosive did a good enough job on the tunnel to make it impossible to get to the bodies. She wondered how the cops had found out so soon.

She pulled out her phone and dialed a number.

"Hello."

"Peter, it's Gabby. Have you guys left for Denver?"

"Not yet. Tina was hoping to see Ramone before we left. Why?"

"I need you to meet me in my office. I have something I need you to do for me. And Peter. Don't mention where you are going to Tina. This doesn't concern her."

Gabriella disconnected the call and walked back to her office. She sat down and clicked on her laptop, then the door opened, and Sylvia De Rivera walked in and closed the door.

Sylvia was in her sixties and had been the chief operating officer for the agricultural division of Velasquez Enterprises for ten years. She had earned the short gray hair and the extra fifteen pounds she hated. She was also Gabriella's closest friend in the company, if she actually had any friends. She walked to the desk, sat down and slid a manila folder across the desk. Gabriella picked it up and opened it.

"We have a problem. Well seven went dry this morning. This drought is killing us, and with the diminished flow in the river right now, we don't have enough water for the horses, let alone the cattle. I've started selling off part of the herd, but no one is paying for premium beef. We're gonna have to take the herd down to about thirty percent of where we were two years ago. We already run less than fifty percent of the horses we ran last year. Twenty-seven calves died this week, and we've got over a thousand acres of dead grain. This is hurting our bottom line. Can you talk to Ramone and see what we want to do?"

"How many wells are still producing?" asked Gabriella.

"Four," said Sylvia, "but the mine is gonna kill those."

"Fuck," said Gabriella. "Okay. Give me a couple of hours to get with Ramone and we'll figure something out."

"Gabby. We're in real trouble here. If we can't replenish the wells, we could lose everything: the herd, the fields, the whole lot."

"I get it. I'll get some answers."

Sylvia stood and walked out of the office. She closed the door. Gabriella picked up her phone and placed a call.

"Yes, ma'am."

"Tony, do we have enough hoses and pumps to get down to the new reservoir in the canyon?"

"Yes, ma'am," said Tony. "Mr. Velasquez had me bring in a bunch of new equipment. I thought he was crazy spending all that money, but it looks like God was watching over him. It turned out to be the right decision."

"Okay, work the crew overtime, but let's get the water flowing. We're gonna need a lot for the rock crushers that Ramone promised the governor. The trucks are supposed to start rolling tomorrow. Run a separate line and start pumping water back into the wells."

"That's gonna take a lot of manpower and time," said Tony.

"Then you'd better get started." She disconnected the call and sat back in her chair. She had a lot to think about now with Ramone gone.

There was a knock on her door and Peter Welker, Tina's husband, pushed open the door. Gabriella waved him in, and he walked in and closed the door. He sat in the chair opposite the desk.

"What's so important I couldn't tell my wife?" he asked.

"I need you to flood the internet with stories about an ecoterrorist group claiming responsibility for the rockslide in the canyon."

"What are you talking about? The governor didn't mention anything specific about ecoterrorists. He said it was a man-made disaster but not by whom."

Peter Welker ran a small IT firm with a handful of small companies as clients. As far as Gabriella was concerned, he was a failure and just living off his wife's money.

She looked across the desk and her expression went dark. She controlled her voice. "What I'm asking you for is very simple. Just do your internet voodoo and convince people it was an ecoterrorist group. Make up some name that sounds eco-y, you know, the Green Army of Satan, or some such shit. You're a smart guy. Figure it out."

"Gabby, why do you want me to do this?" He opened his mouth then sat for a second. "What the fuck did you do? Were you involved in the explosion that caused the rockslide?"

He jumped out of the chair and paced across the office. "Oh, fuck. Fuck, fuck, fuck, fuck, fuck. Shit, we're all going to jail. The whole family. What the fuck did you do?"

Gabriella watched the tirade with amusement. Peter was always a drama queen. From the first day Tina introduced him to the family, she knew he was overreactive. She let him pace for a few minutes, talking to himself and shaking his head like he was having some internal battle between good and evil.

When she'd had enough of his tantrum, she yelled at him. "Peter. For Christ's sake, get a grip. You're a grown man. Stop acting like a kid and sit your ass down before I get up and knock you down."

Peter sat and looked at her. His hands were shaking, and his forehead was covered in beads of sweat. He stared at her. She leaned forward and whispered, "You are the laziest motherfucker I have ever met. You sit around in your country club house, enjoy all the social amenities my sister's money affords you, and waste time instead of trying to make your shitty little business work. So, you listen to me, and you listen good. You either do what I ask, or I will cut off my sister's monthly allowance. Is that plain enough for you to understand? You will have no family income. You will lose your house, fancy cars, trips, and your kids will have to go to public school, and I will make you explain to my sister why the income flow has stopped. What's it gonna be?"

Peter sat there stunned; tears formed in his eyes. "Does Ramone know about this?"

"Yes. It was Ramone's idea. Our family once held the title, by Spanish land grant, to a piece of Colorado the size of Yellowstone. We owned it all. Mineral rights, timber, animals and, most importantly, we owned the water rights to a huge portion of the Colorado and Eagle Rivers. Those rights, as well as the land itself, were stolen from our ancestors. We have been fighting for decades to regain those rights, but the government keeps getting in our way. Our wells are running out of water. We've had to cut our cattle and horse herds to almost nothing. Our fields have dried up, and our mining operation is in jeopardy. The worst part is we just discovered a source of rare earth metals that will make our family, you included, billions of dollars. We asked the state and federal government to allow us to build a reservoir to give us the water we need. We were willing to pay for it ourselves, but they refused and went so far as to tell us that there was no record of us having any rights. Instead, they send the water that rightfully belongs to us to golf courses and resorts in Las Vegas and Phoenix. Our ancestors deserve better. The land on either side of the canyon belongs to us, and we needed the landslide to expose the minerals and give us the water we are entitled to So, we did what the government refused to do. We built our own dam, and now we have our reservoir. And we are doing our civic duty and helping out that weasel of a governor by hauling and crushing all the boulders from the canyon. Boulders that contain the rare earth minerals we found, and now we don't even have to mine for them. They are right there for the picking."

She sat back in her chair and looked at Peter. "What's it gonna be, Peter? Will you help me, or do I call the bank?" She picked up her phone.

"You're insane, you know that. People could have died," said Peter. "You would destroy your sister, our kids and the country's economy to get what you want. You're out of your mind."

She pointed the phone at him.

"All right, I'll do what you ask, but you swear to me right now, on your father's soul, that you will never threaten me or your sister again. And after we are done, you stay away from us."

Gabriella laughed.

"Swear it," said Peter.

"All right, Peter. As you wish. I swear it. Happy now?" He nodded. "Good, then get the fuck out of my office and get busy. I want to see something later today. Do not let me down."

Peter stood and left the office, still shaking. He knew Gabriella had a mean streak; he had seen it before, but this was something else, and he was scared for his family. He also wondered where Ramone was, and that scared him even more.

Chapter Thirty

Gabriella waited until Peter left the building and watched from her office window until his car pulled out of the parking lot. She walked over and closed her office door. She knew she had come down hard on him, but she had to make sure he understood how important this was. She also needed to make sure he never said a word to Tina. Tina would never understand. Tina was all about country club living and volunteering for as many social causes as possible. She enjoyed partying with her friends and living as large as she could. It was a great life for the daughter of a billionaire. It also made her vulnerable, and Gabriella was willing to take full advantage of it.

She walked back to the window and looked out. She wasn't sure if she was looking to make sure Peter was gone or if she was looking out over the pasture behind the building that used to be green and lush and filled with thoroughbred horses. Now the pasture was dead and brown and they had only a handful of horses. She made a silent vow that once she was confirmed as the sole owner of Velasquez Enterprises, she would fix that. She also vowed to take back everything that was stolen from her ancestors.

She walked across the room to the wall safe, checked to make sure no one was watching, opened the safe and pulled out the black semiautomatic pistol. She placed it in her purse, along with the silencer that sat next to it. She added an extra clip to the bag and locked the safe.

Gabriella left her computer running on her desk. She was sending automated emails. She needed to leave a paper trail. She picked up her purse, opened her door and approached her assistant.

"I've got a meeting with the mining department downstairs. I'll be there the rest of the day. Finish what you're working on and call it a day. We'll go over the numbers for the new mine extension tomorrow."

Gabriella walked down the hallway and entered the service stairs at the end of the corridor. She took the stairs, reached the ground floor and, using a key she got from the maintenance office, unlocked the emergency door, opened it, stepped out and locked it from the outside. She walked to where she had parked her SUV, slid in and drove onto an old construction road that was no longer used. It was the long way around, but it kept her from passing in front of the building. She reached the end of the road, turned onto the paved road and headed for the interstate.

Gabriella exited the interstate at Gypsum, followed a long unnamed road and pulled up to the gate. The sign next to the gate read roger burns & sons, but it gave no indication of what the company did. She rolled down her window, pressed the call button and waited. The gate buzzed and slid open. She drove through the gate and parked in front of the small concrete building. She pushed open the door and stepped into the reception area. She let the door close behind her and turned the thumb-turn latch to lock the door.

"Gabriella, come on in," said a gruff voice from the office.

Roger Burns stood up, walked around the desk and kissed her on the cheek.

"This is an unexpected pleasure. What brings you here?" asked Roger.

Gabriella and Roger sat on opposite sides of the desk. She reached into her large purse and pulled out an envelope, which she slid across the desk.

"I need a favor," she said with a grin.

Roger looked at the envelope, picked it up and looked inside.

"Must be a hell of a favor," he said. "What do you need, Gabriella?"

"I need four blocks of plastic explosive and timer blasting caps."

Roger slid the envelope back across the desk. "No can do. I'm still working on covering the tracks from our last business arrangement. Plastic is too regulated, and I can't just hand you four blocks. What do you intend to do with it?"

"That's none of your concern," she said. "You can just write it off to the mining company. What the hell is the problem, Roger? You didn't squirm when I handed you the huge duffel bag of money for the one hundred thousand pounds of RDX. Why are you giving me a hassle over four blocks of plastic?"

"Yeah. I'm having serious concerns about the RDX. My kid is asking all kinds of questions, and I had no idea you would cause so much destruction. You and your brother are insane."

"Are you shaking me down for more money, Roger? Is that what this is about? I told you there'd be much more where that came from once we started production."

"Look, Gabriella. I have no problem taking care of all your blasting needs at the mine, but I am done with this extra crap. I'd like to forget the entire thing with the canyon. It was wrong and stupid for me to get involved. It would be a shame if the authorities found out."

Gabriella picked up the envelope. "Okay, Roger." She opened her purse, put the envelope inside it and pulled out the silenced pistol. She pointed it at Roger, who started to stand up, and shot him in the side. He fell to the floor, and she stood up, walked around the desk and shot him in the head.

She turned and walked to the office door, opened it and walked through. She stepped around the reception counter and pushed open the door to the second office. Keith Burns sat behind his desk. He had on headphones and was tapping keys on his keyboard. He looked up as Gabriella raised the pistol. He raised his hands in a feeble gesture to protect himself, and Gabriella pulled the trigger. The bullet passed through his hand and into his right eye. He fell to the floor, his body shaking for a minute, and then the office was silent.

Gabriella walked out of Keith's office and back into Roger's office. She reached over the dead body and unclipped the key ring from his belt loop. She picked up her purse, walked out and locked the door.

She walked across the lot to the warehouse, keeping the pistol in her hand. She pushed open the door and stepped into the huge metal building. She encountered the first warehouse worker between several rows of demolition equipment and machinery. She never gave him a chance. Her first shot hit him in the knee, and he fell against the tire of an excavator. Her second shot hit him in the head.

She turned and headed for the security area, where she spotted the other worker. He saw her at the same time, saw the gun in her hand and ran towards the side exit. Gabriella dropped into a Weaver stance, aimed and fired one shot into his back. He fell to the ground and slid a few feet. He tried to crawl away, but the second shot to his head stopped that.

Gabriella took the keys she had taken off Roger and tried keys in the security area lock until she found the key that unlocked the large metal door. She slid open the door and walked in. There were large crates of explosives every- where. She laughed, thinking that it would be a terrorist's wet dream to have access to this space.

She knew where to look because she and Roger had been there together a few months back when they started plan- ning the explosion. She walked down an aisle, stopped in front of a wooden box and opened it. She pulled out four bricks of plastic explosives and put them in her purse. She walked to a second aisle, pulled four blasting caps with at- tached digital timers and put those in her back pocket. She walked out and locked the door.

Gabriella walked back to her car. She put her purse on the seat, then went back and opened the office door and walked behind the counter. She pushed the red button that opened the security gate. She walked out, slid into her SUV and drove away from the building and through the gate. She stopped outside the gate, slid out of her SUV and ran back to the office. She stepped inside, hit the button to close the gate, relocked the office and ran back to her SUV. She used Roger's keys to unlock the small gate and stepped through, letting it close. She threw the keys across the street into an empty field, climbed into her SUV and pulled out. She never saw the camera on the light pole twenty feet down the fence.

| **31** |

Chapter Thirty-One

Bax followed Sergeant Reed up twelve miles of the crappiest road she had ever been on. Several times she bounced so hard that she thought she had torn the transmission off the Jeep. The drive was painfully slow, and she hoped Reed knew where he was going, because she was lost.

They came over a slight rise and spotted the source of the smoke. Reed pulled his SUV off to the side and Bax parked alongside him. They slid out of their vehicles and walked towards the pile of smoldering, twisted metal. There was little left that could be identified as a car or truck. Before they walked any farther, Bax pulled out her phone, switched the camera to video and walked around the vehicles, filming as she went.

She stopped filming and walked around the vehicles. This time, she was looking for anything that didn't belong on or in the scorched soil. Reed did the same thing in the opposite direction.

"Nothing," said Bax. "Damn ground is hard as a rock. Not gonna get any useful shoe prints out of this stuff."

Reed nodded, turned, walked a few feet away, stopped, leaned over and kneeled.

"Bax, come take a look at this."

Bax walked over and kneeled next to him. He pointed to a twisted and burned piece of metal. Part of the letters were missing, but there was no mistaking the crest.

"Cadillac logo," said Reed.

"Shit," said Bax. "You want to bet one if not both of these is a Cadillac Escalade?"

"You asked that woman about an Escalade. You think these might be related?"

"I would not be surprised," she said.

She looked over his shoulder, stood and walked a few yards to the pile of rocks that covered the mine tunnel entrance. Reed followed and stopped next to her.

"You think the drivers might be in there?"

"We may never find out," she said. "Would be a waste of time to call search and rescue. This collapse could go back a long way."

Reed smiled. "I might know someone who can help. Mind if I give him a call?"

Bax looked at him. "Seriously?" she said. "Go ahead. If your friend can help, I'll authorize the payment." She was intrigued.

Reed pulled out his phone, pushed the button and said, "Call George."

She could hear the phone ringing on the other end and a gruff voice said hello.

"George, it's Isaac. Gonna need your help with something. It's kind of urgent."

Reed listened. "Yeah. That old mine about twelve miles up God Almighty Road. Might have some folks inside."

Reed listened, thanked George and hung up.

"God Almighty Road," said Bax.

"I grew up around here. That road we came in on doesn't have a name, never did. Folks hereabouts call it the God Almighty Road. Bet you said that a couple of times on the way up."

Bax laughed. "So, who is this George fella?"

"George," said Reed. "Well, he's quite a character. Been working round here for as long as anyone can remember. Must be pushing ninety or so. He started out as a miner; now he's our first call when a mine collapses. He's worked more mine collapses than anyone can count. He's sort of an expert. He's got five sons, big fellas, and they do all the heavy lifting. If anyone can get into the mine, it's George."

"Does he have a business or a company name?" asked Bax.

"Don't rightly know. He's listed in my phone as 'Call George.' That's it."

"How long are we gonna have to wait for him to get here?" asked Bax.

"Told me to give him an hour. He'll be here. No doubt."

An hour later, Bax slid out of her Jeep and heard several vehicles grinding their way up the road. She looked up at the slight rise as an old—make that very old—one-ton flatbed truck crested the rise. An old bulldozer was attached to a trailer behind it, and the flatbed was full of wooden timbers. The truck rolled past her, and the elderly Black man in the driver's seat tipped his hat towards her. Behind the truck came a newer truck hauling a trailer with more heavy equipment.

Bax joined Reed as the first truck parked and the older man climbed down. He shook Reed's hand and introduced himself to Bax. For a frail-looking old man, he had a grip like iron.

"Pleased to meet you, ma'am," he said. He pointed over his shoulder. "Them's my boys."

Bax looked to where he was pointing; standing next to the truck were five middle-aged Black men. She was impressed. These five guys could have been a hell of an offensive line for the Denver Broncos. They were all muscle. The old man whistled, and the younger men started hauling equipment off the second truck.

George walked over to the cave-in. He held a hammer and tapped on some of the rocks. He must have found the right spot because he leaned in closer and put his ear next to one of the boulders. He tapped again and listened. He stood and looked at Reed.

"Doesn't sound too deep. Maybe fifteen, twenty feet. We'll get after it."

He looked at the twisted metal. "You think the drivers are in there?"

"It's possible," said Reed.

"Somebody didn't like those folks much." He laughed and moved out of the way as two of his sons started driving long metal rods into the cave-in. Bax and Reed moved out of the way.

For the next several hours, they watched as George yelled orders and the five younger men, working with extraordinary teamwork, performed each task. They dug nonstop, placed small explosive charges when the rock pile got tight, removed huge boulders and shored up the ceiling as they went.

Six hours after they arrived, George stepped out of the tunnel and waved for them. Bax and Reed slid out of their vehicles and walked to the mine entrance.

"Ma'am, got us two men inside. Both dead. Thought you might want to take a look. Don't look like the cave-in killed them."

Bax walked back to her Jeep and grabbed a long black Maglite, and she and Reed climbed over the few remaining boulders. The first body was closer to the entrance. There was blood on his right thigh and two bullet holes in his chest, one in the side and one in his head. The second body was farther back in the tunnel and had evidence of a knife wound in the chest. George was right. Neither man had died from the cave-in.

Bax asked everyone to step out of the tunnel. She stepped away from the group and pulled out her phone. Since they were closer to Eagle County, she called Sheriff Hartman and asked if he could have his pathologist and forensic team work the site. He told her he'd get his people moving right away and send a couple of deputies up to help secure the site.

She disconnected the call and dialed Buck.

| **32** |

Chapter Thirty-Two

Buck was halfway over Cottonwood Pass when his phone chimed. He looked at the number and hit the talk button on the dashboard entertainment center.

"Afternoon."

"What the hell have you gotten yourself into this time? Ecoterrorists. Fuck, Buck," said Hank Clancy.

Hank Clancy was the special agent in charge of the Denver Field Office of the FBI and one of Buck's closest friends. Hank had been a deputy director until earlier in the year when he fell on his sword and took the blame for a rogue FBI agent. The agent, while working out of the Denver Field Office and fighting Buck at every turn during the investigation of the Christmas Day bombings, caused the deaths of several FBI agents and serious injuries to many others.

Buck had asked the Colorado governor to intervene on Hank's behalf, and as a result, they were able to save his job, but they couldn't prevent the demotion. Hank had a long career with the FBI and was involved in many high-profile cases. And even though his wife wanted him to retire, Hank refused to end his career with a black eye.

Buck laughed. "Not too sure."

"What do you mean? The governor held a press conference and said so. What's going on, Buck?"

Buck filled him in on what they knew so far. Hank listened without interrupting. Buck stopped to take a sip of Coke from the bottle in the cupholder.

"So, if not terrorists, then what?"

"Not sure yet," said Buck. "I've dealt with ecoterrorists before. This feels like something different."

After Buck's wife passed away, he had been called to investigate a fire at a controversial hunting lodge that was being blamed on ecoterrorists. The lodge had been set on fire, Buck later learned, to cover up the murder of a DEA agent, and the lodge fire led to one of the worst wildfires in Colorado history. Buck's investigation led to a group of survivalists selling counterfeit drugs and a billionaire whose companies were pumping hazardous waste into fracking wells. When all was said and done, it had nothing to do with ecoterrorists and was all about the money.

"How so?" asked Hank.

"No upside. What would they hope to gain by blowing up a highway and flooding a canyon? The slide caused more ecological damage to the canyon than the highway ever could. I don't see it."

"Okay, say you're right," said Hank. "Who would stand to gain by closing the highway and flooding the canyon?"

"That's what's got me stuck," said Buck.

"Well, and this is just me spitballing, but what did the landslide do to the canyon? What's different about the canyon today than last week before the slide?"

Buck thought for a minute. "Rocks and water."

"Right," said Hank, "but the canyon always had rocks and water. What's different now?"

Buck thought about the little piece of rock in his pocket that Jeremy Ratzenberger had given him.

"The slide did two things," said Buck. "It created a reservoir in a state ravaged by drought and loosened up the entire top of a mountain."

"Why?" asked Hank.

"Rare earth metals."

"What the hell are you talking about?" asked Hank.

Buck told him about the piece of rare earth metal that Ratzenberger found in the slide area. He also told him about the RDX found in the dirt in the tunnel.

"Now you're getting somewhere," said Hank. "I'm no mining expert, but I bet it's a lot cheaper to pull minerals out of a rock pile than mine for them. Now you need to figure out who benefits."

"Yeah, and figure out who needs a lot of water," said Buck.

"What do you need from me?" asked Hank.

"I'm waiting for the ATF to get back to me with information on who purchased RDX in this area. Can you push them a little?"

"No problem, Buck. I'll put a couple of my folks on it as well. Stay safe and call if you need anything else."

Buck disconnected the call and his phone chimed. He checked the number and answered.

"Doctor, I was just talking to someone about you."

"I hope it was a pleasant conversation, Agent Taylor. Listen, are you anywhere near the east side of the slide area?"

"I'm pulling into Gypsum now. What's up?"

"Can you meet us at the tunnel? Something I'd like to show you."

"No problem, Doc. I'll be there in a few minutes."

Buck disconnected and turned onto I-70 Westbound. He pulled up to the barricade and presented his ID to the trooper on duty. The trooper moved a section of the barricade and Buck pulled through. He drove a couple of miles and stopped outside the tunnel entrance. He slid out of the Jeep, grabbed his backpack and hard hat and walked into the tunnel. He met Todd and Jeremy at the west end. He noticed the water behind the rockslide was only inches from the roadway.

"Okay, Doc. What's going on?"

"Whoever caused this landslide had a specific purpose in mind," said Jeremy. "It's hard to see now that a large chunk of the mountain is in the canyon, but think of the sidewalls of the canyon as a layer cake. Various layers of different types of rocks have piled on top of each other over millennia, all with different densities and properties. It's kind of like different types of snow falling on the mountains: one layer wet, one layer dry and so on until you have the perfect avalanche setup. Take that layer cake and tilt it about thirty-five to forty degrees towards the river—lots of pressure on those layers to stay where they were. Now place a massive explosive charge at the bottom of that slope. The concussive force of the explosion cracks the softer or more brittle layers and then gravity does the rest. Whoever placed those charges knew exactly where to put them."

"Okay," said Buck, not sure where this was going. "But why bring down the mountain?"

"To get to the metals without having to mine them. This canyon is full of rare earth metals. In the short time we've been here, we've found five of the seventeen rare earth metals. That's incredible. If what we've seen is only a part of the find, this could be the largest collection of rare earth metals ever found. It's worth billions and would put the United States ahead of the Chinese in rare earth metal production. Because these metals are now accessible without the high mining costs, they can be produced cheaper and faster. All someone has to do is shovel them up and extract them from the rocks. Someone is going to make a ton of money."

The ground shook, and Buck looked up at what was left of the sidewall of the canyon with concern in his eyes.

"Don't worry, Agent Taylor. Everything above us is stable. More stable than it's ever been," said Dr. Ratzenberger.

"Then what's the vibration?" asked Buck.

"There's a long line of dump trucks on the other side of the slide, along with heavy-duty cranes and earthmoving equipment. They're starting to take down the rockslide. It is a monumental task, to say the least. We spoke to one of the workers, and the governor wants them to create a spillway. If the water gets much higher, the town of Dotsero will be forced to evacuate."

"Okay, Doc," said Buck. "Thanks for the geology lesson. Makes things a little clearer." He looked at the water lapping at the road. "You guys had better clear out before you have to swim out of here."

They shook hands, and Buck headed back through the tunnel to his Jeep. He slid in and headed back towards Gypsum. He needed to talk to Rodney's boss.

He exited the highway and followed an unmarked road for ten miles north of town till he came to a twelve-foot-tall chain-link fence topped by a roll of concertina wire. It looked like a prison. The sign on the gate read roger burns & sons. There was nothing to indicate this was a demolition company.

The large steel gate containing numerous warning placards was closed, but the smaller door to the side of the gate stood open. Buck thought that was odd. He parked the Jeep, slid out, walked up to the security panel and pushed the call button. He could hear it ringing, but no one answered. The little bug in his brain started dancing around. He walked to the back of his Jeep, opened the hatch and pulled out his ballistic vest. He slipped it on, opened the gun safe welded to the floor of his Jeep and pulled out a backup pistol and holster, which he strapped to his thigh. He loaded a couple extra magazines, closed the hatch and walked through the gate.

From their background check on Rodney and Boomer, Buck had learned that Roger Burns & Sons was one of the largest and most respected demolition companies in the world, which seemed not to fit the small concrete building that sat in front of him. The only thing indicating it was an office was the sign above the door that read visitors sign in here.

Buck grabbed the handle and found that the door was locked. He walked around the building, but there were very few windows, all several feet off the ground. He completed his circuit and looked at the two vehicles parked next to the building. Both were locked. He looked at the huge steel warehouse several hundred feet away, but no workers were visible. Buck was on high alert. A warehouse that size should have a large crew working in it, but only two other trucks were in the lot. He returned to the front door, removed a brown folder from his back pocket and pulled out two lockpicks. He worked on the lock for a few seconds, put away the picks and pulled out his pistol.

Buck pushed the door open, and the coppery smell of blood filled the air. "Police, show yourself."

No response. He stepped through the door, closed and locked it. He wasn't sure what was going on, but he didn't want anyone to come in behind him.

Leading with his pistol, he looked behind the small counter in what must have been a reception area. He stepped around the counter and pushed open the office door. The body of a young man was lying on the floor behind the desk. There was a bullet wound in his right hand and his face. It looked to Buck like the victim had raised his hand to protect himself, the bullet going through his hand first.

Buck backtracked out of the office and walked to the second office door. He pushed open the door and found an older man lying on the floor alongside the desk. There was a wound in his back and a lot of blood under his head. Buck backed out of the office, walked through the reception area and opened the door. He stepped outside and pulled out his phone.

Sheriff Al Hartman answered his phone. "Hey, Buck. What's up?"

"Al, I'm gonna need backup, forensics and your pathologist. I'm at Roger Burns and Sons Demolition."

"Shit, Buck. You guys are keeping me busy. Bax just called with the same request, but she's up at an old mine with two dead bodies and a couple of burned-up SUVs."

Buck's phone chimed and he looked at the number. "Bax is calling me. I'll wait for your guys here." He switched calls.

"I just heard. Give me the details."

He listened, disconnected the call and dialed the director. This case had taken a turn, and it wasn't a good turn.

Chapter Thirty-Three

Buck sat in his Jeep and waited for the cavalry to arrive. He had found the button behind the counter that opened the gate and pushed it. Back in his Jeep, he read through the investigation file and added notes from his conversation with Dr. Ratzenberger and the details of what he found at the demo office.

He looked in the mirror as two Eagle County Sheriff's Department SUVs pulled through the gate, followed by the coroner's van.

Effective in 2024, the Colorado legislature passed HB24-1100. The act required a coroner of a county with a population greater than 150,000 who was elected on or after November 5, 2024, to be either a death investigator certified by and in good standing with the American Board of Medicolegal Death Investigators or a forensic pathologist certified by and in good standing with the American Board of Pathology.

Unlike in the medical examiner system, and since the coroner did not have to be a doctor, in smaller counties, coroners would contract with a licensed forensic patholo-gist to handle any investigations that required an autopsy.

These forensic pathologists were trained doctors who split their time among several jurisdictions to keep costs down. Many forensic pathologists were current or former medical examiners, and several were retired, working part time to keep their hands in the game.

Dr. Charlene Maxwell slid out of the coroner's van and walked up to Buck, standing next to his Jeep. Her assistant slid out of the passenger seat, walked to the back of the van and pulled out new packages of Tyvek coveralls, booties and masks.

Charlene shook hands with Buck. "Looks like you get me, Buck," she said with a smile.

"Charlene, good to see you."

Dr. Charlene Maxwell was heavyset with black hair tied in a ponytail. She'd received her medical training at the University of California and had served as the assistant medical examiner for Los Angeles County. When she retired two years ago, she moved to Avon, Colorado, to be near her grandchildren. She now volunteered as the backup forensic pathologist for Eagle County. She was a cheerful woman, and she was enjoying her retirement.

"You guys are keeping us busy today." She punched Buck in the arm. "Good to see you, Buck. Wanna tell me what we've got?"

She put on the Tyvek suit her assistant handed her while Buck described the scene. She pulled on her gloves and put on her mask.

"Give me a few minutes," she said, and she and her assistant stepped through the door.

Buck called over the two deputies. Deputy Kritch was a short Black woman with a firm grip and beautiful eyes. Deputy Crandall was White, tall and well built. They both looked like they had spent some time in the military. Buck asked Crandall to stand guard while the pathologist worked and asked Kritch to follow him. They walked towards the warehouse. They stepped up to the door, which stood open. Buck looked at Kritch.

"Deputy, I believe this is an explosives warehouse. If we run into a problem, check your line of fire. I'd like to avoid blowing up half the county."

Kritch nodded, pulled her pistol and held it in the low ready position. Buck pulled his pistol and pushed open the door, moving right while Kritch moved left. The warehouse was huge. Part of it contained various vehicles and equipment used for the demo business, and there was a separate fenced-off space towards the back with a caution sign over the door.

Buck pointed towards the left and Kritch stepped away, pistol forward, while Buck moved down the first row of equipment. He found the first body propped up against the tire of a small excavator, a bullet hole in his knee and one in the side of his head. Buck kneeled and checked for a pulse, even though he knew it was pointless. He'd started moving when Kritch yelled for him.

Buck walked towards a small service door next to the fenced secure area. Kritch was standing next to a young man with long blond hair now caked with dried blood. He was lying on his chest and had a wound in his back and one in the back of his head.

"Looks like he was trying to get away when he bought it," said Kritch.

"Yeah," said Buck. Kritch made the sign of the cross.

They spent the next half hour clearing the building and then walked back to the office to give Dr. Maxwell the news that they had two more bodies.

Sheriff Al Hartman had arrived while Buck and Kritch were clearing the warehouse. He stepped out of the office, removed his nitrile gloves and shook Buck's hand.

"Pretty bad day," he said. "Is this all related to the rock-slide?"

"It's looking more and more that way," said Buck.

"Forensics is finishing up at the mine site. I'll wait till they get here. You've got enough to do. I'll let you know if we find anything useful."

"We need to inventory the explosives and see what's missing and we need a sample of the RDX if they have any," said Buck. "You okay if I call Franklin and his team to assist?"

"No problem, Buck. I called Roger's other son. He's on his way. He can do the inventory. What a fuckin' shame. Roger was a pain in the ass sometimes, but he would give you the shirt off his back. What a waste."

Buck pulled out his phone and dialed the director.

"Buck."

"Sir. Gonna need that chopper back."

"What's going on?" asked the director.

"Just found four bodies at a local demolition company. All were shot earlier today. I'm gonna need Franklin and his team."

"Buck, Bax just called me because she couldn't reach you. Are her two bodies related to yours?"

Buck looked at his phone. "Shit, Bax. She called while we were clearing the warehouse. I need to call her back. Has she identified the bodies?"

"Pathologist just got there. Give her a call and I'll call Franklin and get the chopper ready. Buck. What the hell is going on?"

"I think someone is cleaning house. I'll call you when we know more."

"Bax," said Buck as she answered her phone. "Sorry. We were clearing the demo company warehouse. Have you ID'd the bodies?"

"Yeah," said Bax. "We have a problem. The bodies belong to Ramone Velasquez and a guy named William Heinrick."

Buck was quiet. He turned to Sheriff Hartman. "Al, can we hold on to the deputy you sent with Bax? I don't want her making the notification on her own."

Sheriff Hartman nodded.

"Okay, Bax. Once the pathologist confirms the IDs, go ahead and make the notification. Take . . ."

"Sergeant Reed," said Bax.

"Take Sergeant Reed with you. Al said it's okay. You're in good hands. I've known Isaac for a long time."

"Okay, Buck. What are you gonna be doing?"

"As soon as Franklin arrives, I'm heading back to Glenwood Springs. Call Paul and have him start deep background on the Heinrick guy." He paused for a second. "What the hell were they doing at an old mine tunnel, and how did they end up dead?"

"Maybe Gabriella Velasquez can tell me."

"Okay. Bax. Stay in touch." He disconnected the call and clipped his phone back onto his belt.

Two hours after Buck called the director, a CANG Blackhawk helicopter flew up the valley, crossed over the security fence and landed in the yard between the office and the warehouse. Franklin and two of his forensic techs climbed out of the chopper, grabbed their gear and waved to the pilot as the chopper lifted off and headed back to Grand Junction.

"Buck, what have we got?" asked Franklin.

"Two bodies in the office, both shot; two bodies in the warehouse, also shot. The pathologist has cleared the bodies. Once you guys are finished, the paramedics will transport them to Avon for autopsy. Check in with the forensic team from Eagle County and see where they need you. Bag up all the electronics and I'll get those to Paul. I'll get the bullets at the autopsy."

"You got it, Buck. Why don't you get out of here for a few hours and get some food and rest? You look beat."

"Thanks, Franklin. I'll check in later." Buck walked to his Jeep, slid in and pulled out of the parking lot. He knew a great little restaurant in Gypsum, so he decided to head there. He'd catch a couple of hours of sleep in his Jeep and then head back up to hook up with Franklin. Tomorrow was going to be a rough day.

| 34 |

Chapter Thirty-Four

Bax pulled to a stop in front of the massive house. Sergeant Reed pulled in next to her. She slid out of her Jeep and looked at the house. It was a smaller version of the corporate office building: exposed steel beams and posts, local rock that helped it blend into the hillside, and massive panes of glass on all sides. There were two stone fireplaces at either end of what looked like a great room and with all the lights on, the house glowed in the darkness. Bax checked her watch. It was late, but there was never a good time to deliver this kind of news.

Sergeant Reed stepped next to her. "You ready?" he asked.

Bax nodded and walked up the sidewalk and the stone steps to the front door. She paused and listened. The sound of an argument came through the two massive front doors. Two women, she thought to herself. She pushed the doorbell and heard footsteps heading towards the door. The door swung open.

Gabriella stood in front of her, wearing jeans and a large University of Colorado sweatshirt. She was barefoot and her red hair hung loose. She held a large half-full wineglass.

"What?" she asked, then realizing who it was, she changed her tone.

"Agent Baxter, Sergeant Reed," she said.

"Evening, ma'am," said Bax. "May we come in?"

Gabriella gained her composure. "It's quite late, Agent Baxter. Can't this wait till morning?"

"No, ma'am. I'm afraid it can't."

"Well, if you must, please come in." She stepped aside, and Bax and Reed stepped into the largest entry foyer Bax had ever seen. The floors were polished granite, and the stairs to the second level were black steel and varnished wood. She looked through the door to a massive sitting area with several wall-mounted televisions, huge leather couches and two massive stone fireplaces. A massive black metal-and-glass chandelier filled the center of the room. The over-all effect was stunning.

Gabriella stepped through the door into the sitting area, and Bax and Reed followed. Standing near one of the fire-places were two people: a man in his forties, wearing jeans and a T-shirt, and a woman who was a younger version of Gabriella but without the years of stress on her face. Gabriella introduced them to her sister, Tina, and her hus-band, Peter Welker. Both nodded, never extending a hand. Tina's cheeks were red, and it was obvious that she was one of the people involved in the argument.

Gabriella sunk onto one of the couches and looked at Bax.

"Folks, there's no easy way to say this. Your brother Ramone's body was found at the scene of a tunnel cave-in earlier today. We just received confirmation of his identity from the coroner. You have our deepest condolences."

Tina's hand went to her mouth, her eyes filled with tears and she wobbled. Reed, who was closest, stepped over and eased her onto the couch. Peter Welker never moved and looked at Gabriella. Bax wondered about his reaction.

Gabriella, always in control, looked at Bax. "That's not possible. There must be some mistake."

"Why do you say that, ma'am?" asked Bax.

"I would have heard about a cave-in at one of our mines. I've heard nothing. Where did this happen?"

"An old mine at the top of God Almighty Road," said Reed.

"Why the hell would he be up there? That mine was abandoned twenty years ago, at least. He was supposed to be looking at security for a new mine we are preparing to open. He was with Dutch. Shit. I need to call Dutch." She pulled her phone from her back pocket.

"Who is Dutch, ma'am?" asked Bax.

"Dutch Heinrick. He's our director of security."

She pushed a few buttons, but Bax stopped her.

"Ma'am, would Dutch also be known as William Heinrick?"

Gabriella froze. "Yes. Why?"

"Your brother's body was found near another body, which we've identified as William Heinrick."

Tina shook. "Oh my god."

"Ms. Velasquez," said Bax. "We need to ask you some questions, if that's all right. I know you are in shock, but it will help us catch the person who did this."

"Did this," said Peter Welker. "You said they were killed in a tunnel collapse. What do you mean, who did this?"

"I never said they were killed in a mine collapse, sir. Ramone Velasquez was stabbed to death, and Mr. Heinrick died from multiple gunshot wounds. It appears from the crime scene that Mr. Velasquez was stabbed by Mr. Heinrick, who was then shot several times by someone else. We recovered the knife and two pistols at the scene. We believe the collapse was triggered to conceal the murders."

"That's ridiculous," said Gabriella. "My brother and Dutch were as close as brothers. They were raised together, and who would have triggered the collapse?"

"That's what we are investigating to find out. We suspect there was a third party at the scene. When did you last see your brother?"

Gabriella stood and paced. "This morning at breakfast. Right afterward, he went to meet Dutch. This makes no sense, Agent Baxter. Dutch was a part of the family. There must be another explanation."

"Dutch was a psycho," said Tina.

Gabriella stared at her sister, who had recovered from the initial shock.

"Why do you say that?" asked Bax.

Bax noticed Gabby shake her head, but Tina continued.

"He was always sneaking around when we were younger, and when he got back from the army, he was even nuttier. He was always playing with the knife he carried, and once, when I was home from college, I watched him beat up one of the union reps. The guy almost died. Ramone paid the guy off, and it was never reported to the authorities. That's how it worked. Ramone would need something done and that crazy fuck Dutch would make sure it got done."

"Tina, that's enough," said Gabriella. "Please excuse her, Agent Baxter. This has been a shock to all of us. Now, if you'll excuse us."

"Just a couple more questions, ma'am. Where were each of you today?"

Peter Welker stepped forward. "You can't believe we had anything to do with this?"

"Mr. Welker, we need to know to remove you from our suspect list. So, if you please."

Welker, looking annoyed, said, "I met with Gabriella at the office this afternoon, and after I was here doing work. We were supposed to head back to our home in Denver, but Tina wanted to speak with her brother, so we stayed."

Tina looked up and stared at Peter, the news of the meeting with Gabriella catching her off guard. She took a deep breath. "I was here with the boys all day. We rode horses this morning and then we watched two movies this afternoon. The first two of the *Lord of the Rings*."

"I was in my office all day except for a meeting with the mine engineering team from one to four. You can stop by the office and check my email and calls."

"We'll be sure to do that," said Bax. "So, you have no idea why your brother and Mr. Heinrick were at the old mine."

They each shook their head.

"Ma'am," said Bax. "Did Mr. Heinrick have any family we can contact, and did he drive one of your Escalades?"

"Dutch has—sorry, had no living family, and yes, he drove one of our Escalades. Why?" asked Gabriella.

"We found two burned-out vehicles at the crime scene. It was the smoke from the car fires that attracted the attention of someone who reported it."

Bax looked at Reed, then back at the group. "Thank you all for your time, and again, you have our deepest sympathies."

Gabriella led the way back to the front door and opened it, and they walked through and headed for their vehicles. The door closed behind them.

"What did you think, Isaac?"

He stopped next to her Jeep as she opened the door. "I think Tina was surprised, as was her husband, who seemed oblivious. Gabriella was hiding something."

"I agree. I also got the impression that Tina was not aware of the meeting between her brother and Gabriella," said Bax. She looked at her watch. "I need to head back to Glenwood and get a few hours of sleep. Thanks for hanging around with me all day. I hope your wife won't be mad."

Reed laughed. "My wife's been married to a cop for a long time, Bax. She's never complained once in all that time. She's my rock."

They shook hands, slid into their vehicles and drove away from the mansion.

Chapter Thirty-Five

"WHAT DID YOU DO?" Tina had fire in her eyes. Maybe the wine she had been drinking gave her the confidence to question her sister, or maybe it was years of living under her and Ramone's thumbs.

"Did you kill Ramone and Dutch?"

Gabby walked across the room and got in her face. "What the fuck did you say? How dare you accuse me of something like that?"

"You didn't even flinch when that cop told us Ramone was dead. What did you do, tire of him being the boss and take him out?"

"You listen to me, you entitled little bitch. Don't you ever question me again about anything concerning this company. Just return to your cozy little country club lifestyle and stick your head back in the sand where it belongs."

"Or what?" asked Tina. "What are you going to do, take away my money from the trust? Well, understand this, you bitch. You can't touch it. Dad set it up so as soon as I turned twenty-five, I had sole control over my trust. He did that for all of us. So, fuck off!"

Gabriella slapped her across the face and Peter jumped. She looked at Peter. "You'd better get hold of your wife before I put my fist through her face."

Peter walked towards Tina, and she glared at him. "Don't you fucking come near me, you piece of shit. If you think you control me, you've got another thing coming. I'll cut you loose so fast your head will spin. And why the fuck were you meeting with her today?"

She looked at Gabriella. "I don't know what kind of crap you two are involved in, but I'm gonna find out, and if you ever touch me again, I will fucking kill you."

Tina picked up her glass of wine and strode out of the room. Peter looked stunned. She had never spoken to him like that in all the time they had been married. He stared at Gabby.

"What the fuck are you looking at, you weak fuck?"

Peter took a sip from the beer bottle he was holding. "Gabby, what have you done? Is this why you needed me to spread the false story about the eco group?"

"I didn't do anything. And how dare you even ask me a question like that? My brother and his best friend are dead, and all you and that idiot wife of yours want to do is attack me."

"Look, Gabby. I don't know what's going on," said Peter. "But I will stand behind you. Did you kill your brother?"

"You have to be the stupidest man alive. You and my sister belong together. I have done nothing since our father died but support this family and work to make us stronger.

Now that we're on the precipice, you all question what I'm doing. You never cared before. Why would you care now?"

"You still haven't answered my question," said Peter.

"And I'm not going to. I find it insulting and you intolerable, and don't think for one minute I can't take control of Tina's money. So, hear me and hear me good. I want you and your family out of my house before breakfast. If I come down and you are still here, there will be hell to pay. Now get out of my face."

Peter looked at her like he wanted to say something else but decided that retreat was the better part of valor. He set his empty bottle on the table and walked out of the room.

Gabriella walked to the end of the room and opened the sliding glass door that led to the enormous granite patio. She stood against the low rock wall and sipped from her glass.

"What the hell is going on?" she asked herself.

She thought about all the things she had done for her little sister while they were growing up, and it pissed her off that Tina would ask her if she killed their brother. She sipped wine and listened to the cattle mooing in the distance. She thought back on the questions Agent Baxter had been asking and wondered how much they thought they knew. There was no evidence that could connect her to Ramone's death. She had picked up all the shell casing. Tomorrow she would dispose of the gun. More important, there was nothing to connect her to the explosion and rockslide in the canyon. Ramone and Dutch handled all the details, including dealing with the geologists and that slimy Roger Burns.

She finished her wine, stepped inside and walked to the bar. She poured herself another glass of wine, went back outside and sat on the wall. She looked up at the Milky Way. It was all perfect.

| 36 |

Chapter Thirty-Six

Buck woke up to a ringing in his ears and rubbed the sleep out of his eyes. Not that there was much there. He hadn't slept that long, and it took him a while to fall asleep. He should have laid the back seat down and crawled into his sleeping bag, but he was too tired, so he tilted back the passenger seat and closed his eyes. Now he was stiff.

He reached for the phone on the center console and noticed it was still dark outside. He answered the phone.

"Taylor."

"Buck, it's George. Hope I didn't wake you."

"No, you're good. What's got you up so early, George?"

"Haven't been to bed yet," said George. "A group hit the internet and took responsibility for the bombing in the canyon. It's all over the net."

Buck was now wide awake. "Who are they, and what do we know about them?"

"That's why Mel and I have been up all night. Prior to this evening, when their first post hit the internet, we'd never heard of these guys. They claim to be called the Earth

Survival Federation, but they don't exist anywhere before tonight."

"Can you backtrack their IP thingy and see who made the post?" asked Buck.

George laughed. Buck was definitely a tech dinosaur. "That's what we've been doing. The guy thought he was smart. He routed through servers in Europe, Asia and then off into the Pacific Islands, but we finally got him. The poster's name is Peter Welker, and we traced him to an IP address in Denver."

"What do we know about him?" asked Buck.

"He owns a small IT company. The odd thing is he lives in an expensive part of Denver. The old money country club section. He has no mortgage and no debts that we can find."

"Why's that odd?" asked Buck.

"Because according to last year's tax filing, he paid taxes on business income of less than sixty K."

"Lifestyle and income don't jive. Family money?" asked Buck.

"Mel's going deeper into his background."

"George, is there a link between this guy, Welker, and the Earth Survival Federation?"

"Nothing, but he did a good job creating the organization. It even included pictures of other eco-bombings they said they were responsible for and an entire manifesto on using violence to save the planet. Many of the bombings we know for certain were not committed by them. I uploaded it to the investigation file in case you get bored and can't sleep. The pictures were pulled off the internet, and the manifesto was probably AI-created."

"What the hell was this guy's game? Why go through all that trouble to create a fictitious ecoterrorist group? Did he make any demands?"

"No demands that we could find. We'll probably discover he's some bored rich guy living in his mother's basement."

Mel came on the line. "Hey, Buck. He put up another post. This time, he's demanding ten million dollars and the release of Rodney Toobin. He's threatening to blow up a bridge this time."

"Nothing in the demand about wanting any eco-related items, just the release of Toobin?" asked Buck. He looked at his watch. It was too early to call the prosecutor. He needed to see if she had made any progress with Rodney Toobin and his new public defender.

"Yeah, pretty strange," said George.

"Mel, wake up a judge, get a warrant, and then call Denver PD and ask them to raid this guy's address."

"Will do, Buck."

"Hey, George. Could you do me a favor? Go into the Denver tax rolls and see who owns the property."

"Okay, Buck. Hold on for a minute."

Buck raised the passenger seat and looked at the clock on the entertainment system. He had gotten a full two and a half hours of sleep. The open sign in the restaurant window came on and Buck realized he was hungry. The restaurant was closed by the time he got to it last night or early this morning, so he hadn't eaten since breakfast yesterday.

George came back on the line. "Tracked the owner through a bunch of corporations. Looks like the owner is a corporate entity called CMV Trust Incorporated. We'll need a warrant to get into the financials."

"Okay, George. Ask Mel to call me when the raid is set up with Denver SWAT."

Buck disconnected the call, slid out of his Jeep and buttoned his Carhartt ranch jacket. There was a light dusting of snow on the Jeep. He walked to the restaurant, pushed open the door and listened to the little bell above the door ring. He stepped inside and slid into the first booth. He faced the door.

The waitress, a stern-looking woman with gray hair in a tight bun and a name tag on her white blouse that read pam, walked up to the table.

"You sleep in the lot last night? Was gonna call the cops," she said.

Buck slid his badge off his belt and laid it on the table. Pam looked at the badge and almost smiled.
"Can't be too careful. What'll ya have?"

Buck ordered a large glass of Coke and the scrambled egg platter with bacon, sausage, home fries and a side of French toast.

Pam left to put in his order and returned a minute later with his Coke. He looked out the window and noticed it was lighter than when he'd walked in. He checked his watch. It was still too early to start making calls. The platter landed in front of him, and he thanked Pam and dug in. Several people walked in and took seats. They looked like miners or ranchers. He ignored them and ate his fill. Pam seemed to know their names, so they were local.

Buck had just finished his meal and sat back to enjoy the feeling of not being hungry when his phone rang. He looked at the number.

"Hey, Max. What's got you up so early?"

"Buck Taylor, how's my favorite cop?" said Max Clinton. "Didn't wake you, did I?"

"No, Max. You're good."

"Excellent. I wanted to get you the ballistics reports as soon as they hit my desk. The team worked all night, so here it is, hot off the press. The pistol found near Ramone Velasquez was a match for the slug taken out of Heinrick's side. The slug in Heinrick's thigh, the two in his chest and the one in his head did not come from that gun, but they were all a match. They were also a match for all the wounds at the demolition company. Even though the pistol that was found on Heinrick hadn't been fired, we ran a check on it as well. We got a match for two unsolved murders in Garfield County from five years back, and it was a match for the bullet removed from the body of Timothy Woodman. I'll upload the shooting files for those victims. So, it looks like Heinrick was a busy man and you've got a third shooter."

"Thanks, Max. Tell the team, the next time I'm in the front range, dinner is on me."

"You got it, Buck. You're a good man, Buck Taylor. God will watch over you."

Buck disconnected the call and had just decided he needed to make some calls, too early or not, when his phone chimed.

"Mel."

"Hey, Buck. The judge faxed the warrant to Denver PD and SWAT is rolling."

"Thanks, Mel. Great job."

Buck disconnected and dialed the director.

"Mornin', Buck."

"Sir, I need you to wake up a few people." He gave the director a short summation of the past couple of hours. "Can you have one of our folks hook up with Denver SWAT? I just texted you the address, and we'll need forensics and a cyber team there as well."

"No worries, Buck. I'll call you from the residence."

Buck left money on the table, finished his Coke and headed to his Jeep. The evening clouds were breaking up and it looked like it was going to be a nice day. He slid into his Jeep and headed back to the demolition company.

| **37** |

Chapter Thirty-Seven

Paul pulled his Jeep into the parking lot in front of the *Garfield County Examiner*'s office in Glenwood Springs. The *Examiner* was a small local newspaper that had been around since right after the Civil War. Paul was getting nowhere with the background on the Velasquez family, so he decided to go old school.

Paul had received a call last night from the state patrol shooting investigator and was cleared to return to work. The shooting had been ruled a "good" shooting. Paul always hated that term. A man was dead. There was nothing good about it, and that was something he would need to live with for the rest of his life. Paul had always expected, when he got into law enforcement, that events like those the day before would happen, and he was prepared for when they did, but that didn't change the fact that his bullet ended that guy's life; good or bad, he had still killed a person.

He packed that feeling away as an old pickup truck pulled into the lot. A gray-haired man with a beer belly slid out of the truck, walked up and unlocked the door to the news-

229

paper. Paul slid out of the Jeep, grabbed his backpack and walked to the door. He pulled open the door, and the smell of decades of ink filled his nostrils. It reminded him of the paper route he had as a boy, back in Dallas.

"Help ya?" asked the gray-haired man behind the counter.

Paul held up his badge and ID. The man looked at them and then looked at Paul. "What can I do for CBI this morning?"

"I'm wondering if you have back editions of the paper here on-site? I'm trying to track down some information."

"Internet not helping you?" asked the man.

"As much as I hate to admit it, yeah, not having much luck. Hoping you can help me out."

"What kind of information are you looking for? I may be able to send you in the right direction."

"It's kind of sensitive, so if you could just point me in the right direction, that would help," said Paul.

The man looked at him for a moment. "Been doin' this for forty years next fall, and have never revealed a source or compromised an investigation."

Paul looked into his eyes and saw the sincerity. "So, I can trust you?" asked Paul. The man nodded. "Okay," said Paul. "I'm looking for information on the Velasquez family." Paul hoped he hadn't made a mistake.

The man stood there for a moment. "Ramone and Gabriella. There's a pair, all right. What are you looking for?"

"Any information on where they got their money, lawsuits they may have filed, complaints against or filed by them."

"Yeah," said the man. "I can help ya with that. Come on around the counter and let's get started." He held out his hand. "Stewart Weston," he said.

Paul shook his hand. "Paul Webber, it's nice to meet you."

"Okay, formalities aside. Grab that chair, Paul, and slide it over here."

Stewart sat behind a desk covered with papers and files. He made room for Paul and clicked a button on his keyboard. His computer monitor came to life.

"We digitized the files back to about 1905. Anything back further than that and we'll need to dig into the graveyard in the back. So, let's start here."

He clicked some keys, and after a minute, the screen filled with a list of articles from the paper. He ran his finger down the screen and clicked on a file. He turned the monitor so Paul could read along.

"Two years ago, we did a story about the family when they donated the new football field at the high school. Since it was a philanthropic piece, we left out a lot of the things we found." He clicked another folder. "These are the reporter's notes. Here you go."

He pushed his desk chair out of the way and stood. "I'll be in back if you need me."

Paul thanked him, pulled out his laptop and opened it next to the keyboard. He opened the investigation file and clicked on the background tab. He started a new file for both Ramone and Gabriella, and he started reading.

Two hours later, he sat back in the chair. He took a sip from the bottle of water Stewart had set on the desk next to him and rubbed his eyes.

"Think you got what you need?" Stewart asked.

"Yeah, more than I expected," said Paul.

"Can I ask you a question—off the record, of course?" asked Stewart. "Just old reporter curiosity."

"Sure," said Paul.

"Do you think the Velasquez family had something to do with the rockslide?"

Paul looked at him. "Tell you what. If anything comes of this, I'll give you a call before anyone else finds out."

"Enough said," said Stewart.

Paul placed his laptop back into his backpack, shook Stewart's hand and thanked him for the help. He buttoned up his coat and walked out the door. A brisk wind had come out of the north, and Paul felt like the temperature had dropped twenty degrees. He looked at the clouds forming in the west and slid into his Jeep.

He started the Jeep to get warm, pulled out his phone and dialed. Buck answered right away.

"Paul. I got the call from the director a few minutes ago that the shooting team cleared you. You good?"

"Yeah," said Paul. "Listen, Buck. I played a hunch and just walked out of the local newspaper in Glenwood Springs. Found out some interesting information about the Velasquez folks."

"Hold on, Paul. I'm pulling into the demolition company parking lot. Give me a sec."

Paul heard the crunch of gravel through the phone and waited.

"Okay, Paul. Newspaper office, huh?"

Paul laughed. "Yeah, but we weren't getting anywhere online, and then I remembered that during the background check, we noticed that Velasquez Enterprises owns several large media and internet companies. I wondered if their online profiles were being cleaned up."

"And what did you find?" asked Buck.

"Over the last eighty years, the Velasquez family has sued the state of Colorado and the federal government forty times. For as long as anyone can remember, they have claimed that all the land they own and a significant portion of the land in Garfield and Eagle Counties and beyond belongs to them based on a land grant issued by the king of Spain in 1590. They have never been able to produce the grant, and no one has been able to verify its validity. That led to much speculation in the early days about how they acquired so much land. More important, two years ago, they filed a lawsuit because the Army Corps of Engineers and the Interior Department refused to allow them to build a dam on the Colorado River. The petition said they needed more water for mining and agricultural operations and that they held the water rights to over ten miles of the Colorado River and a lengthy portion of the Eagle River.

"The reporter doing the investigation confirmed that they own water rights to the Colorado, but not the Eagle, and those rights were only for about a mile of the river.

That lawsuit involved Colorado, Utah, Arizona, Nevada, California, Mexico and several Native American tribes. Based on the land grant, according to their attorneys, they were entitled to fifteen percent of the water in the river. Their attorneys have appealed that decision seven times, and they have appealed to the U.S. Supreme Court."

Buck was quiet as he thought about what Paul had told him. "Do you think they would be rash enough to destroy the canyon to get their way?"

"Well," said Paul. "The reporter noted that the family was ruthless, going back to the original Velasquez, and that anyone who crossed them met with swift Western justice. She also noted that on at least two occasions over the last century, the family had built small diversion dams along their stretch of river, and both times, the dams were removed by force and the family fined."

"Shit, Paul," said Buck. "Okay, meet me at police headquarters at noon. We need to talk to Rodney Toobin again. ADA Garvey sent me a text earlier, but I've got a couple of things to finish up on this side first."

Chapter Thirty-Eight

Buck slid out of his Jeep and walked into the small office at the demolition company. Sheriff Hartman was standing in the doorway to the office behind the counter, talking to Franklin and a younger man. He waved Buck over.

"Buck," said the sheriff. "This is David Burns. He's been helping us sort through his brother and father's paperwork."

David Burns was over six feet tall and had a bald head and mustache. He had bags under his eyes, but he stood tall, walked over and shook Buck's hand.

"My condolences. What have we got so far?" asked Buck.

"David finished the physical inventory about an hour ago," said Franklin. "It looks like they are missing four bricks of plastic explosives and four digital timer blasting caps, but that's not the worst of it."

Buck looked at each man. "Okay, what's the worst of it?"

Sheriff Hartman looked at David. "My brother was concerned about some missing explosives, but he told me the night before last that when he brought it up to Dad, he was shut down and told not to worry about it, but he was worried about it. I spent a lot of time last night going through his computer, and there is a lot to worry about."

"What are we talking about?" asked Buck.

"Over the last eight to ten months," said David, "little bits of RDX went missing. Not enough to trigger a federal investigation, but it adds up, and it appears that gradually, almost one hundred thousand pounds of RDX went missing. Oddly, we don't use that much RDX, but Dad bought it in such small quantities that no one noticed the loss. We have records of it coming into the company but none going out. All I can tell you is that it's not in the warehouse."

"Roger Burns also shipped a lot more TNT to Velasquez Mining, over that same period, than he ever shipped before."

David looked at Buck. "Agent Taylor, was my father involved in whatever caused the landslide in the canyon? Is that what got him and my brother killed?"

"It's possible," said Buck. "With the security system on the gate, your dad would have had to let in the killer, which means it was someone he knew."

"Did you check the camera?" asked David.

Buck looked from Sheriff Hartman to Franklin to David. "Did you guys find a camera?"

They shook their heads. David stepped behind the desk, sat down and clicked some keys on the keyboard. "Keith was worried that one of the employees might have been stealing the RDX, so one day, while Dad was out of town doing an estimate to bring down a small office building, he had a security company install the cameras. There's one in the warehouse and one watching the gate. Here you go."

Buck and the sheriff stepped behind him and looked at the monitor. "Can you run that back twenty-four hours?" asked Buck.

David clicked a few keys, and they watched the camera feed. "Okay, this was yesterday morning. According to the log, six teams of blasters left the yard at around eight a.m."

They watched all six trucks leave the yard. Two hours later, a black SUV pulled up to the gate. The gate rolled back, and the SUV pulled forward and parked in front of the building. A woman slid out and stepped through the office door.

"That looks like Gabriella Velasquez," said David. "I wonder what she was doing here? Dad didn't have any meetings on his calendar."

They watched the camera feed. Ten minutes after entering the office, Gabriella stepped out and locked the door. She walked across the lot and entered the warehouse using a key.

"What the hell," said David. "She has no business being in the warehouse."

A few minutes later, the door flew open, and Gabriella walked out of the warehouse. She walked over, unlocked the office, went inside and came out. She slid into her SUV and drove towards the gate, which was sliding open, and she drove through and stopped. She climbed out of the SUV, ran back to the office, unlocked the front door and went inside. Less than fifteen seconds later, she came through the door, relocked it and ran towards the gate that was now closing. She walked through the small gate and appeared to throw something towards the other side of the road, then she climbed into the SUV and drove off.

Franklin raced out the door and called his two techs, and the three of them ran towards the open gate. They spread out and searched the area on the other side of the road.

Buck looked at David, who was sitting in stunned silence. He looked up at Buck, and tears filled his eyes. "I don't understand," he said. "Dad has worked with those people for his entire business life."

Sheriff Hartman rested his hand on David's shoulder. Words failed him.

"David," said Buck. "I know this is hard, but you said there were two cameras. Can you bring up the tape from the second camera?"

David looked up, nodded and clicked a couple of keys. The interior of the massive warehouse filled the space. He ran the tape until he reached the time stamp when Gabriella entered the warehouse. He slowed the feed. It wasn't as close a view as he would have liked, but they watched as Gabriella cold-bloodedly shot both workers and disappeared into the secure explosives area, exiting the warehouse a few minutes later.

Buck pulled his business card out of his back pocket and handed it to David. "David, can you email me both tapes?"

David wiped the tears from his eyes, opened the email program and sent Buck the tape. Buck's phone chimed with the incoming email. Buck thanked him. He signaled for the sheriff to follow him, and they gave David a few minutes alone.

Once outside the office, Buck said, "The office pictures don't show her shooting Burns and his son, and the warehouse pictures are too far away to show her face clearly. When taken as a whole, we can show intent and action, but her defense attorney will have a field day with this. I'll run it by the DA's office and see what they think. Can you make sure David gets home safely?"

"No worries, Buck. I still can't believe that this is real."

"Yeah. No kidding. Has the flooding reached Dotsero yet?"

"No. Velasquez Mining has hooked up a bunch of huge pumps, just this side of the tunnel, and they are pumping a massive amount of water back into their wells." The sheriff stopped. "Is that what this is all about? Water?" he asked.

"Not entirely, Al, but I think it's all about money."

Al nodded, and they watched Franklin approach, holding up a clear evidence bag.

"The office key ring," said Franklin. "I'll get this to the lab as soon as I can."

Buck pulled out his phone, called the number the chopper pilot had given him and asked him to fly the chopper back and pick up Franklin and his team.

He hooked his phone back onto his belt, shook hands with Franklin and the sheriff and said, "Al, I'll let you know what the DA says, and if it's a go, I'll bring you in on the arrest." The sheriff nodded, and he turned to Franklin. "You and your team did good. Get some rest."

Buck slid into his Jeep and backed out of the lot. His phone rang, and he looked at the number. He pushed the green button.

"Yes, sir."

| 39 |

Chapter Thirty-Nine

"Buck," said the director. "We're standing in the middle of the residence, and the only ones here are two housekeepers. They told us the family is out of town visiting relatives, but they don't know where. I checked some mail we found on the kitchen table, and it's addressed to Christina and Peter Welker. I've got cyber going over a desktop computer we found in an office in the basement, but there's no laptop. The housekeepers told me they don't have cell numbers for Christina or Peter, which I think is a lie. They're both pretty shaken up."

Buck pulled over to the shoulder and stopped his Jeep. He pulled his laptop out of his backpack and opened it. He pulled up the DMV website and entered the name Christina Welker. Christina's driver's license popped up on the screen, and he enlarged it. The address was the same as where the director was now standing. He looked closer at the picture. There was something familiar about the woman. He looked at the red hair, and a thought flashed through his mind.

"Sir, are there any photos in the house? Family photos?"

"Hold on, Buck. I'll put you on video." The screen switched to the director's face, and Buck clicked the video button on his phone.

The director held his camera, walked into the living room and panned the phone over a collection of pictures on the wall. Buck watched the video feed. The camera passed over one large group photo.

"Sir, can you go back to that last big group photo you passed?"

The director backed up and held the camera in front of the picture. Buck enlarged his screen and looked at the photo. It showed Christina Welker standing beside a man about her age and two young boys. Next to them were two people that Buck recognized. He opened the driver's license picture and looked at the name. Christina M. Welker.

"Sir, I think I know where Peter Welker is," said Buck. "The two people on the left of the picture are Ramone Velasquez and his sister Gabriella. Bax met the younger sister. She goes by Tina. It makes sense now."

"What does, Buck?"

"The title on the house," said Buck. "CMV Trust. According to Christina Welker's driver's license, her middle initial is M. Christina M. Welker was formerly Christina M. Velasquez. I know where we can find Peter Welker."

"What do you need, Buck?"

"A couple of troopers would be nice. If they're in Eagle County, that would help. I'll text you the address and I'll meet them at the entrance to the driveway. Can you text me a copy of the warrant?"

Buck's phone chimed; he opened it and looked at the warrant. He returned to the DMV website and punched in Christina's and Peter's names. They had three cars registered to them: a new Mercedes AMG, a two-year-old Ford Explorer and a one-year-old Lexus GX 550 Luxury. Buck jotted the information in his notebook. The director came back on the line.

"You're in luck. Got two troopers in Avon. They're cutting their lunch break short and heading your way."

"Thanks, sir. I'll let you know how we make out."

He disconnected his phone, made a U-turn and headed towards Gypsum. He turned onto I-70 Westbound and headed for Dotsero. He exited the highway and followed the road to the entrance road leading to the Velasquez residence. He pulled to the side of the road, where he could keep an eye on anyone leaving the property, and waited for the troopers. Ten minutes later, two state patrol SUVs stopped behind him. He slid out of the Jeep and walked back to the SUVs.

Trooper Hallie Perez was medium height with black hair pulled up in a bun. Trooper Corporal Mike Graybar was older than Perez, tall, with a bald head. Buck shook their hands and explained the plan. He would take Trooper Graybar with him to make the arrest. Perez would block the entrance with her patrol unit and stop anyone leaving the property.

Buck walked back, slid into his Jeep and pulled away from the curb. Trooper Graybar followed in his SUV.

Buck drove to the front of the house and parked in front of the black Lexus sitting in front of the massive doors. The back hatch was open. Trooper Graybar parked alongside the Lexus.

Buck slid out just as the front door opened and two teenage boys sprinted for the Lexus. They stopped in mid-stride when they saw Buck and the trooper. Peter and Christina Welker, carrying small suitcases and backpacks, stepped through the door and stopped.

"Mr. Peter Welker, please keep your hands where we can see them," said Buck. The trooper stood off to Buck's side and had his hand on his pistol. Peter Welker stood frozen.

"Ma'am," said Buck. "Please come down the stairs and stop next to the SUV."

Christina Welker walked down the stairs and stopped where Buck had indicated. She set her suitcase down and let her backpack drop from her shoulders.

"Officer, what's going on?" asked Christina.

"Ma'am. Please, stand where I indicated." He looked at Peter. "Mr. Welker, please drop the backpack next to your suitcase and walk down the stairs slowly."

Christina started to object, and Buck held up his finger to silence her. She did not look pleased, but she stood quietly. Once Peter reached the bottom of the stairs, Buck walked over and placed him in handcuffs.

"Mr. Welker. I'm Buck Taylor with the Colorado Bureau of Investigation. We have a warrant for your arrest for a series of internet crimes, the least of which is interfering with an ongoing investigation."

"What did my husband supposedly do?" asked Christina, glaring at Buck.

"Your husband posted stories on the internet, posing as an ecoterrorist group and taking claim for the explosion in the canyon. He also demanded ten million dollars and the release of a prisoner we have been speaking with. We raided your home in Denver this morning and are seizing a computer and other items related to the case."

"You raided my home," said Christina. "How dare you? Do you know who I am?" Spittle flew from her mouth as she spoke.

Buck had found over his time in law enforcement that whenever anyone started a conversation with "Do you know who I am?" they weren't as important as they thought they were.

She stopped and looked at her husband. "What the fuck, Peter?" She looked over at her two sons and apologized for her language. "Did you do what he says?"

Buck held up his hand and pulled a laminated card out of his pocket. "Mr. Welker, before you say anything, I am going to read you your rights."

Buck read the Miranda warning and asked Peter if he understood his rights. Peter nodded and softly said yes. He refused to look at his wife.

"Trooper, please place Mr. Welker in your SUV and take him to the Garfield County Sheriff's Office. Mrs. Welker, I would suggest you get your husband an attorney."

Christina didn't answer and glared at her husband. She turned to the two boys.

"Back inside. We're not going anywhere."

Buck handed her his business card. He walked back to his Jeep, slid in and pulled out of the parking area. He followed the trooper to the end of the driveway, thanked them and headed back to Glenwood Springs, following the trooper. He called the director and told him he had Welker in custody. He had just turned onto Cottonwood Pass Road when his phone rang. He checked the number and answered.

"Buck Taylor."

"Agent Taylor, this is Captain Lloyd Fisher, Nevada State Police."

"Captain, what can I do for you?"

"We just picked up one Jack Mortensen off your BOLO."

"That's great, Captain. Where did you find him?"

"He got stuck in a flash flood in the Humboldt National Forest near a little town called Carvers. BLM rangers found him trying to dig his truck out of a ravine that was full of mud. I guess he'd been camping in the area and didn't know about rain and ravines in the desert. Anyway, they also got a copy of the BOLO and once they got him unstuck, they called us."

"Where are you holding him, Captain?" asked Buck.

"We've got him set up in a motel in Tonopah. I got one of my folks watching him and we've got his truck. What do you want us to do with him?"

"I'll send someone to get him. Can you keep him for a day or two?"

"No problem. The BOLO said he's wanted as a material witness. What's his deal, if you don't mind my asking?"

"He might have seen the men who murdered his wife two days ago, and he could have information related to the explosion and rockslide on I-70 in Glenwood Canyon."

"Damn. Murdered his wife, huh? That sucks. I heard about that canyon rockslide. Hell of a mess. Ecoterrorists?"

"Nah. So far, it looks like good old-fashioned greed."

"Well, I hope you get the bastards, and don't worry about Mr. Mortensen. We'll keep him company until you can get here."

"Thanks, Captain."

Buck disconnected the call and dialed the director.

"Hey, Buck."

"Sir, I just got a call from the Nevada State Police. They have the other geologist, Jack Mortensen, in custody. I'd like to send Bax to interview him. Can we arrange a charter?"

"Go ahead, Buck, and good work on Welker."

Buck disconnected the call and dialed Bax.

| **40** |

Chapter Forty

Bax hung up from her call with Buck and didn't waste any time. She needed a charter pilot, and she knew just who to call. Mack Price answered on the second ring. She explained what she needed, and Mack told her he was just puttering around the hangar and to head on over. Bax hung up, grabbed her backpack, ran out of the B&B and slid into her Jeep. She left the parking lot and headed for the Grand Junction Airport.

Mack Price landed his Beechcraft King Air 250 on the end of the runway at the Tonopah Airport like he was landing on a cloud. He throttled back the power and rolled onto the taxiway, stopping outside the local fixed base operator (FBO). Bax always liked flying with Mack. He was personable and funny, and his white hair gave her a sense of security. Mack was five foot ten and rail thin. He wore his leather bomber jacket with pride, having spent twenty years flying jet fighters, first in Korea and then in the early years of the Vietnam War. After his hitch in the Air Force, Mack started his own charter operation and, with almost fifty thousand hours of flying, was one of the most experienced pilots Bax knew.

Mack told her he would camp out at the FBO until she was ready to head home, and if she needed to stay overnight, he was okay with that. His next charter wasn't for another seventy-two hours, so he had time to wait for her. She thanked him with a big hug and headed out the front door to the waiting Nevada State Police SUV.

The young Native American trooper spotted her coming out of the terminal and stepped away from his SUV with his hand extended.

"Agent Baxter, Ron Yellow Knife."

They shook hands. "Nice to meet you, Ron. Please call me Bax."

"Yes, ma'am," he said. "You made good time. Do you need to stop to eat or anything before we head to the hotel?"

"No, thanks, Ron. Let's get this over with."

They slid into the SUV, and Ron pulled out of the parking lot and headed west on U.S. Highway 6. He asked about the bombing and the rockslide, and Bax gave him a quick debrief.

"So, you think this fella might have been involved?" asked Ron.

"We'll know in a little while."

Ron drove into Tonopah and turned off U.S. 6 onto South Erie Main Street. They drove for a couple of blocks, and he turned into the parking lot of the Sundowner Motel. He drove through the lot and parked next to another state police SUV. Bax slid out of the passenger seat as the door to unit 108 opened and another trooper stepped out. He introduced himself as Charlie Givens, and they shook hands.

"You want me to stay inside with you?" asked Charlie.

Bax laughed. "I'll be fine, Charlie. Thanks for asking."

He stepped aside, and Bax walked into the room and closed the door. Jack Mortensen sat on the edge of the bed. He looked up as Bax entered. She walked over, shook his hand and introduced herself. She pulled a laminated card out of her back pocket and read him his Miranda rights. She told him that he was not under arrest, that reading him his rights was for his protection, and that at any point during the interview, he could stop and ask for an attorney. He told her he understood them.

"Mr. Mortensen, do you want to waive your right to an attorney and talk with me? The captain told me you were willing to return to Colorado if needed."

"Am I being charged with anything?" he asked.

"Right now, you're a material witness. That could change once this interview is over."

He sat for a few minutes, mulling over the question. "Can I ask you something? Is my wife okay?"

Bax looked at him. "No, sir. I'm sorry to have to tell you, but your wife was found dead in your home. You have my deepest condolences. That was the primary reason we issued the notice on you. We wanted to talk to you about what, if anything, might have led to your wife's death."

Tears formed in his eyes, and he wiped them with the back of his hand. "I figured they wouldn't hurt her if I wasn't around and she didn't know anything. Did Heinrick kill her?"

"Why do you ask?" asked Bax.

"Because those two goons work for the demolition company, and they do anything he asks."

"We're not sure who murdered her, but we have one of the demo guys in custody."

"What about the other one?"

"He was killed in a standoff with police," said Bax.

Jack got quiet again. He rubbed his face with his hands and looked at Bax. "We're in big trouble, aren't we?"

"Who is we, Mr. Mortensen?" asked Bax.

"Tim and I. Tim Woodman. We work together at Velasquez Mining."

"Mr. Mortensen. Tim Woodman was murdered the morning following the rockslide. I'm sorry."

"Oh, fuck," he said. "That's why they were at my house. To kill me too. Instead, I got Betty killed." Tears ran down his face, and he covered his face with his hands. Bax let him cry.

Mortensen had a good cry, and when he finished, he wiped his eyes and said, "If you hand me my backpack, I'll give you something that explains everything."

Bax stepped over to the backpack, opened it, looked inside for any weapons and handed it to Jack. He opened a small side pocket and handed her a silver thumb drive. "This was our insurance policy, Tim and mine. Once we understood what we had been working on and realized the scope of the plan, we decided we needed to put all the information somewhere safe. You'll find emails, texts and all our research on there. Should be enough to prosecute everyone involved."

He stood up. "Will you excuse me? I feel sick." Jack stepped around her, walked into the bathroom and closed the door. The gunshot made her jump, and she ran to the door with her pistol drawn just as the two troopers pushed open the door with guns drawn. Bax slammed her foot into the door and the lock blew apart. She stepped into the bathroom and found Jack sitting in the bloody tub with blood all over the walls. A small pocket pistol was lying in the tub next to him. She reached down, checked for a pulse, looked at the two troopers and shook her head.

Ron clicked the mic hooked to his collar and requested a supervisor, paramedics and the medical examiner. Within fifteen minutes, the parking lot was packed with local and state emergency vehicles.

Captain Fisher and Tonopah Police Department Detective Allison Marsh took control of the scene. Five hours after arriving in Tonopah, Bax was leaning against the trooper's SUV when Detective Marsh, a pretty blonde with blue eyes and a pleasant demeanor, leaned against the hood next to her.

"Looks like he had the little twenty-two in a boot holster. The troopers never checked since he was being looked at as a material witness, not a suspect," she said.

Bax shook her head. "I fucked up. I should have checked. I checked his backpack when he asked for it, but I never checked him."

"No one's at fault here, Agent Baxter. I read all your statements. It was a tragic accident, and that's what my report will say. He had been in that room for seven hours before you got here. He could have shot himself at any time. Did you at least get the answers you came looking for?"

Bax held up the thumb drive. "I hope so." She slipped the drive into a small evidence bag she pulled out of her pocket and sealed it.

Detective Marsh pushed off the hood and extended her hand. "I've got a lot to do. You're free to go, Agent Baxter. If I have any questions, I'll give you a call."

She stepped away, stopped and turned. "I hope you catch the bastards that blew up that canyon." She turned and walked away.

Bax walked over and spoke with the two troopers and Captain Fisher. Since they had all given their statements, there was no issue with speaking to one another. Bax thanked them for their help and asked if she could get a ride back to the airport. Captain Fisher asked Ron to drive her, and they shook hands. She pulled out her phone as they walked towards the SUV and called Mack, who told her he'd be ready when she got there.

It was a long, quiet flight back to Grand Junction.

Chapter Forty-One

Buck stood talking to Sheriff Weaver when Janine Garvey walked in.

"Buck," she said. "Do you make all this extra work for all the people you work with? I haven't done this much running around in months."

They all laughed. "Yeah, sometimes," said Buck. "How did you make out with Rodney Toobin and the public defender?"

"That was the number two thing on my list for you. The first item of business is Peter Welker, and how is he connected to all this?"

Buck explained about the internet posts claiming responsibility and the extortion demand for the ten million dollars and the release of Rodney Toobin. He then told her about his connection to the Velasquez family.

"Fuck," she said. "My older sister went to school with Gabriella Velasquez. She can be a real bitch when she wants to be. This is not going to be fun. Should we go talk to him and see what he needs?"

Buck removed his holster from his belt and handed it to the sheriff. He and Janine walked to the first interrogation room, and the sheriff turned on the recording equipment, walked over and stood in front of the small one-way window.

Buck pushed open the door and stood aside so Janine could enter. She took a seat, and Buck followed. He set his backpack on the floor, pulled out his laptop and opened it. He pulled the laminated Miranda warning card from his back pocket and set it on the table. He looked at Peter Welker, who looked pale under the fluorescent lights and the light green color of the walls. He had red eyes, messy hair and appeared on the verge of tears.

"Peter, I'm going to read you your Miranda rights again. If you remember, we did this at the time of your arrest, and you haven't spoken with anyone up to this point. Is that correct?"

"Yes, to both," said Welker.

Buck read the warning off the card and placed it back in his pocket. He asked Peter if he understood his rights, and Peter replied that he did.

"Peter," said Buck. "You have not asked for an attorney. Are you willing to give up your right to have an attorney present and speak with us?"

Welker looked confused. "My wife was supposed to call our attorney, but she refused, and when I called him, he told me he could not represent me in this matter. I feel like I've been abandoned. What do I do?"

"Mr. Welker," said Janine. "If you would like, I can call a public defender before we speak. He could represent you for this interview, and you can work out your attorney issues after this interview is completed."

"I guess that would be okay. I don't know."

Janine excused herself and left the room. Peter looked at Buck, and Buck held up his hand. "Peter, you need to sit there and be quiet until the lawyer arrives, okay?"

Peter nodded, and Buck placed his laptop into his backpack and left the room. Paul was talking to the sheriff, and Buck walked over.

"We ran a background check on Peter Welker, and he came back clean, not even a speeding ticket. He runs a small IT company, and his tax returns indicate he doesn't work very hard at it. His income hasn't changed in three years, and if it weren't for the missus, he'd be living in someone's basement. We found one account in his name, and he has less than a grand in it."

"What about Christina?" asked Buck.

"Christina receives a large check each month from a private bank in the Caymans. No debts, and assets of almost five hundred million. It doesn't look like she is involved in any Velasquez enterprises. She never held a job that we could find, and she graduated from Bryn Mawr College with a degree in finance. She and Peter have been married for eighteen years and have two sons."

Janine walked back into the bullpen area. "Spoke with a friend of mine. She was finishing up an arraignment down the street. Should be here in ten minutes or so."

"Okay," said Buck. "While we wait, fill me in on Rodney Toobin."

She sat on the edge of the desk. "He told me that his involvement was only holding Mrs. Mortensen until Dutch arrived, but he admitted to roughing her up a bit. Nothing sexual, according to him. The order came from Dutch and his boss, which we can no longer verify since Dutch Heinrick and Roger Burns are dead. He said he knew nothing about the trailers full of explosives that blew up in the canyon. He told me that loading the trailers must have happened after hours at the Burns & Sons warehouse, and neither he nor Boomer was involved."

"What about the murder of Betty Mortensen?" asked Paul.

"He admits to being there when she was killed, but he said that Dutch pulled out the knife and slit her throat before they could even move. That's how the blood got his boots."

Buck laughed. "Shit, everyone who can corroborate his story is dead, and the only evidence is a few specks of blood on his boots. What did you offer him?"

Janine looked offended. "How do you know I made him a deal? I might want to take this disaster to court, maybe all the way to the Supreme Court." She laughed, and they all joined her. "I offered him five years for accessory. He jumped at it. He wants to talk to you before we arraign him."

Buck looked surprised. "Wonder what that's all about?"

Janine shrugged her shoulders. "Maybe he wants to apologize for threatening to blow you guys up."

The door opened, and a middle-aged woman with dark hair and tortoiseshell glasses walked in. She was tall, stocky and dressed in a tan pantsuit with a dark brown blouse. She walked up to the group and held out her hand.

"Gloria Cordova," she said. She shook hands with everyone and asked to see her client. Janine led her to the interrogation room and then turned off the recording equipment. They sat and waited. After a half hour, Gloria stuck her head out the door and announced that Peter was ready. Buck and Janine gathered their backpacks and notepads and headed inside.

Janine took her seat and pulled out her laminated Miranda warning card. "We've done this twice, but for the benefit of counsel, I will read Mr. Welker his rights." She read from the card and asked Peter if he was ready to answer some questions. He replied yes, and she looked at Buck.

"Peter, can you explain to us why you posed as an ecoterrorist group and posted several messages online, taking credit for the bombing in the canyon?" asked Buck.

"No comment," said Peter.

"Can you tell us why you demanded ten million dollars and the release of Rodney Toobin?"

"No comment," he said.

"Who ordered you to post those things online?" asked Buck.

"No one," said Peter.

Janine looked at Peter. "Peter, let me explain something to you. We have a trail that leads from those posts all around the world and back to your laptop. We have your laptop and have found all the posts. Right now, you're not giving us much to work with, which surprises me, since your own wife refused to call your attorney. If you're trying to protect her, we will keep digging until we can connect her to several murders and the bombing in the canyon. Since by virtue of the posts, you have admitted to bombing the canyon, I am going to recommend that you be charged with those crimes as well as the subsequent murders, and then I am going to go after your wife. I will also be seeking life in prison without the possibility of parole. You will die in prison."

Peter looked stunned and looked at his attorney. Gloria held up her hands. "You told me you wanted to cooperate, Peter. What changed your mind in the last ten minutes?"

"I've got nothing further to say," said Peter.

Janine grabbed her notepad. "Interview concluded at five fifty-eight p.m." She walked out of the room, followed by Buck and Gloria. She turned to Gloria.

"Glo, what the hell?" she asked.

"I have no idea," said Gloria. "I explained that you could charge him with internet fraud but that there was no corroborating evidence showing he had anything to do with the murders or the bombing of the canyon. I told him he needed to find a good lawyer and I could recommend a few. That's it."

"Buck," asked Janine. "What do you think?"

"I think he's scared, but not of us. I think he's scared of what could happen to his family. I have no idea how his wife's trust is set up, and that's way above my pay grade, but I think he's afraid that Gabriella Velasquez will shut off the money tap."

"Makes sense, I guess," said Janine. "So where does that leave us?"

"We have nothing to connect him to the bombing or any of the murders. The guy's never been in trouble a day in his life, and his background says he's too lazy to do this on his own. Someone put him up to it, and that means we're stuck."

"Glo," said Janine. "Can you cover his arraignment and then you can pass him off to someone else?"

"No problem," said Gloria. "See you in court." She grabbed her shoulder bag and headed for the door.

Janine grabbed her backpack. "Let's go see Mr. Toobin and see what he has to say."

| **42** |

Chapter Forty-Two

Bax and Paul were sitting in the common room at the B&B when Buck walked in. The table was covered with Chinese takeout boxes. Buck grabbed a plate and started scooping. He wasn't sure when he had eaten last, but his body and his mind were telling him it was time. He pulled a chair up to the table and looked at Bax.

"Rough day, huh?" he asked.

Bax nodded as she filled her mouth with noodles. She chewed, swallowed and set her fork down.

"I screwed up," she said. "Mortensen is dead because of me."

Buck set his fork down next to his plate. "How could you have stopped it? I read the detective's preliminary report. You checked his backpack when he asked for it. He wasn't suspected of any crime but might have been a witness to his wife's murder. His involvement in the bombing was unknown when we put out the BOLO. We were worried about his safety. What would you have done differently?"

Bax thought for a minute while Buck wolfed down several pieces of orange chicken. "Well?" he asked.

She looked up at him. "You're not going to let me wallow in my own self-pity, are you?"

Buck laughed. "No, not when you did nothing wrong. I'm more concerned with the fact that he could have taken out you or his state police protectors. Since he didn't, case closed."

Paul pushed his plate aside and placed his laptop on the table. He had the thumb drive installed in the USB connector. "Before we start, how did you make out with Welker and Toobin?"

Buck pushed his plate aside too. "Welker is a dry hole. I think he's more afraid of his sister-in-law than he is of us. I think he'd be willing to go to jail to protect his family."

"That's a hell of a hold someone has over him," said Bax.

"Money is a hell of a motivator, especially money like that family has," said Buck. "Toobin, on the other hand, worked out a deal with Janine Garvey. He's gonna take five years for being an accessory to the murder of Betty Mortensen. Said it was Dutch Heinrick that slit her throat, and he and Boomer had no idea it was going to happen. Pled ignorance of loading the truck or setting the charge."

"You believe him?" asked Paul.

"Yeah, I do. I met with him alone tonight. He's scared to death of Gabriella Velasquez and told me that Heinrick was nuts, but Gabriella was off the charts. He said he overheard Roger Burns on the phone with her and Roger was confirming account details for a bank transfer. That was two weeks before the bombing. He said he and Boomer wondered why they received so much RDX in the warehouse, but Burns wasn't the kind of guy you questioned about his business. And here's the strange part. He said Roger Burns had hired four illegals to load two trailers that Ramone Velasquez purchased and that Dutch watched over them. He said once the truck left the warehouse, he never saw those four guys again. He gave me a spot on the Burns property where they could be buried. Al Hartman has a team headed up there at first light."

"Fuck," said Bax. "It's getting hard to keep track of how many people have died with this case."

"Yeah, but one person who hasn't is Gabriella Velasquez. Okay, Paul. What did Dr. Mortensen's thumb drive have to tell us?"

Buck stood, walked into the kitchen, returned with a plastic trash bag, loaded all the empty containers and plates into the bag and set it by the kitchen door. He sat down, and Paul turned his laptop so they could all see.

"There are a lot of geological reports in here talking about the quality and potential quantity of the rare earth metals found, and thoughts on where to mine to reap the most benefit. The reports suggest that the largest quantity of metals is on the ridge overlooking Glenwood Canyon. Lots of reports from lawyers about how to claim the land as theirs as part of that Spanish land grant. It seems several law firms all agreed that any lawsuit would lose. There is another report from a water engineer stating that there was insufficient water to support a new mine and that several of the wells on the Velasquez property had stopped producing.

He suggested that they needed either a new reservoir or another source of water."

Paul took a sip of his coffee. "The email strings are strange." He pulled one up. "Here is one. This one asks Mortensen and Woodman if it might be possible to fracture the canyon face. The problem is we only have part of the string. It's like part of it has been wiped away or moved elsewhere."

"Is it possible that the rest of the string is on Woodman's laptop?" asked Bax.

Buck pulled his phone from his belt and dialed a number. "Hey, George."

"Hi, Buck. What's up?"

"George, have you been through the emails on Woodman's laptop? Anything odd or missing?"

"There are no email strings on the laptop. We've been going through the reports, et cetera. I thought maybe he was too careful to keep emails on his laptop. He might have them stored on a flash drive or external hard drive. Why?"

"We're looking at his partner's emails, but we only get part of the string. Mortensen told Bax this was their insurance policy, but there's nothing incriminating on it. Just a bunch of geological reports and stuff from some lawyers."

"Sounds like they have some things hidden someplace else," said Mel, who joined the conversation. "What about the wife? Might she know?"

"I'll call you back," said Buck. He disconnected the call, looked up a number on his phone and dialed. It rang several times.

"Hello," said Mrs. Woodman.

"Hi, Mrs. Woodman, Buck Taylor from CBI. I hate to disturb you so late, but I have a question that maybe you can help me with."

"Okay, Agent Taylor. I will certainly try."

"Ma'am, did your husband have a secret spot in the house or garage where he might hide a thumb drive or an external hard drive?"

"I'm not sure, Agent Taylor. Can I reach you at this number?" she asked.

"Yes, ma'am."

"Good. Let me check a few places and I'll call you back if I find anything." The call disconnected, and Buck looked at Bax and Paul and shrugged. He stood, walked into the kitchen and came back with a full bottle of Coke. He sat and read through some of the reports that Paul had highlighted. Fifteen minutes later, his phone rang.

"Ma'am," he said.

"Agent Taylor, I might have what you are looking for."

"I can head over there now and pick it up if that's okay."

"This may sound a little paranoid, Agent Taylor, but ever since my husband's death, I feel like I'm being watched. I know it's probably just me, but I've arranged with a neighbor to help me leave the house unnoticed. Can we meet at the summit of Cottonwood Pass? I can be there in about forty-five minutes."

"I'll be there, Mrs. Woodman. And thanks."

Buck clipped his phone back onto his belt. "You guys keep working on the laptop."

Buck stood and headed out to his Jeep, slid in and headed to Cottonwood Pass Road.

| 43 |

Chapter Forty-Three

Gabriella parked her SUV in the driveway and was pissed off before she even exited the vehicle. Her sister's SUV was parked in the driveway. She couldn't believe it. She had told them in no uncertain terms to be gone by breakfast, and here she was getting home after a long day at the office, hoping to have a nice stiff drink and a little dinner and chill out.

She slid out of the Escalade, walked up the steps and pushed open the massive front door. The glass full of whiskey slammed into the doorframe next to her head and shattered, covering her with alcohol. She ducked.

"What the fuck?"

Tina was standing at the entrance to the great room.

"What the hell have you gotten my husband involved in, you bitch?"

Gabriella dropped her shoulder bag, slammed the door and wiped the liquor out of her eyes.

"What the hell is wrong with you, Tina? Are you out of your tiny little mind? Look at me." She spread her arms, displaying the wet spots all over her blouse.

"That wet blouse is gonna be the least of your worries when I get through with you."

Tina stared daggers at Gabriella and balled her fists. Gabriella had never seen this side of her sister, and she was both impressed and frightened.

"What the hell is wrong with you?" asked Gabriella.

"Peter was arrested today," said Tina. "And it's all your fault."

Gabriella picked up her bag and pushed past her sister, stepping into the great room and walking to the bar. She dropped her bag on the floor, picked up a bar towel and wiped her face. She poured herself a drink and turned to face her sister.

"What the hell are you talking about?" she asked. "Why was Peter arrested? Must be a mistake, since he's never done anything in his life except mooch off this family."

"Did you threaten him with my trust fund?" asked Tina. "Wouldn't be the first time."

"I have no idea what you're talking about. I've never threatened him."

"You never had to," said Tina. "Just being you scares the shit out of him. What did you get him involved with?"

Gabriella finished her drink and poured another. She stepped around the bar and sat on the leather couch.

"What was he arrested for?" she asked.

"He posted things online, posing as an ecoterrorist group and taking credit for the bombing and rockslide in the canyon. He demanded ten million dollars and the release of one of the clowns who works for the demo guy. What did you and Ramone get him involved in?"

Gabriella tried to keep her hand from shaking as she sipped her drink. "This is not good," she thought.

"I have no idea why your husband did what he did. Maybe he got tired of living under your money and wanted some of his own. He's always been a lowlife, ever since you brought him home from college, like a stray puppy. Who knows what goes on in that warped mind of his."

Tina stared at her for a few seconds and then a light bulb went off. Tina could always tell when Gabriella was lying, no matter how hard she tried to hide it.

"You lying sack of shit," said Tina. "What did you do? Did you and our crazy brother cause that landslide?"

Gabriella jumped up and pointed at Tina. "Our brother is dead. You watch how you talk about him. We had nothing to do with the rockslide. How dare you?"

"How dare I?" asked Tina. "He's been trying to regain our water rights and land for as long as I can remember, as did Dad and Granddad. They all failed." She paused for a second. "Is that what this is all about, a land grab? You couldn't do it legally, so you did it underhanded? Is that why Ramone and Dutch are dead?" She raised her hand to her mouth and stared at her sister.

Gabriella downed her drink in one swallow, walked over, poured herself another and downed that one. Tina had always lived in her own little world and never showed the slightest interest in the family business. Suddenly, she was aware of what had been going on. Gabriella was shocked and uncertain how to respond.

"Ramone and Dutch died because they were careless and entered an old mine they had no business being in. It had nothing to do with me," said Gabriella.

"You killed them," said Tina. "I can see it in your eyes. You've never been a good liar." Tina turned away from her and then turned back. "How many other people have died because of your scheme? My god, Gabby, you blew up a highway and dammed a river with a rockslide. What the fuck is wrong with you?"

Gabriella finished her drink and poured another; she was slurring her words as she staggered around the bar. "Anything we might have done, we did to save this family. Our fields are drying out because our wells are going dry, we have almost completely lost the cattle and horse business and we need more water to open a new mine. We are on the precipice of a huge mineral find, which will make us incredibly wealthy."

"We're already incredibly wealthy," said Tina. "When is it enough?" She looked at Gabriella. "You're insane—both you and Ramone. Dad would be turning over in his grave if he knew what you did, and then you had the nerve to get my husband involved. I should call the police right now and have you arrested."

Gabriella, as drunk as she was, moved with lightning speed, crossed the floor and smashed her fist into the side of Tina's head. Tina's head snapped back, and she fell over the couch and landed on the floor. Gabriella stood over Tina, who was trying to move.

"You go ahead and call the cops," said Gabriella, "but know this, you little bitch. If you do, I will not only cut off all your money, but I will kill you and your kids. You'd better think about that."

Gabriella picked up her bag and staggered out of the room and up the stairs to her bedroom. Tina rolled onto her back and raised her hand to her face. She was going to have a hell of a black eye. She was hurt, but more than anything she was stunned. Even when they were kids, Gabriella had never physically hurt her, no matter how mad she had gotten. She was afraid for her own safety, but she was more concerned with the safety of her kids. She sat up, raised her arms and lifted herself up using the back of the couch. She walked over to the bar, found a bar towel, filled it with ice and held it against her cheek. Her ear was ringing, and she could sense the headache coming on. She needed to do something. She poured herself a drink and headed towards the back of the house to Ramone's office.

Before heading back, she stopped at the bottom of the stairs and listened. She heard no noise coming from Gabriella's room. She walked through the kitchen and slid into Ramone's office, closing and locking the door. She sat behind his desk and opened his laptop. She may not have been interested in the family business, but she listened whenever she was around and knew a lot more than anyone thought. She also knew Ramone's passwords, and it took only three tries before she had access to his computer. She listened to ensure no one was coming and clicked open a file.

For the next two hours, Tina read emails and geology reports, all aimed at bringing down a mountain. She sat back, stunned and appalled that her family, so rich in history, could have stooped so low as to commit this horrible crime against the people of Colorado and against nature.

Tina opened drawer after drawer until she found what she was looking for. A small silver thumb drive. She plugged it into the laptop, erased what was already on it and downloaded the documents. She prayed the downloads would be completed before Gabriella came down the stairs.

The task completed, she pulled out the thumb drive. She now had to decide what to do with the information. She had a thought and dug into her back pocket and pulled out a business card. CBI Agent Ashley Baxter had given her the card when she first came by the house to let them know Ramone had died from a knife wound and had been found with that creep Dutch in a long-abandoned mine that had been collapsed to hide the crime.

She walked out of the office, removed her running shoes and climbed the stairs. She stopped when she saw Gabriella's shoes and shoulder bag lying outside her bedroom. She listened at Gabriella's door and heard drunken snoring coming from within. This was typical Gabriella.

She kneeled and opened the bag, hoping to find Gabriella's laptop, but what she found was more chilling. She lifted the small black handgun with the short silencer attached to the end of the barrel out of the bag and stared at it. She was right to be afraid of her sister.

Tina was no fan of guns, but she, along with her siblings, were taught early on how to use and respect guns of all types. She stuck the pistol in her waistband and covered it with her sweatshirt.

She walked down the hall and checked on her two sons. She hated to wake them, but she was afraid to leave them in the house alone with Gabriella. She had learned some things during the past couple of hours that made her see her sister and brother in a whole new light, and it wasn't pretty.

She tapped the boys on their shoulders, and they opened sleep-filled eyes. They protested, but she held her finger to her mouth and whispered for them to dress quickly. She waited in the hallway, watching Gabriella's door, praying it didn't open.

Dressed and sleepy, the boys followed her down the stairs and out to her SUV. They slid in and buckled up, and Tina turned around in the driveway and headed for Glenwood Springs. She figured the sheriff might know where to find Agent Baxter.

| 44 |

Chapter Forty-Four

Buck pulled to the side of the road at the summit of Cottonwood Pass and turned off the engine. He opened the door and slid out of the Jeep. It was a beautiful night with almost no wind, and the Milky Way looked like you could reach up and touch it. The temperature had dropped, and Buck could feel some moisture in the air. Snow would come soon, and he was sorry that it would put a crimp in the governor's plans, but he knew the governor would press on anyway. He had set a huge project in front of a massive army of federal, state and local workers and would not rest until they achieved his goal.

Buck looked in the distance and saw two sets of headlights farther down the road on the east side. It looked like one set was in a field off the road. The bug in his brain kicked him in the side of the head and a chill ran up his spine.

Buck jumped into his Jeep and pulled off the shoulder. He cruised down the empty road until he was a couple hundred feet from the cars and hidden by a small rise. He pulled over, stopped the Jeep, slid out and softly closed the door. He worked his way over the rise.

One vehicle, a dark SUV, was parked on the road. The second SUV, lighter in color, was several yards off the road, tilted to one side. There was someone lying on the ground in the field alongside the SUV. Another person was crawling around the seats, looking for something. Buck made his way into the field and moved closer. He paused and listened.

"Where the fuck is it, bitch?" asked the person looking in the SUV. He stopped looking and approached the person on the ground. He grabbed the person on the ground, pulled them up by the collar and punched them in the face.

"Tell me where you hid it and I might let you live," he said, then he hit them again.

Buck had seen enough. He pulled his pistol and held it down at his side. "Police," he said. "Don't move a muscle."

The man dropped the person to the ground and started to stand up. As he did, he grabbed a pistol off his belt and spun towards Buck's voice, but Buck had moved five paces to his left. The bullet went right where Buck had been standing fifteen seconds before but flew through empty air. Buck fired twice, and the man slammed into the SUV and slid to the ground.

He walked over, pistol at the ready, and approached the man on the ground. He kicked the gun away, pulled his handcuffs and cuffed the man's hands together, then he checked for a pulse. He stood and stepped over to the person on the ground. It was a woman he had seen before. He pulled out his phone, but he had no service, and he put his phone away.

He took off his coat, folded it into a pillow and placed it under Mrs. Woodman's head.

"I'll be right back. I need to get my sat phone from the car." He patted her hand and raced to his Jeep, where he pulled the sat phone out of a case in the back. He punched in a number from memory, and he could hear the phone connect to the closest satellite and ring.

"Sheriff Weaver, who is this?"

"Paul, Buck Taylor. I'm about two hundred yards from the Cottonwood Pass summit. There's been an accident. A woman's hurt, and I was involved in a shooting."

"Are you all right?" asked the sheriff.

"Yeah," said Buck. "Suspect is dead, and the woman is hurt badly. I've got to go. Send everyone."

Buck grabbed a water bottle and ran back to the SUVs. He kneeled next to Mrs. Woodman, raised her head and gave her a sip of water.

"Mrs. Woodman, can you tell me what happened?" He pulled a handkerchief from his pocket, soaked it with water and wiped the blood from her face.

Mrs. Woodman asked for another sip of water, drank and looked at him. She was pale, and her body was shaking. Her voice was strained.

"I hoped I had avoided them, but I guess they were on to my deception." She swallowed and winced, gasping for air. "I saw the same car several times in the past couple of days, which is why I made an exit plan. It didn't work."

"What was he looking for, ma'am?"

"A small black USB drive. Did he find it?"

"I don't think so. Where is it?"

She coughed and placed her hand on her chest. "I put it in the washer fluid container under the hood. It's in a plastic bag."

Buck could hear sirens coming from both directions. He laid Mrs. Woodman on the makeshift pillow and walked to the SUV. He reached in, popped the hood and stepped around to the front of the vehicle. He opened the hood, pulled a flashlight out of his pocket and lit up the engine compartment. He spotted the washer fluid reservoir on the left side, popped the top open, stuck his two fingers into the reservoir and felt a plastic bag. He gripped it with his two fingers, pulled it out and let the fluid drain off the bag. He shined the flashlight on the bag and found the drive was dry. He walked back over to Mrs. Woodman and held up the bag.

She looked at the bag and smiled weakly. "Tim told me if you plug it into his laptop, all would be revealed. I don't know what that means, but Tim enjoyed being mysterious." Tears flowed down her one open eye.

Several Garfield County sheriff's SUVs pulled to a stop and turned their searchlights on the SUV in the field. Sheriff Weaver, followed by several deputies, ran down the slope and approached Buck. He looked at the body on the ground and the body next to the SUV. He pointed to the body by the SUV.

"You check for ID?" asked the sheriff.

"I didn't want to disturb the crime scene," said Buck.

Two paramedics raced down the slope and checked Mrs. Woodman. They ran back to the ambulance, grabbed a wooden backboard and carried it down the slope. Buck and the sheriff walked over.

"She gonna be all right?" asked Buck.

"She's beaten up pretty good, but I'm worried she might be bleeding internally. We need to get her to the hospital ASAP."

They rolled her onto the backboard, and with the help of two of the deputies, they carried it to the ambulance, placed her on the gurney inside and raced towards the emergency room at Valley View Hospital in Glenwood Springs.

A white van with a Garfield County logo on the door pulled to a stop, and two Tyvek-clad technicians walked down the slope. Sheriff Weaver called them over and gave them instructions. They headed back to the van, pulled two boxes out of the back and headed for the stuck SUV.

Buck stepped aside with the sheriff and gave him a quick debrief. After finishing, the sheriff asked, "Did you find the USB drive?"

Buck held up the sticky wet bag. "Yeah, I need to get this to the team and get them working on it."

"Who the hell would have done this to her?" the sheriff asked. "Did she say anything?"

"Only that since her husband's death, she felt like she was being watched. She was sharp enough to work out using a neighbor's car so she could get away unseen. Good plan, it just didn't work."

"Poor lady," said the sheriff. "She's had a hell of a week." He looked serious. "Buck, what the hell is going on? We've got a lot of bodies stacking up."

"Yeah," said Buck. "I'm hoping whatever is on this drive will help us figure this out."

One tech walked over with a cardboard evidence box. Buck pulled his pistol from his holster, popped out the magazine and jacked the round out of the chamber. He placed everything in the box, and the tech sealed the box, signed the tape and handed Buck a receipt.

"We'll get that back to you as soon as possible. I called the DA, and Sima is on the way up here. Sima was calling your director to see if he could send up the chopper. I'll wait here for her and the DA's shooting team. Why don't you head back and get that USB drive figured out?"

They shook hands, and Buck accepted his handcuffs from one of the techs. He walked to his Jeep, opened the hatch and opened the gun safe in the back. He took another pistol from the safe, placed it in his holster, closed the hatch and slid into the Jeep. He made a U-turn on the road and headed back to Glenwood Springs. They still had a lot to do, and he would be out of commission for a day at least.

| 45 |

Chapter Forty-Five

Tina Welker had made good time on Cottonwood Pass Road until she got near the summit. Traffic had slowed almost to a standstill—there wasn't usually this much traffic on the road at this time of the morning—and she noticed all the emergency vehicles parked on the shoulder of the narrow road. She spotted an SUV in a field off the road. She figured it was some flatlander not used to driving on mountain roads who wasn't paying attention on the dark, curvy road and drove off the edge. She stopped as a deputy held up her hand and waited while an ambulance pulled onto the road and headed west with lights and sirens. Someone must have been hurt in the accident.

Tina followed the ambulance at a safe distance and, once on Highway 82, turned and headed into town. She pulled into the parking lot for the Garfield County Sheriff's Office and parked in a visitor's space. She and the boys slid out of the SUV, walked across the lot and pushed open the front doors. As she stepped through the door, an alarm sounded and the deputy behind the desk pulled his pistol and pointed it at her.

"Hands where I can see them," he yelled. "On your knees."

Two more deputies came through a side door with guns drawn. Tina had no idea what was happening but fell to her knees. The boys did the same thing. With two deputies holding guns, the third deputy holstered her weapon and stepped up to Tina.

"Hands on your head," she said. Tina placed her hands on her head, and the deputy cuffed her right hand, pulled it behind her and cuffed the left one. She then patted her down.

"Gun," she said as she ran her hands down her back. She pulled a rubber glove out of her pocket and pulled out the pistol with the glove.

Tina realized what had happened. She had forgotten all about the gun in her waistband when she entered the building. "That's not mine. I brought that to give to Agent Baxter from CBI."

The deputy at the desk put his pistol back into his holster, dialed a number and spoke with someone on the phone. While he was talking, the other deputies checked the boys for weapons and then had them sit in the visitors' chairs. Tina was helped up and placed in one of the chairs.

The side door opened, and a tall Black sergeant walked through the door. He stepped up to Tina.

"Ma'am, I'm Sergeant Reed. You told these deputies that you were bringing the pistol to Agent Baxter. May I ask what this is all about?"

Tina composed herself. "My name is Christina Welker; you guys arrested my husband earlier, and I have information and that gun for Agent Baxter."

Reed looked at the growing bruise on the side of Tina's face, then recognized her. "We met yesterday at the Velasquez home, did we not?"

Tina looked at him. "Yes, you were with Agent Baxter when she came to tell us that my brother had been killed."

Reed smiled. "Ma'am, who hit you, and why were you armed?"

"I'm sorry, Sergeant, I forgot I had the gun. I took that out of my sister's purse. I think it's the gun that killed my brother. I also have a thumb drive for Agent Baxter."

"Deputy, please uncuff Mrs. Welker," said Reed. "Mrs. Welker, please follow me. Deputy, why don't you take the boys to the lunchroom and see if you can find a couple of soft drinks and maybe some snacks." He held open the door, took the pistol and the glove and led them through it. The deputy and the boys turned right, and Tina followed Reed to a small conference room and he asked her if he could get her anything to drink. She told him that a black coffee would be great, and he stepped out of the room and closed the door. He pulled out his phone, looked at his contacts and dialed a number.

"Sergeant, what's up?" asked Bax.

"Hope I didn't wake you, but Tina Welker just walked through the door with a thumb drive and a silenced pistol and asked to see you."

Bax was now wide awake. "Okay, we'll be there in fifteen minutes."

She disconnected the call, and Reed put his phone away and went in search of a fresh pot of coffee. It had been a strange night, and as morning approached, it had gotten stranger.

Twenty minutes later, Bax and Paul walked through the front doors of the sheriff's office and were buzzed through to the back. They found Sergeant Reed and Tina Welker sitting in a conference room. They walked in and dropped their backpacks on the floor. Bax looked at Tina.

"Mrs. Welker, what happened to your face?"

"Gabby punched me," said Tina, speaking in a whisper.

Bax pulled out a chair and sat opposite her. "Why?"

"She got drunk. I accused her of getting Peter involved in the rockslide thing. Then I accused her of killing Ramone and Dutch and she lost her temper and hit me."

Reed slid two evidence bags over to Bax. She picked up the first one, opened the bag and looked at the thumb drive. She held it up in front of Tina.

"I was mad, so after she passed out, I went into Ramone's office and got into his laptop. I copied several files that I think might implicate my brother and sister in the explosion that caused the rockslide." Bax slid the drive over to Paul, who opened his laptop and plugged it in.

She picked up the second bag and looked at the silenced pistol. "Tina, want to tell me about the pistol?"

"I found that in my sister's shoulder bag. She had dropped it in the hallway outside her room, and I looked in it, hoping I might find her laptop. I found the gun instead."

"And you think she used this to kill Dutch Heinrick and your brother?"

"Yeah. She's crazy, and she practically admitted blowing up the canyon over some mineral find. I couldn't believe what she was saying until I got into Ramone's laptop, then I got scared, took the gun and the files and raced here with my sons. I'm afraid of what she'll do when she realizes we've gone." Tears flowed down her cheeks.

Bax stood and signaled for Reed to follow her, and they stepped into the hallway and closed the door.

"You think she's legit?" asked Reed.

"She seems scared, and that bruise. I doubt she did it to herself. I'm worried though that as evidence, we may be in a bad place, since we have no way of proving the provenance of the gun and the drive. I tried to call Buck, but his phone went straight to voice mail."

Reed looked surprised. "You hadn't heard. Buck was involved in a shoot-out up on Cottonwood Pass tonight. I guess he was meeting the wife of that geologist who was murdered, but someone forced her off the road. The guy beat her to a pulp. Buck got into a shoot-out with the guy and killed him. Sheriff said they should be here shortly so Buck can give a formal statement. ADA Garvey and the state patrol shooting investigator are on their way."

The door opened, and ADA Janine Garvey walked in and shook hands with Bax and Reed. She looked at them with a curious expression. "Why are you here?" she asked.

Bax filled her in and explained about the thumb drive and the gun. "I was going to call you. I need a read on the legality of the drive and pistol as evidence."

She smiled. "You state guys sure lead interesting lives. Let's go talk to Mrs. Welker."

She followed Bax and Reed back into the conference room and introduced herself to Tina. She sat opposite her, pulled a small digital recorder out of her shoulder bag and had her repeat everything she had told Bax earlier. She asked her where she found the items in question, and she asked her about the title to the house.

"The house is in a trust. The three of us are named in the trust, and if something were to happen to one of us, the other two retain ownership through the trust."

"Okay," said Janine. "So, with the death of your brother, you and your sister share ownership through the trust, correct?"

Tina nodded and said, "Yes. That's how our father wanted it set up. We all share everything equally: the house, the ranch, almost everything. Ramone got seventy percent of the business and Gabby got thirty. With his death the business goes to the remaining siblings, fifty-fifty."

Bax looked over at Paul, who was clicking on the keys. "Paul, anything good?" she asked.

He slid his laptop over to her, and Bax advanced the images so she and Janine could look at them. After a while, they sat back and looked at Paul.

"There's a lot of information there—not enough to make a case against Gabriella Velasquez, but I can work with this. Since Mrs. Welker is part owner of the house and with her brother's death, she technically has access to everything in the house that belonged to her brother, I think we are okay on the drive. The gun might be harder since it was in Ms. Velasquez's bag, but Mrs. Welker will testify that the bag was in a common hallway, where there is no expectation of privacy. It's something we'll let a judge decide on. We need to confirm that this is the gun that was used to kill Mr. Heinrick."

Bax picked up the evidence bag containing the pistol and stepped out of the conference room. She'd just pulled her phone out of her back pocket when Buck and Sheriff Weaver walked through the door, followed by the state patrol shooting investigator. Buck was on his phone. She stepped in front of him.

"You okay?" she asked.

"Hold on, sir," said Buck into the phone, "Bax is here." He turned to Bax. "I'm fine," he said. "What are you doing here?"

"Long story. Is that the director on the phone?"

Buck nodded, and she held up her hand and Buck handed her the phone.

"Sir, can you get the chopper up here as soon as possible? I need to get a piece of evidence to the state lab fast."

"I can," said the director. "They're still in Grand Junction. Let me make a call and I'll call Buck back."

She returned the phone to Buck and explained what had been happening while he was up on the pass.

Buck pulled an evidence bag from his pocket containing another thumb drive and handed it to her.

"Mrs. Woodman almost died and may still to get this to us. Her husband told her it works in conjunction with his laptop—no idea what the hell that means, but see if Paul can figure it out. I'm gonna be tied up with the shooting investigator for a while. Nail down Mrs. Welker's interview, and if you think you can use the information, get her husband back in here, and let's see if you can break through his fears."

She nodded and headed towards the conference room, and Buck followed the state patrol investigator into one of the interrogation rooms and shut the door.

| **46** |

Chapter Forty-Six

Gabriella Velasquez woke up with a massive headache and only a vague idea of what happened between her and Tina the night before. She was still wearing the clothes she had come home in, and her right knuckles were bloody and swollen. She remembered yelling a lot but little else. She slid her legs off the bed, waited for her head to catch up, stood and wobbled.

She stripped off her clothes and jumped into the shower, her head clearing. She got dressed and opened the door. Her purse was lying on the floor in the hall next to her shoes, and she kneeled to pick it up. It was lighter than she expected, and she looked inside, dumping the contents into a pile on the floor. Her pistol was gone.

She ran down the hall to the guest rooms and pushed open the door to the room Tina had been using. The bed was made, and it looked like the room hadn't been used. Her suitcase was gone from the closet. Gabriella ran to the room the boys were sharing and pushed open the door. They were also gone, but the beds had been slept in and the sheets were lying partially on the floor.

Panic set in, and she ran down the stairs, through the kitchen, and entered Ramone's office. His laptop was sitting on the desk, but it was open. She sat behind the desk and entered his password. The screen opened, and she read the file that appeared on the screen and her heart sank. Contained in the emails that made up the file were notes on the purchase of large quantities of RDX and a timeline outlining the plan to peel off small amounts of RDX over time and store it for later use. The file also contained the purchase agreement for two used trucks and two sixty-foot trailers.

She glanced in the corner of the screen, and there was a small note approving the removal of a storage device. Fury raged in her, and she threw the laptop against the opposite wall. It smashed into several pieces.

"That little bitch," she said to no one. "When I get my hands on her, I'll kill her and then I'll kill her sons. Fuck."

She stood behind the desk and tried to calm herself down. She thought about everything that had happened, and she took a deep breath—then thought about the fact that all this information was on Ramone's laptop. She hadn't kept any information on her laptop. There was nothing connecting her to the explosion in the canyon or the purchase of the RDX and the semis. Ramone and Dutch had handled the geologists and the wife. So, there was nothing there. As far as the pistol was concerned, she could plead self-defense. She had to shoot Dutch to protect her life, and he had an explosive device that went off and buried him and Ramone. She figured she might be in the clear on everything. She was breathing a little easier. Everything was going to be okay.

But everything wasn't okay. Had she not destroyed Ramone's laptop, and had she looked at the other files that Tina had copied, she would have found a large number of videos. And had she watched those videos, she would have realized that Ramone had placed a small high-tech camera in one corner of the bookcase in his office. A camera that had recorded the images and the sounds of them plotting with Roger Burns to blow up the canyon. She would have seen herself on the video handing Roger a leather duffel bag containing fifteen million dollars and him counting the cash out on the desk before agreeing to load the RDX, TNT and aluminum powder into the two trailers that Ramone had purchased. There was even a recording of her and Dutch talking about killing the geologists, the drivers and the guys loading the trailers.

It seemed Ramone had decided to be overcautious and make videos of all their meetings and conversations, and Tina had found the recordings in the cloud and copied them onto the thumb drive. Gabriella was far from in the clear.

Oblivious and feeling better, she went to the kitchen and ordered a breakfast of scrambled eggs, bacon, fruit and coffee. She was still pissed at her sister, but she would deal with that once everything else had passed. She pulled out her phone and checked her messages. One text message was marked urgent. She opened it. It said the bird had left the house, and he was following to intercept.

She checked the time on her watch. The text had come in at 1:00 a.m. She replied with one word: STATUS.

She finished her breakfast and checked her phone. He should have responded by now. She wondered what was going on. Once she took over the company, she had decided she was going to fire a lot of incompetent people. She needed to surround herself with the best and the brightest, not those idiots Ramone had hired. She would start with the members of the board.

Forgetting all about her headache, she grabbed her bag, opened the front door and headed for her SUV. She stopped and looked at the sky. It was a glorious day, and it was only going to get better.

| **47** |

Chapter Forty-Seven

"Who the hell was this guy?" asked George.

Bax, Paul and Sheriff Weaver sat in the conference room with George and Mel on speaker.

"This software would make James Bond envious," he said. "You sure he was a geologist and that he didn't work for the NSA?"

"So, the software on the drive did work in conjunction with his laptop?" asked Bax.

"You've all heard of steganography, right?" asked George. The sheriff shook his head.

"Hold on a minute, George," said Bax. She turned to the sheriff. "Steganography, in its simplest form, is when you use a computer program to hide something inside something else. For instance, you want to hide child porn so no one can find it. You use a program, and you embed the porn in the picture of, say, a beautiful sunset. Only you and the people you trust know the porn is there, and when they want to look at the porn, they open this program, enter a password and it converts the sunset picture back into the porn."

"Shit," said the sheriff. "The older I get, the weirder the world becomes. Okay, so this geologist used this stega-whatever to hide pictures inside other pictures."

"Also, files and reports," said George. "And the encryption is top-notch. Keep an eye on your screen."

They could hear George click a few keys, and the pictures and file folders on Tim Woodman's laptop screen melted in a swirl of vibrant colors, and in their place were new files, reports and pictures. Paul opened the first file and found a transcript of a conversation between Woodman and Ramone and Gabriella Velasquez. After a few minutes of reading, the sheriff sat back and said, "They did. They talked about blowing up the canyon to make it easier to get to a new find of rare earth metals. I still can't believe it. These people have lived here since the beginning. They've supported the local economy for years and, just like that, they decide to blow up the canyon."

Paul had continued reading. "Here's a conversation between Ramone and Gabriella where they talked about killing two birds with one stone—access to the minerals, and damming the Colorado River and returning the water to its rightful owner. There are also financials here showing that their wells were drying up, and they were selling off huge parts of the cattle and horse herds. These people were desperate."

The door opened, and Buck stepped into the conference room.

"How'd the interview go?" Bax asked.

"There won't be any problem. The investigator and Janice are talking to the DA right now, and I should be good to go in a couple of hours. Anything on the guy I killed?"

Bax handed him a sheet of paper. "Ex miner hurt working on one of the Velasquez mines. Large influx of cash into his account over the last couple of days. We checked his phone. One text to Gabriella Velasquez's cell phone. Telling her he was following someone and would intercept. Gabriella replied several hours later, asking for status. The money this guy received came from a trust fund that appears to belong to Gabriella. The director has financial crimes working on that."

"What about Tina Welker and her sons?"

"We've got them stashed away in a hotel out of town with two deputies keeping an eye on them," said Bax.

Buck's phone chimed, and he looked at the number and answered.

"Hey, Max."

"Hey, Buck. How's my favorite cop? How the hell do you get into these jams?"

"You know me, Max, just lucky."

"Yeah. Okay. Enough small talk. Back to work," said Max. "The gun that Bax sent us this morning matches the bullets we retrieved from Mr. Heinrick. It was also a match for the bullets retrieved from Roger Burns, Keith Burns and the two guys you found in the warehouse, Jerry Medina and Edgar Nunez. We found two sets of prints on the weapon. The first two were a thumb and forefinger on the end of the magazine. Those are a match to the elimination prints Bax sent of Christina Welker. The others are a full right hand set and match Gabriella Velasquez. She was printed ten years ago after a bar fight. No charges were ever filed, and the case went away."

"That's great, Max," said Buck. "Upload the reports to the investigation file, and thanks for the rush job."

"No worries, Buck. You're a good man, and God will watch over you."

Buck disconnected the call and hooked his phone onto his belt. "Okay," he said. "We can connect Gabriella to the murders, which is enough to put her away, but can we connect her to the destruction in the canyon?"

Paul looked, but George responded first. "With all these encrypted files from the geologist and all the files Mrs. Welker gave us, yeah. Without a doubt, we can connect her and her brother to the bombing. Her name and image are all over these files and videos."

Buck's phone chimed, and he looked at the number. "Buck Taylor."

"Agent Taylor, this is Dr. Walsh over at the hospital. I wanted to let you know that Mrs. Woodman died ten minutes ago from her injuries. The beating left her with significant internal bleeding. We tried our best but were unsuccessful."

"Thanks, Doc. I appreciate you letting me know."

Buck disconnected the call. "Fuck," he said, and he walked out of the conference room. He walked over to the refrigerator in the corner and pulled out a bottle of Coke, dropping a five-dollar bill in the donations cup. He stood looking out the window.

Bax walked over and stood next to him. "You gonna be okay?"

He was silent for a minute and took a large sip from the bottle. "Yeah. I wish I had gotten to her sooner. It was only by luck that I spotted the two sets of headlights and felt like something was wrong. She was afraid."

"Sounds like you did all you could. The damage was most likely done before you even got to her. Nothing else you could have done," said Bax.

He took another swallow. "Do me a favor and see if Janice is still in the building."

Bax walked away, and Buck finished the bottle of Coke and threw it in the recycle bin. He walked back to the conference room just as Bax and ADA Garvey came around the corner. They followed him into the room.

"Bax, please open the investigation file and see if Max has uploaded the ballistics report. Sheriff, can you have someone bring Peter Welker to the interrogation room?" asked Buck.

"Okay, Buck," said Janice Garvey. "What are we looking at?"

Bax opened the report. "The bullets from the gun Mrs. Welker brought in are a match to the murders of Heinrick, Roger and Keith Burns and the two warehouse workers."

Buck took over. "How confident are you on the admissibility of the pistol? Everything hinges on that."

"Well, let's look at what else we have," said Janice. "We have a video of her entering and leaving the demolition company trailer at the same time the pathologist says the murders took place. We have a grainy video of a woman who fits Gabriella's description killing the two warehouse workers. The only tie we have to the murder of Heinrick is her prints on the gun and the bullet match. She could claim self-defense, but we can get around that."

The sheriff stuck his head in the door and nodded.

"Paul, pull up the files from the computers and review those while I go talk to Peter Welker," said Buck. He walked out the door and followed the sheriff to the interview room.

Peter Welker looked like he hadn't slept in days. He was pale and drawn and his hair was a mess. Buck sat across from him and opened the recording app on his phone.

"Peter, I need to remind you that you are still under oath. Do you understand?" asked Buck.

Peter responded he did.

"Do you want me to call the public defender?"

Peter said no.

"Peter, this morning your wife came into the station and gave us a gun and a thumb drive. There is evidence on the drive that implicates Ramone, Gabriella and several other people in a plot to blow up the canyon. The gun is registered to Gabriella and has been linked to five murders."

"Is my wife okay, and my sons?" Peter asked.

"Yes. We have them tucked away in a safe house close to here with two guards. Your wife is sporting a black eye courtesy of her sister, but other than that, she is fine."

"Gabby hit her? Can I see her?" asked Peter.

"Not just yet, but I will arrange for that to happen as soon as possible. Peter, your wife took a huge risk bringing that pistol and the information to us. She's frightened and knows that Gabriella will seek revenge if she can. The only protection for your family is to make sure that Gabriella goes to prison and never gets out. Can you be as strong as your wife and help us protect them?"

Peter put his face in his hands and cried. Buck and the sheriff sat back and waited. After a few minutes, Peter looked up and wiped his eyes on his sleeve.

"Gabriella forced me to post those things on the internet. She wanted to take the focus off her, Ramone and the company."

"How did she force you?" asked Buck.

"She threatened to shut down Tina's trust fund. She said she could do it with one phone call to the bank. I've been a shitty provider for my family, and if it weren't for the income from the trust fund, we'd be living on the street. I'm a failure, and she used that against me."

"Did she order you to ask for the ransom or the release of Rodney Toobin?" asked Buck.

"No, that I did on my own. I figured nothing would come of the demands, so I just ad-libbed. Guess that was pretty stupid, huh?"

"Peter, would you be willing to testify to all this in court?"

"Yes," Peter answered without hesitation. "Whatever it takes to protect my family."

"Thanks, Peter. Sit tight and someone will come get you."

Buck turned off the recording app, and he and the sheriff stepped out of the room then walked to the conference room, where Paul and George walked Janice through the evidence.

He placed his phone on the table and hit the play button. They all listened to the interview with Peter. When the interview ended, Buck put his phone away. Janice looked deep in thought.

"The evidence against Gabriella for the bombing is a little light. She covered her tracks. We have her discussing the explosion, her talking with the geologists, she, Ramone and Roger plotting and the payoff to Rogers. We don't have her pushing the button, but I think we can make a conspiracy charge stick. This woman is smart and knows how to hide her involvement, but I can work with that. The murders are a no-brainer. I would take those to a grand jury any day of the week. Package it all up and I'll take it to Judge McAllister and see if we can get an arrest warrant. Sit tight."

Bax filled out the warrant and search request while Paul in the office and George and Mel on the phone packaged the documents into a file the judge could understand.

Buck went to find an office so he could grab a few hours of sleep.

Chapter Forty-Eight

Gabriella was wrapping up a meeting with the vice president of the livestock division when her phone rang. The meeting had gone well, and she was pleased with what she heard. The pumps that Ramone had purchased were well on their way to restocking the aquifer, and they were receiving lots of praise in the press for keeping the water from flowing over the highway and backing up into Dotsero.

She had also found out earlier that her trucks were moving tons of debris from the canyon, and the crushing work was well underway. Gabriella was feeling good until the call.

"This is Gabriella," she said.

"Cops are coming for you," said the male voice on the other end of the phone. "They have a warrant for your arrest for five counts of murder."

The caller disconnected, and Gabriella stood there, staring at the phone in her hand. She was stunned and raced down the hall to her office and shut the door. Panic set in. Where did they come up with five counts of murder? She thought to herself. Then she stopped moving. "That son of a bitch Roger," she said. "I'll bet that fuck had a camera in the office and the warehouse. Shit."

She grabbed her coat off the rack by the door, put her laptop in her shoulder bag and opened her door. She told her assistant she was going home and wouldn't be back. She strolled through the building, entered the elevator, pushed the button and exited into the lobby. She checked out with the security guard at the reception desk and walked to her SUV. She pulled out of the parking lot, took the dirt road from the office to the house, parked out front and ran up the stairs. She pushed through the front doors and ran up the stairs to her bedroom, where she grabbed a bunch of clothes out of the closet and drawers and filled a large suitcase. She gathered her necessities, threw them in a carry-on and dragged everything down the stairs.

Once outside, she put the suitcases in the SUV. She had no idea how long she had until the cops arrived, but she needed to get going. She planned to head towards Vail, then jump on Highway 9 at Silverthorne, head north to US 40, and stay on that until she reached Salt Lake City. From there, she would catch a flight to Houston and then Europe. It didn't matter where in Europe. Her money would ensure a warm welcome wherever she went as long as they didn't have an extradition treaty with the United States.

She slid in, started the SUV and turned around in the driveway. She stopped and slammed her hands against the steering wheel. She was growing more panicked and pissed off.

"That fucking Tina," she yelled at the top of her voice. "You bitch. I will make you suffer."

She mashed her foot down on the gas pedal and roared down the driveway. Halfway down, she jammed on the brakes and skidded to a stop. Beyond the trees, she could see two Eagle County Sheriff's Office SUVs blocking the driveway. She pounded on the steering wheel. She needed a new escape plan. She couldn't go back to the house. Then she remembered the old access road that led to the mine complex. She hadn't been on the road in years and had no idea if it was still passable. The last time she was on it, Ramone had torn the transmission off his old truck after hitting a rut that seemed to swallow the truck. It was her only chance, and she had to take it. She turned the SUV around and headed back the way she came but continued past the house for half a mile and turned onto a road that was nothing more than two ruts in the hardscrabble. She headed up the mountain.

Chapter Forty-Nine

Bax stepped into the office and tapped Buck on the leg. He opened his eyes and stretched.

"The judge signed the warrant application," she said. "The sheriff has called out the regional SWAT team, and I've asked Eagle County to put a couple of deputies on her driveway. We don't know if she is at the office or the house, so we thought we'd hit both simultaneously."

Buck yawned. "Good work. Let's go get her."

They grabbed their backpacks and headed for the parking lot, where the sheriff gave the teams their orders. Paul and Sergeant Reed would lead one SWAT team to the office, and the rest would head for the house.

The sheriff walked over to Buck. "Janine called a little bit ago. She spoke with the shooting investigator, and you've been cleared. It was a good shoot." He handed Buck the evidence box with his pistol, and Buck took it and thanked him. Buck and Bax grabbed their ballistic vests and put them on.

"We've closed Cottonwood Pass from this direction, so we should have no trouble getting through," said the sheriff. "Let's roll."

They each headed for their vehicles, and the long procession headed down Highway 82 and turned onto Cottonwood Pass Road. The drive over the pass was quick and uneventful, and the teams split up when they got to Dotsero. Buck, Bax and the SWAT team followed the sheriff and headed for the house.

They pulled up to the entrance to the driveway, and the sheriff spoke with the two Eagle County deputies. He walked back to Buck's Jeep.

"They think she tried to come down the driveway about fifteen minutes ago. They didn't see the vehicle but saw a cloud of dust. She must have gone back to the house."

The deputies pulled their vehicles out of the way, and the procession headed up the driveway and stopped fifty feet from the front doors. There was no vehicle in sight, but the front door was sitting open. The sheriff's radio chirped.

"Reed to the sheriff."

"Go ahead, Sergeant."

"Security at the office has her leaving the building an hour ago. We have begun searching and will report back if we find anything."

"Ten-four, Sergeant." The sheriff looked at Buck and Bax standing next to him. "Looks like it's us."

Buck sent the SWAT team in to clear the house. They found the two housekeepers and a cook in the back servant's quarters, but they had no idea where Gabriella had gone. In the driveway, Buck asked the SWAT leader to deploy the drone. They stood back as the drone was set up on the driveway and then the SWAT leader launched it.

Buck pointed beyond the house, and the drone headed in that direction. Fifteen minutes into the flight, they spotted the black SUV sitting at the bottom of a small rise. It was tilted at an odd angle and appeared to be stuck. There was no sign of Gabriella. Buck slid into his Jeep, followed by Bax and SWAT, while the sheriff and three deputies began a search of the house.

Buck followed the road past the house, and a half mile down, he spotted two ruts in the hardscrabble. He turned and followed the ruts. Two miles later, he stopped and exited the vehicle. The SWAT team spread out across the field and took up positions where they could see the SUV.

Buck followed the SWAT leader, who pulled out a pair of binoculars and scanned the SUV. He handed the binoculars to Buck.

"Looks like someone in the driver's seat," he said.

Buck looked and agreed.

"What do you want to do?" asked the SWAT leader.

"Stay tight. I'm gonna see if I can get her attention."

The SWAT leader nodded, and Buck walked back to the two ruts and walked towards the SUV.

"Gabriella Velasquez. Buck Taylor with CBI. I'd like to talk to you and see if we can work out a way where we all go home tonight. What'd'ya say? Can we talk?"

Buck moved in a little closer. "Come on, Gabriella. Let's talk about this."

Still no response from the SUV.

Buck had taken two steps when he saw the driver's window roll down. Gabriella held her hand out the window, and for the second time in three days, Buck was confronted with a situation, only this time it wasn't a stick of dynamite. Instead, Gabriella held a six-inch block of plastic explosives with a blasting cap stuck in the end.

Buck signaled for the SWAT team to back up and spotted Bax over his left shoulder. He walked back to her.

"You think she'll do it?" asked Bax.

"Haven't got a clue," he said. "She knows she's stuck and can't go anywhere. She might be desperate enough."

Buck waved over the SWAT leader and pointed to a ridge perpendicular with the driver's window.

"Let's put a sniper up on that ridge. Have him work around behind us and stay behind the hills until he reaches that spot. Let's see if he can get confirmation that it is Gabriella Velasquez."

The SWAT leader keyed his mic and called one of his officers over. They discussed the position and the sniper headed over a slight rise before he headed for the spot Buck had pointed out. Buck ordered everyone to move back fifty feet and stepped forward.

"Gabriella, what do you want?"

"I want to be left alone," she shouted through the window. "Go away."

"You know we can't do that, Gabriella, so why don't you put down the explosives and slide out of the SUV? No one will hurt you. I promise."

"You can't help me, Agent Taylor. My family is either gone or has turned against me. I have no one to turn to, and I did it all for them."

"Let's go back to the sheriff's office and talk about it."

"Too late for talking, Agent Taylor."

The explosion blew Buck back twelve feet from where he was standing, and he landed hard on his back. Bax, far enough back not to get hit with the blast wave, ran to his side and kneeled next to him.

Buck had a nasty gash on the side of his head and was covered in blood. He was unconscious but breathing. The SWAT leader called Dispatch and requested an air evac. One of his officers, a trained medic, pulled a pressure bandage from his medical kit and applied it to Buck's head. They waited for the chopper that seemed to take forever, and Bax breathed a sigh of relief when they heard it coming over the canyon. It landed in the field, and the SWAT team carried Buck to the helicopter, which took off as soon as the doors were closed. Bax stepped next to the SWAT leader and looked at the burning wreckage of the SUV. He looked at Bax.

"Hell of a day, Agent Baxter. Hell of a day."

| 50 |

Epilogue

Buck spent four days in the ICU at Valley View Hospital and then two weeks in a regular room. He had a concussion, assorted cuts and scrapes, four fractured ribs and one of his ribs had punctured a lung. The gash on his head required fourteen stitches. He was lucky he had survived.

He was sitting on the edge of the bed when Bax pushed open the door and stepped into the room. "You look a hell of a lot better than yesterday," she said.

Buck smiled. "Feel better."

During the past couple of weeks, Bax had filled him in on progress in the investigation. The DA had worked a deal with Peter Welker. Since his actions didn't hurt anyone, the DA offered him three years of probation and no jail time. He pled guilty to a misdemeanor and had to stay away from computers for the entire length of his probation. He didn't hesitate to accept the offer. Also, the local paper, the *Garfield County Examiner*, was the first to report on the investigation. Seemed like they may have gotten a call before all the big guys did. Buck smiled, and Bax laughed.

"Spoke to Al Hartman this morning," said Bax. "They found four bodies buried a hundred yards behind the warehouse in a trash pit. There were no IDs, but the best guess would be that they were the guys Burns hired to load the trailer. All were shot."

"A lot of people died because of greed," said Buck. "Damn shame."

Bax nodded.

"Oh, some good news. Tina Welker has agreed to keep the pumps running until the spillway is finished. That should happen in the next two weeks. Her mining folks are working around the clock to clear enough boulders to get the water flowing over the dam. She also agreed to give the state fifty percent of the profits from the sale of the rare earth minerals. The governor is pleased under the circumstances. She plans on making some significant changes to the business."

"I heard from one of the nurses that there is an entire city of construction housing up on the pass and that they have already expanded eight miles of the road to four lanes." Buck looked at the snow falling outside the window and the six inches that covered the parking lot.

"Yeah, just in time," said Bax. "You know the governor better than anyone. Once he sets his mind to a plan, nothing gets in the way. He's got the Feds jumping through hoops trying to get him everything he needs and wants."

They both laughed. Buck stood up, walked to the closet, pulled down his coat and put it on—with Bax's help and a little wincing. He figured he was going to be sore for a while. He stopped before leaving the room.

"I had this weird dream that PIS came to visit me while I was in the ICU. They had me so doped up because of the pain that I must have dreamed it, right?"

Bax laughed. Buck sat in the wheelchair the nurse left in his room and Bax pushed. They passed through the door and moved down the hallway to the elevator. Buck stopped at the nurse's station, shook hands with the three nurses on duty and thanked them for all they had done for him.

Bax pushed the call button for the elevator, and when the doors opened, they rolled inside and she pushed the button for the lobby. When the door opened, Buck was surprised to see the director and the governor standing in the lobby talking to a well-dressed man wearing a camel hair coat. The governor walked over, and Buck could see sadness in his eyes. Buck stood and they shook hands, and the governor waved over the man they had been talking with.

"Buck, this is FBI Director J. Michael Ferranti."

Buck shook the director's hand. Ferranti had been the acting director of the FBI for the past six months and had been confirmed by the Senate just a month before. He was young, in his mid-forties, with wavy black hair and an olive complexion. He was as tall as Buck, and his handshake was solid.

"Buck, nice to meet you," he said. "I've heard a lot about you."

Buck looked from Director Ferranti to the governor to Kevin Jackson. "What's going on?"

"Buck," said Ferranti. "I've got some bad news, but I wanted you to hear it from me. Hank Clancy was killed last night."

Buck stood in disbelief. Bax raised her hand to her mouth and looked astonished. "How?" asked Buck.

"It was all so senseless. Hank stopped for gas last night on his way home from the office. A man and a woman in the parking lot got into a heated argument, and the guy punched his wife several times. When he punched their five-year-old son, according to the store manager who was on the phone with 911, Hank moved to intervene, but before he even got to them, the husband pulled a gun, shot his wife and son and then turned and shot Hank. The wife and Hank both died at the scene. The little boy is in critical condition, and when the husband realized what he had done, he put the gun in his mouth and shot himself. We're all heartbroken."

Buck was silent, and tears filled his eyes. He had known Hank Clancy a long time, and they had been through a lot together.

Director Ferranti continued. "I met with Hank's wife this morning before coming here, and she told me how close you and Hank were. I knew all about your relationship and didn't always agree with how you and Hank worked together, but you can't deny the results. She told me you were a man who could be trusted. She also asked me if you would be one of the pallbearers. I'll get you the details as soon as I know them.

"I want you to know that I disagreed with the way Hank was treated by my predecessor. To that end, as of this morning, I have reinstated him posthumously as the deputy director of the Denver field office. I have also removed all the information regarding that unfortunate incident during the Christmas bombings investigation that got him demoted.

He will be buried with all the respect and honor he is so rightfully due."

"Thank you, sir. He would be pleased to know that," said Buck, wiping tears from his eyes. "I'll call Victoria in a day or two and tell her I will be honored to be at the funeral."

Director Ferranti reached into his jacket pocket, pulled out a business card and handed it to Buck. "I'm not sure I can replace Hank, but I'd like to try. The number on that card is my personal cell phone. Few people have that number, and I always answer it. I have been in law enforcement my entire adult life, as were my father, grandfather and great-grand-father. For too long, we in the FBI have thought ourselves superior to everyone else. Hank broke that mold with you, and I value that relationship. If you need anything, please call that number. I promise you I will do whatever I can to work with you and your team."

They shook hands, and Director Ferranti buttoned his coat and headed out the door into the snow. Buck looked at the director and the governor.

"Not bad, Buck," said Director Jackson. "Can't hurt to have the FBI director on speed dial. Sorry about Hank, Buck. He was a good man."

The director shook his hand and walked out the door, leaving him, Bax and the governor. "I'm gonna get the car," she said, wiping tears from her eyes and walking out behind the director.

"Buck," said the governor. "I'm sorry for your loss. Our loss. Hank was a good friend to Colorado, and he will be missed. This was a tough case. I still can't believe how low the Velasquez family sunk. I have known Ramone for over twenty years and always liked him. You guys did great work. Now go home and get some rest. We'll talk soon."

Buck followed the governor through the door and stepped over to Bax's Jeep. She put his go bag into the back and held the door while he gingerly slid into the passenger seat. She slid into the driver's seat and looked at him. "I'm so glad you survived," she said and put the Jeep in gear and pulled out into the snow.

ACKNOWLEDGMENTS

A special thank-you to my daughter Christina J. Morgan, my unofficial collaborator.

Thanks to my editor, Laura Dragonette, whose efforts helped turn my manuscript into a polished novel. Her help is greatly appreciated. Any mistakes the reader may find are solely the responsibility of the author.

Special thanks to my daughter Stephanie Morgan, my beta reader. Stephanie has read every novel in its rough stages and rarely gets to see the completed product. Her insight and critique have been critical to making sure the stories make sense.

Also, I would like to thank my family for their encouragement. I have been telling them stories since they were little, and I always told them that someone should be writing this stuff down. I decided to write it down myself.

I want to thank my closest friend, Trish Moakler-Herud. She has been encouraging me for years to write my stories down. I hope this will make her proud.

A special thanks to my late wife, Jane. She pushed me for years to become a writer, and my biggest regret is that she didn't live long enough to see it happen. I love her with all my heart and miss her every day. I think she would be pleased.

Finally, thanks to the readers. Without you, none of this would be important.

ABOUT THE AUTHOR

2019 Pacific Book Awards Best Mystery Finalist . . . *Crime Delayed*

2020 Pacific Book Awards Best Mystery Winner . . . *Crime Denied*

2020 Chanticleer International Book Awards: 1st Place Blue Ribbon, CLUE Book Awards for Suspense, Thriller Fiction . . . *Crime Denied*

2021 Chanticleer International Book Awards Finalist, CLUE Book Awards for Suspense, Thriller Fiction . . . *Crime Conspiracy*

2021 Chanticleer International Book Awards Finalist, Book Series, CLUE Book Awards for Suspense, Thriller Fiction . . . Crime Series, The Buck Taylor Novels

2022 Chanticleer International Book Awards Finalist, CLUE Book Awards for Suspense, Thriller Fiction . . . *Crime Exploded*

2022 Chanticleer International Book Awards Finalist, CLUE Book Awards for Suspense, Thriller Fiction . . . *Crime Spree*

2023 Chanticleer International Book Awards Finalist, CLUE Book Awards for Suspense, Thriller Fiction . . . *Crime Scene*

2023 Chanticleer International Book Awards Series Finalist, Mystery & Mayhem Book Awards . . . *Crime Series*

Chuck Morgan attended Seton Hall University and Regis College and spent thirty-five years as a construction project manager. He is an avid outdoorsman, an Eagle Scout and a licensed private pilot. He enjoys camping, hiking, mountain biking and fly-fishing.

He is the author of the Crime series, featuring Colorado Bureau of Investigation Agent Buck Taylor. The series includes *Crime Interrupted, Crime Delayed, Crime Unsolved, Crime Exposed, Crime Denied, Crime Conspiracy, Crime Unknown, Crime Exploded, Crime Spree, Crime Family, Crime Scene* and *Crime Victims.*

He is also the author of *Her Name Was Jane,* a memoir about his late wife's nine-year battle with breast cancer. He has three children and four grandchildren. He resides in Lone Tree, Colorado.

OTHER BOOKS BY THE AUTHOR

Dear Reader, thank you for reading this novel. Please enjoy the other books in this series and follow Colorado Bureau of Investigation Agent Buck Taylor and his team as they investigate new and sometimes unusual crimes in the Colorado mountains. Each novel is a separate story, and they can be read in any order, but you might find it more enjoyable to read them in order.

Happy Reading,
Chuck Morgan

"Crime Interrupted: A Buck Taylor Novel by Chuck Morgan is a gripping, edge-of-the-seat novel. Right from page one, the action kicks off and never stops, gaining pace as each chapter passes." Reviewed by Anne-Marie Reynolds for Readers' Favorite.

Finalist . . . 2019 Pacific Book Awards Best Mystery
"This crime novel reads like a great thriller. *The writing is atmospheric, laced with vivid descriptions that capture the setting in great detail while allowing readers to follow the intensity of the action and the emotional and psychological depth of the story." Reviewed by Divine Zape for Readers' Favorite.*

"Professionally written in the style of a best-selling crime novelist, such as Tom Clancy, Crime Unsolved: A Buck Taylor Novel by Chuck Morgan is a spellbinding suspense novel with an environmental flair. *Intriguing subplots of fraud, survivalist paranoia and murder weave their way through the fabric of the plot, creating a dynamic story. This is an action-filled, stimulat-*

ing tale which contains fascinating details that are relevant in our present climate." Reviewed by Susan Sewell for Readers' Favorite.

"Chuck Morgan has a unique gift for plot, one that makes Crime Exposed: A Buck Taylor Novel a hard-to-put-down book. *From the start, readers know what happens to Barb, but they become curious as they follow the investigation, wondering if the characters will find out what happened to her. The descriptions are filled with clarity, and they offer readers great images. The prose is elegant, and it captures both the emotional and psychological elements of the novel clearly while offering vivid descriptions of scenes and characters. This is a fast-paced thriller with memorable characters and a criminal investigation that is so real readers will believe it could happen." Reviewed by Romuald Dzemo for Readers' Favorite.*

Winner … 2020 Pacific Book Awards Best Mystery

2020 Chanticleer International Book Awards: 1st Place Blue Ribbon, CLUE Book Awards for Suspense, Thriller Fiction

"It's really progressive to see a female serial killer portrayed with such intelligent writing and depth of character, and the cat and mouse chase dynamic is thrown off nicely by the switching of genders. What results is a really enjoyable thriller and crime mystery novel, and overall Crime Denied is certain to please fans of both hard-boiled detective tales and action/adventure crime novels." Reviewed by K.C. Finn for Readers' Favorite.

2021 Chanticleer International Book Awards Finalist, CLUE Book Awards for Suspense, Thriller Fiction . . . *Crime Conspiracy*

"This makes for a truly dynamic story where anything is possible, and a hero you can root for even when it looks like all is lost." Reviewed by K.C. Finn for Readers' Favorite.

"This is a book you can't put down, which will entertain you on many levels, and at times make your skin crawl; the kind of book that remains in your thoughts long after you finish reading." Reviewed by Steven Robson for Readers' Favorite.

*"I read Crime Unknown in one sitting. The plot is intense and the main character, Agent Buck Taylor, is a hero like no other.** This book has everything a thriller needs to be and more. I thought I knew the story at the beginning. Buck will solve a tricky murder case, I thought. But Chuck Morgan adds a twist to this story that expands it and makes it one of the most enjoyable books I've read in this genre. I loved that the lead was such an awesome well-rounded fellow but that he also had a support team who were just as important to the story." Reviewed by Maureen Dangarembizi for Readers' Favorite.*

"Crime Unknown is a thoroughly enjoyable read and I would not hesitate to recommend this book to fans of the crime genre and those looking for a gateway in." Reviewed by K.C. Finn for Readers' Favorite.

2022 Chanticleer International Book Awards Finalist, CLUE Book Awards for Suspense, Thriller Fiction... *Crime Exploded*

"Action-packed and fast-paced, I was sucked into the story the moment I opened the novel. The author built the story to perfection. Chuck Morgan gave just the right amount of suspense, mystery, and action to keep readers' attention on Buck and his team. There was never a dull moment in the story. The narrative ran smoothly until the end; it followed the development of the story and the pace set by the characters. I enjoyed the twists and turns. What I loved more than anything else in the plot was how calculating Buck was. He was smart; he didn't let the FBI discourage him and kept his head in the game. The action gave me an adrenaline rush. Absolutely brilliant!' Reviewed by Rabia Tanveer for Readers' Favorite.

2022 Chanticleer International Book Awards Finalist, CLUE Book Awards for Suspense, Thriller Fiction . . . *Crime Spree*

"*It is one of the best crime novels I have read in a long while, with real characters developed in a way to let you get to know them intimately, understand them, and appreciate their strengths and weaknesses.* The plot is tight, exciting, and tense, with plenty of action, and it will grip you from the start. The bizarre storyline is enthralling, written in descriptive prose that lands you right in the middle of the action. Forget sleep; once you pick this book up, you won't want to put it down until it's finished. Fantastic story, and highly recommended for fans of high-octane crime thrillers." Reviewed by Anne-Marie Reynolds for Readers' Favorite.

"Crime Family is the tenth book in the Buck Taylor series. Chuck Morgan had me hooked from the first page until the end. *There was never a dull moment with all the action; one chapter flowed into the next. The story was fast-paced and kept me on the edge of my seat. I kept turning the pages to find out what would happen next. I was intrigued, and with all the twists and turns, I could not predict what was looming. The characters were well-developed. Each had a background description, and it was fun getting to know some of them. The story was excellently written with a fitting ending." Reviewed by Alma Boucher for Readers' Favorite.*

"Crime Scene is a must-read for lovers of mystery sleuth and murder tales with a touch of conspiracy." Reader's Favorite review.

"Crime Scene has a carefully designed intrigue that deepens with every unforeseeable turn of events, and a dynamic narrative." Reader's Favorite review.

"This is a great book. Holds your attention and you don't want to put it down. I would recommend this book to anyone who loves a good crime novel." Amazon review.

"Spellbinding, gripping, powerful, and relevant are just a few words that come to mind after turning the last page of Crime Scene: A Buck Taylor Novel, book 11, by Chuck Morgan." Amazon Review.

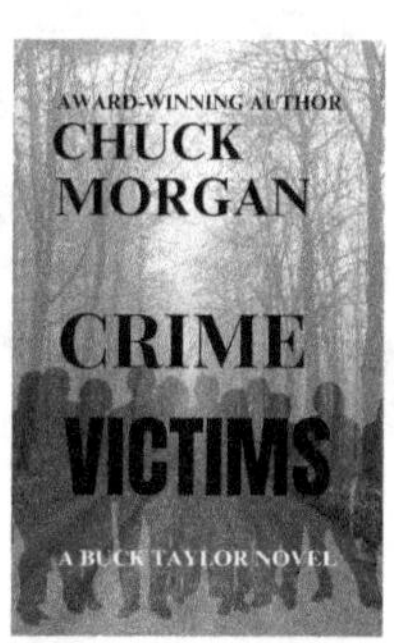

"A riveting plot and good pacing keep the reader in suspense as Buck Taylor and his team establish evidence beyond a reasonable doubt. The author sustains interest by skillfully showing the art and intuition involved in crime investigation and the science behind it, as well as the elements that can delay or confound it. There are a lot of quirky characters in the novel and the author gives them mannerisms, voices, and descriptions that make them distinctive and realistic. The details and descriptions of the work

and everyday life of the players are both pleasantly appealing and revolting, depending on the scenario. What's most captivating and intriguing about the character development is the backstory of the unhinged characters and how the author uses them as part of the perplexing trail of a horrendous crime. Themes of sadism, cruelty, grief, forensics, police procedures, and even a little bit of romance can be found in this installment of the Buck Taylor series. Highly recommended for crime story fans who especially enjoy the information as well as the twists, turns, and the untangling of intricate and cold case crime sprees." Reviewed by Carmen Tenorio for Readers' Favorite.

www.ingramcontent.com/pod-product-compliance
Lightning Source LLC
Chambersburg PA
CBHW070611300726
48975CB00006B/1786